Warwickshire County Council

2 2 AUG 2022			

This item is to be returned or renewed before the latest date above. It may be borrowed for a further period if not in demand. **To renew your books:**

- **Phone the 24/7 Renewal Line 01926 499273 or**
- **Visit www.warwickshire.gov.uk/libraries**

Discover • Imagine • Learn • *with libraries*

Warwickshire
County Council

Working for Warwickshire

Phil Whitaker is the author of two previous novels, one of which won the Mail on Sunday/John Llewellyn Rhys Prize, a Betty Trask Award and was shortlisted for the Whitbread First Novel Award. The other one was joint winner of the Encore Award for best second novel. He lives in Oxford with his wife and children, and divides his time between writing and his work as a forensic medical examiner and GP.

THE FACE

When Ray Arthur, a retired detective, is killed mysteriously in a road accident, his daughter Zoe is shattered. Her need to understand his life — and the strange circumstances of his death — sends her home to Nottingham, the city in which she was born and her father grew up. She tracks down Declan, a former police artist and a one-time friend of her father's. Through their fraught encounters, a terrible picture of guilt and betrayal emerges.

PHIL WHITAKER

THE FACE

Complete and Unabridged

ULVERSCROFT
Leicester

First published in Great Britain in 2002 by
Atlantic Books, London

First Large Print Edition
published 2003
by arrangement with
Atlantic Books
Grove Atlantic UK Limited, London

British Library CIP Data

Whitaker, Phil, *1966 –*
    The face.—Large print ed.—
    Ulverscroft large print series: general fiction
    1. Psychological fiction
    2. Large type books
    I. Title
    823.9'14 [F]

    ISBN 0–7089–4808–1

Published by
F. A. Thorpe (Publishing)
Anstey, Leicestershire

Set by Words & Graphics Ltd.
Anstey, Leicestershire
Printed and bound in Great Britain by
T. J. International Ltd., Padstow, Cornwall

This book is printed on acid-free paper

For SP, LP and BR.

And in memory of two influential people,
Margaret Hotine and Julian Clarke.

Your face, my thane, is as a book where men
May read strange matters. To beguile the time,
Look like the time; bear welcome in your eye,
Your hand, your tongue; look like the innocent flower,
But be the serpent under't.

Shakespeare, *Macbeth*

False face must hide what the false heart doth know.

ibid.

Prologue

December

Holly and I had come to an understanding. I would open an envelope and offer it to her; she would grasp the edge of the card inside. Once she'd managed to pull it out she would examine the picture, pointing at cats and robins and Father Christmases. Then she would give it a chew. Each card would be passed back with an emphatic 'Da!' In return I'd be allowed a few seconds to wipe off the saliva and scan the message inside. But before long she would start rocking and bouncing and whining, hand held out for the next.

Without exception the greetings were breezy — To Zoe, Paul and Holly, Happy Christmas, Don't drink too much! The words 'so sorry must be grim this time of year' didn't feature at all. Yet the sentiment was there, I felt, in all the Lots of loves and the rows of kisses, in the jokey phrases and the red-nosed reindeers.

It made me think about Dad, the way he would loop lengths of string beneath the picture rails in the lounge. Never ribbon or tinsel, always plain string. There wasn't any point, he said, you couldn't see what was under there once you'd finished. It was an inconsequential memory, a glimmer of the Dad I had always known, standing on a chair, a bundle of Christmas cards in hand, hanging them like washing. The image that had blocked all others in the weeks since the inquest — his hands clutching the steering wheel as he smashed into the concrete wall; not knowing whether at that moment his face had been crazed by horror or stilled by a determination to die — had begun, at last, to give way.

I slid the next card off my dwindling pile. A glance at the front showed two postmarks, a London one smudgily overlapping the original. And there was his name, Ray Arthur, written in elegant fountain pen. The rest of his address was covered by a post office sticker with an instruction for the sorting office: Redirected mail — treat as first class. I stared at it, momentarily paralysed. I hadn't had any post for him for weeks, and even then nothing personal. Now there was this. Holly let out an indignant squeal. I looked at her, hurt in her eyes that Mummy should have forgotten her part in the game. I edged a thumb under the flap and ripped the envelope. She tugged and tugged till eventually the card came free, exactly like every other one she'd helped me open that morning.

★   ★   ★

That day, the day it happened, the only constructive thing I did was find his address book. I know other people crumple in heaps, swallow pills, sit sobbing or staring out the window, but I was gripped by a powerful need to tell, to make people hear. As I walked out of the hospital — Paul talking, his words swirling like tickertape — my eyes flicked from face to face. Nurses, visitors, porters, pyjama-clad patients swam up and flashed past. People chatting, people mulling, people hurrying, people *alive*. Wanting to grab them, shake them, force them to look at me. Ray Arthur, my father — *listen*, will you — my precious bloody dad is dead.

Paul drove me. He didn't think it was a good idea but he took me anyway. I made him wait in the car. I knew what I was looking for, a black book, the cover scuffed, the corners of the pages worn smooth from years of being turned. Alone in my childhood home I searched round, taking in the emptiness and the quiet. I don't know why but I imagined I was Dad, walking from room to room. I didn't hum like he would have, but

I could hear him doing it, the low, semi-tuneless soundtrack that accompanied his quests for missing keys, wallet, watch. His lunch things were on the side in the kitchen, plate freckled with breadcrumbs, the red rind off a piece of Edam perched on the rim. His mug was half-full of tea, bag floating. The Thomson Local was on the phone table in the hall, open at roofing contractors, several ads biro-starred. I finally found the address book in the utility. For some reason he'd tucked it under the elasticated edge of the ironing board cover. As soon as I had it I left, pausing only to switch off the answer phone in the hall. I couldn't bear the thought that someone might call before I could break the news, that they would hear him speak his pre-recorded spiel and leave a message as though he were still alive. Better that the phone should ring and ring.

Paul's mum had taken Holly over to Farnham, an hour's drive away. He asked if I wanted to come. The prospect of having to be daughter-in-law, mother, wife, was intolerable. I said no, suggested that he stay for supper while he was down there and wait till Holly was ready for bed before heading home. I told him I loved him, loved Holly, but I needed time alone. He nodded, said nothing. Back at the flat, I nipped in to fetch some pyjamas for him to change her into. When he pulled away, leaving me standing on the pavement, I waved. His hands stayed on the wheel. He may, or may not, have seen me in his rear view mirror, I couldn't be sure.

Alone in the flat, the silence was absolute. I put Dad's address book on the desk, shied away from it like it could hurt me. I turned the TV on, flicked through all five channels before switching it off again. I tried music, tried eating, but nothing was right. In the end I phoned Sarah. I thought it would help, an old friend to talk to, someone who knows me well. It wasn't her fault — she was shocked, it was awful, she was very sorry to hear — but the longer it went on the more I struggled to breathe. Cardboard cut-out phrases uttered to every single bereaved person there ever has been. I grew angry — not with her, with everyone who had overused the language, blunted its meaning, rendered it completely inadequate now the time had come for my own dad to die. I cut the call short, telling her I was sorry, I had to go.

The steady whine of the computer, the staccato crackles from the hard disk, the flurries of my keystrokes. I went through methodically, entering addresses from Dad's book into a merge file. Every now and again

I'd be ambushed, a particular name summoning up a memory that would blur the screen. I skipped the people I knew — relatives, neighbours I used to call uncle and aunt — I would inform them in person. But there were dozens of names I'd never heard before. The more I discovered the more demoralized I became. I had no way of telling whether they were once close friends or merely acquaintances, people he'd met on a holiday and promised to look up but never did. That was the point at which I first felt the implacability of his absence. If you've got cancer, at least you get some warning, a chance to organize your affairs. He'd gone in the click of a finger, one minute driving along the A40, the next nothing. Even the simple question of where he'd been going that afternoon, what had caused him to be driving along that stretch of road, was unanswerable. I closed the address book with its meaningless entries, person after person I had never known, and left the computer to put itself to sleep.

I hadn't drunk since just after I discovered I was pregnant with Holly. The first gin and tonic had surprisingly little effect. By the time I'd finished the fourth my head and limbs had turned to mush.

★　★　★

I was hungover and only half-awake when the phone went the next morning. I took the call before the second ring, instantly alert, the same vertiginous feeling as when the policewoman had appeared the previous afternoon. The coroner introduced himself and explained he was phoning personally because he'd known Dad quite well in the past. He was sorry to hear what had happened. The inquest would open on Wednesday morning at ten. I would need to attend but my evidence at this stage would be concerned solely with identification. Once that was formalized he would adjourn and my father's body would be released. He'd let me know the date for the hearing proper, once all the reports he required were in.

Paul's side of the bed was rumpled, Holly's cot was empty and there was a note on the floor in the hall. Paul hoped I was OK, I wasn't to worry about work because they weren't expecting me, he'd leave early and go to the nursery on his way home. I hadn't registered either their coming in or their leaving. I had never, in the whole of Holly's year-long life, missed giving her breakfast, getting her ready for the day ahead. I should have been grateful. Instead there was the same suffocating guilt I always have when falling short of perfect motherhood. I shook

9

my head, cross with myself. My hungover brain kicked back, hard. Shrugging off my dressing gown I shut myself in the shower, closed my eyes, and let hot water needle my scalp until the pain began to recede.

★ ★ ★

Ray Arthur, redirected mail, treat as first class. The day after Dad died I used the computer to send a form letter to every one of the unknown names in his address book. The trickle of condolence cards I received dried up within a week. Months later, one Christmas card. There were two postmarks, a London one from the redirection, the other partly obscured but definitely Nottingham, where Dad lived and worked in the early days. I waited a long time, watching Holly's absorption as she examined the card, a pressure building in my head. Finally she handed it back. 'Da!' A nativity scene reproduced from the Royal Academy collection. Inside, the same ink pen writing as on the envelope. To Ray, Happy Christmas, Declan (Barr).

I fetched Dad's black book from the desk drawer and went through the Ds and Bs. I hadn't missed anyone. There was no sender's address. I retrieved the envelope and started to put the card back. It snagged on something. I felt inside and drew out a piece of paper. Holly started to grizzle.

'Just a minute, poppet.'

The pitch increased, became a cry. I remembered, too late, that it was her job to pull things out of envelopes.

'Paul!'

He appeared at the door, bleary in his boxers.

'Can you take her?'

He looked at me for a second before coming across to whisk her away to the kitchen. 'Come on, tiger, let's give your mum some peace.'

The paper had a row of torn perforations on one edge. The entire sheet was taken up by a pencil drawing of a man, a woman and a child sitting on a grassy bank. The slope led up to a cottage, a rib cage of rafters visible where the tiles had caved in. The woman was off to one side. The way her arms were wrapped around her made her look as though she was cold. Between her and the others was a giant stone toadstool. There was something on top of it, too vaguely sketched to be identifiable. On the other side, the man had the child perched on his knee.

The faces were good likenesses — outstandingly so. Even if they hadn't been, the poses and the background were sufficiently familiar that I would instantly have recognized the photograph from which the picture had been drawn. It had been on Dad's mantelpiece for as long as I could remember. The woman was my mother. I don't think she was feeling cold, I think she was always like that. The giant toadstool beside her was an old stone seat; on it, a toy rabbit called Snowy. The cottage was the house in which, many years before the photo was taken, my father had been born. The man with the child was Dad. And the child with the man was me.

Declan

Before I say anything, you must understand: everything happened long ago. We're talking three decades — half a lifetime, for Christ's sake. The world was completely different, you can't judge it the way we do today. The regrets I've had these past months. They come at me like brigands in the night, clutching their coshes and knives. Round and round my head, again and again; not even whisky can chase them away. I keep telling myself: If I had my time again I would do things differently. And myself tells me back: Oh aye, you would, would you? And I know I wouldn't. I'd be back in that world, I'd be the me of thirty years ago, and I would do every last thing exactly the way it happened the first time around.

The world was the same fucked-up place we inhabit today, it just didn't seem that way. Maybe it was because I was young. I was in my late twenties, I could still say I was on course. On course for what? Yeah, right. All the hopes and dreams. The stuff that never, in the end, came true. The stuff that weathered and crumbled and flaked, and blew to the ground on the wind. The reverses and the losses, the messy compromises, the guilty-not-guilty of it all, they have at last fitted me for life. But it is not the life I ever thought I would live.

I wasn't a fool. Neither was your father. Ray's ignorance, if that was what it was, had as much to do with things being unspoken. I'm sure I'm right about this. Back then there were so many taboos. It's like, I remember — before I left Liverpool for art school, this was — one of my friends' mums, Mrs Carragher, coming to the door one afternoon. I answered her knock, I remember smiling and starting to say hello, like it was a nice surprise, her calling round. But her face was serious, wrong. She didn't return my smile, didn't come in when I stepped back from the door, she just asked in a flat voice if Ma was there. I stayed in the hallway while they talked, keeping in the background, perversely thrilled by the gravity of the mood. It was a friend of theirs, another woman with three kids all younger than me. She was dead. The words seemed to hang in the air, it took an age for them to clear. Ma didn't react, she just stood stock still. Then she asked what had happened. Mrs Carragher looked at me, nodded her head slightly. I was waved away. I didn't say anything, I just started up the stairs. But I still heard the unspeakable word, how it came out in a cross between a whisper and a hiss. *Cancer.* As if it was a scandal. As if the woman who had died had turned out not to be one of them after all.

It's only an example but maybe it helps. Your father wasn't stupid; no way was he corrupt. It was just that he lived in a certain world, of shared assumptions, of sturdy furniture and fresh wallpaper. Yes, the carpets and rugs and linoleum were lumpy and awkward to walk on, all the shit that was hidden under there. But people did their best to keep their balance, no one making any remark, every one of us pretending, acting — believing — that the ground beneath our feet was level and sweet and even.

I don't know if you'll make another trip to Nottingham. Maybe you will one day, when your daughter is older, when you have moved further through your life. I may be long dead. Even if I'm alive you won't come to see me — not after last time, the way I treated you. For which I am sorry. I couldn't answer your questions. Not then. Perhaps, as I tell my story, you will understand.

You had come to visit the places your father had lived, that was what you told me, even if it wasn't the whole truth. You sounded embarrassed, didn't go on to explain yourself,

15

as if you were worried I would think you mad. You needn't have been. I understand the lure of geography, of architecture. Every street in this city, every building, every alley, every park and playground, harbours stories that ache to be told. But you need a guide, someone to show you. Someone who can whisper incantations to the ghosts that haunt the bricks and cement, the grass and the trees.

If ever you do return, let me tell you the places you should see. As you walk, try to imagine the Nottingham we lived in. I have no desire to burden you. Whether I speak or not, the names Hunter and Scanlon will soon be bitterly familiar. The only consolation is that you should hear the truth from someone who was there. At times you might be tempted to doubt my account, question my motives. You should not. Speaking here, as in a confessional, I have no cause to lie. I have long since forgiven what your father did to me.

Inquest

'This inquest was opened on the thirtieth of October and adjourned. Before I reconvene, I should explain one or two procedural points for the benefit of the jury. Firstly, your presence here should not be taken to imply that this is a trial. No one is accused of any crime, we are here simply to establish, as best we can, the circumstances touching on the death of Raymond John Arthur. Ordinarily, I act alone in arriving at a verdict. However, in cases where important consequences may arise I am empowered to appoint a jury to act in this capacity on my behalf. This I have done. Your task is to consider the evidence. In so doing you may become aware of the effects your verdict may have. I must ask you to put these to one side. Your deliberations should be based solely on the evidence and must not be swayed by other considerations.

'I shall conduct the initial examination of each witness. At the conclusion of my inquiries there will be an opportunity for questions from the representatives of interested parties. The Royal Mutual life assurance fund and the Insignia motor insurance group are both represented by Mr Nigel Forshaw QC. The family of the deceased is represented by Mr Toby Johnson. May I remind counsel that this is a coroner's court and I do not expect adversarial questioning.

'I now call the first witness.'

[He takes the stand.]

'Would you please give the court your full name.'

'David Michael Burrage.'

'You are a consultant pathologist at the Queen Charlotte hospital?'

'I am.'

'Did you conduct a post-mortem examination on the deceased, Raymond John Arthur?'

'I did.'

'Would you please give the court a summary of your findings.'

'Yes, I conducted the examination on the twenty-fourth of October in the autopsy suite at Queen Charlotte's. The deceased was a sixty-year-old Caucasian male of average height and build. There was external trauma, most notably severe bruising across the anterior chest and right shoulder. This was in a pattern consistent with driver seat-belt injury, commonly seen in deceleration incidents. There were also crush injuries to both legs and a deep, four-centimetre laceration to the forehead directly above the left eye, with no underlying skull fracture. Internally, the main findings were in the thoracic cavity where a tear of the aortic root had resulted in massive mediastinal haemorrhage and cardiac tamponade. Put simply, the main artery supplying blood to the body had been torn at the point where it leaves the heart. This had resulted in uncontrolled blood loss, some of which had gathered in the fibrous sack which surrounds the heart, compressing it and preventing it from beating.'

'And in your opinion, this was the cause of death?'

'It was. Whether death resulted from blood loss or constriction of the heart is impossible to say. In either case, the disruption to the aortic root was the principal cause.'

'Doctor Burrage, in your view, would these injuries be consistent with the apparent mechanism of death, namely a high speed road traffic accident?'

'There was certainly nothing to suggest otherwise. I conducted a thorough microscopic examination of the aortic valve and wall, but could find no evidence of prior valvular disease, aneurysm, or medial necrosis, which might have led to spontaneous rupture.'

'And the laceration to the head, can you make any comment on that?'

'Again, the laceration was consistent with trauma sustained in a road traffic accident, arising as a result of the head striking the steering wheel or similar structure.'

'The seat belt would not have prevented this?'

'Ordinarily yes, but in a high velocity head-on impact the front compartment of the car will concertina under the weight of the engine block. The crush injuries to the legs were also consistent with this.'

'And the laceration could not have been caused prior to death?'

'Well, in fact, it was — as were the other injuries I have described. Death was not instantaneous, it would have taken several minutes for the internal bleeding to have compromised vital circulation. However, the degree of bruising and associated tissue reaction was the same for all injuries, so I have no reason to doubt that the head wound was caused around the time of the impact.'

'Thank you. Now, Doctor, you will be aware that this was a single vehicle accident. Were there any findings in your examination that might help explain this?'

'There are a number of conditions that can cause a driver to suddenly lose control. Most common would be simple tiredness, but a heart attack or stroke, or a fit or sudden disturbance of heart rhythm could all precipitate an accident. I found no evidence of thrombosis in the coronary or cerebral circulations, and the widespread micro-haemorrhages in the brain were a result of deceleration injury rather than evidence of a primary haemorrhagic stroke. I cannot rule out either a cardiac arrhythmia or an epileptic seizure, although I understand there was no prior history of either of these.'

'So you found no medical condition that could explain why the deceased might lose control of his vehicle?'

'No, sir, although I must stress, I cannot rule this out.'

'I see. And did you also perform toxicological tests?'

'Of course. We routinely check for alcohol and a battery of drugs, both illicit and prescription.'

'And what were your findings?'

'Alcohol was not present. Regarding drugs that might have affected driving performance adversely, only one was identified. I under-stand that the deceased was being prescribed a medication called amitriptyline by his general practitioner. Tests confirmed the presence of this drug but the levels in the blood were well within the therapeutic range.'

'And amitriptyline can affect driving?'

'It can. Common side effects include drowsiness and impairment of cognitive function. These are more likely in the early stages of taking the drug, or in the days following a dose increase. The longer someone is taking the medication the more these side effects tend to resolve. Nevertheless, the label on the bottle will always contain a warning about the potential to affect driving.'

'I see. So, in your opinion, the presence of this medication contributed to this accident?'

'No, it's impossible to be so categoric. I am merely saying that it might.'

'Thank you. Mr Forshaw?'

[Mr Forshaw stands.]

'Doctor Burrage, am I to understand that you identified, in the body of the deceased, a drug that can impair driving ability?'

'That is correct.'

'And anyone taking this drug would be warned not to drive?'

'They would be warned that driving might be affected. That is not the same thing.'

'No, quite. No further questions.'

[Mr Forshaw sits. Mr Johnson stands.]

'Doctor Burrage, regarding this medication you identified. In fact, you have absolutely no idea which particular side effects, if any, the deceased might have experienced, have you?'

'No.'

'Is it possible for people taking this medication to be perfectly able to drive?'

'It is, yes. I was merely making the point that some people can be affected.'

'And just to clarify: you cannot with any certainty rule out a medical condition that might have caused sudden loss of control of a vehicle.'

'No, I can't rule that out, although I found no evidence — '

'Furthermore, something as simple as tiredness could explain what happened?'

'Yes.'

'Thank you, Doctor. No further questions.'

[Mr Johnson sits.]

'Doctor Burrage, thank you very much for your time. That is all the court requires of you. If you could sign against your name on the clerk's list, you may leave.'

Part One

February

Paul wakes first. I open my eyes to find him sitting on the side of the bed, facing away. He is stretching his arms above his head, fingers interlocked, palms upwards. As his back arches, the contours are thrown into relief: twin columns of muscle, the spine forming a long trough between them. He holds the stretch and groans — both pleasure and dismay — then relaxes with a sigh. In the travel cot beside me, Holly's breathing is soft and regular. I can count on the fingers of one hand the times Paul has woken before her. I can't remember him ever doing so without the intervention of an alarm.

The bed creaks as he stands. In the half-light, I watch as he crosses the room. Twice weekly five-a-side, sporadic running, it's enough to keep him in shape: sleek quads, the swell and taper of the calves. Not bad for thirty-two. The boxers are ones I gave him — I forget the occasion — midnight blue with tiny white dots that are meant, perhaps, to be stars. He hasn't worn them in ages, these days preferring the hug of Calvin Kleins. Through the loose cotton I can make out an

27

impression of his buttocks and for a moment I try to remember how they feel beneath my hands.

The curtains are draped from ceiling to floor, rippled folds of velvet. He parts them, admitting a sliver of morning sun. I feel a flicker of optimism. Yesterday, the weather was foul. Don't set out unless your journey is essential — that was the advice on traffic and travel. Freak conditions, gusts up to storm force, flooding in the Midlands and the West. But we saw no accidents, and although the Leicestershire fields had turned to lakes, the M1 itself had managed to keep its head above water.

The brightness gives me an excuse to stir. I fake a quiet yawn.

'Morning.'

Paul glances over his shoulder.

'Sorry, did I wake you?' He too keeps his voice low.

'Not to worry.'

I flip the duvet to one side and slide out of bed, checking on Holly. She's blissful, face serene, one hand resting on Pooh Bear, her constant bed friend. Cool air on my bum makes me conscious of my T-shirt; I tug the hem down as I go. Joining Paul at the window I peer through the gap between the curtains. A clear day, stonewashed skies, dazzle from a low sun. It hardly seems possible after yesterday. Outside it will be crisp, fresh, far colder than it appears from behind glass. Invigorating. I lay a hand on Paul's shoulder, rest my head against it. I hope he too sees something cheerful, promising, in the upturn in the weather.

'I'm sorry about yesterday.'

He leans his head against mine. 'Yeah. Me too.'

We are looking out over the city. Steel and glass, Victorian redbrick, sixties high-rise. There is a surprising amount of greenery. Between two tall office blocks I can see part of a large slate-grey dome. A white windmill juts above distant terraces. Faced with a London skyline I could have a pretty good stab at the landmarks, but here the meaning of everything is unknown. Yesterday evening, head in the map trying to guide Paul to the hotel, I paid little attention to the darkened, rain-lashed city in which we'd arrived. This is the first time I've really seen it.

I was born here. Not a trace of an accent, and I don't remember a single thing about it, but this is where my life began. Name, Zoe Arthur. Nationality, British. Place of birth, Nottingham. How many times have I entered that on forms and never given it more than a passing thought? Nottingham. If it meant anything it was Robin Hood country, the place that broke the miners' strike, the team that rivalled Liverpool — my club as a star-struck teenager, though I was more interested in the players than the football. Now, I am here. I hold the thought, allow myself a few seconds to weigh it.

The hotel is on the inner ring road, directly below us is a large roundabout. Cars queue up, sprint forward, break free of the bottle neck and stream on their way. If roads are arteries then cars are corpuscles, constantly resisting the tendency to clot. Scenes like this are going on in every city and every town. Looked at from my vantage point, the triple glazing muffling the noise, I am reminded that I've left my own life behind. It is strange to think of it continuing, somehow, in my absence. This is an interlude, something from which I shall return. I am here because of Dad. I am here because of me. I am here because surely, somewhere in this city, is the answer to the infernal doubt Dad's inquest seeded in my mind.

'Well,' Paul says. 'Nice day for it.'

He glances back at the cot. 'Do you want to grab first shower, while the going's good?'

'No, you go.' I remove my hand from his shoulder. 'I'll make some coffee.'

He starts towards the en suite. At the door

he hesitates. 'How are you, anyway?'

'Oh, you know,' I tell him.

He reciprocates my half-smile, and comes back over. We slip arms round each other, pull close, hold the hug for a long while. It feels good, like a homecoming. At the same time it's tinged with sadness; it reminds me how rare these moments have become. His work, my work, most of all Holly. Never a moment to ourselves. Paul draws a deep breath. When he exhales, the air ruffles my hair and is warm against my ear. In the travel cot, Holly begins to stir.

★ ★ ★

When I was a girl I didn't really know what Dad did. I knew he was a policeman, but as to what that involved, I wasn't capable of understanding. I think that's true of most kids. Your dad is a pilot, a percussionist, a prime minister. They're just labels to explain the long hours he's away from home, words that conjure up an uncomplicated vision of what goes on while you, the child, are not around. Dad whizzing about in a plane. Dad banging on a drum. Dad running the country.

Dad didn't have a uniform. We would leave in the morning, me with my blazer and

31

satchel, him wearing an ordinary suit. He'd drop me off at primary school — a single father among the crowd of mums — then go on to work. Most days he'd be there again in the afternoon, the sky-blue Variant sitting with its engine idling just along from the gates. I would see the car, the open driver's door, Dad crouched on the pavement miming a hug with his outstretched arms. When we got home he would park me in front of the TV while he disappeared upstairs to finish what he'd been doing. Sometimes, if he had to go back to the office, he'd drop me at a friend's house and collect me later — often not till eight, nine in the evening. Those friends saw a lot of me in the Christmas and Easter holidays too; in time I gained a whole set of aunties and uncles to replace the ones I'd lost. Only at weekends and in the summer did Dad become a full-time parent.

He used to be a proper policeman when we lived in Nottingham. He started out in uniform then joined CID several years before I was born. The move to London enabled him to take up a post with the major crime unit. He loved the job, but it meant uncertain demands, away from home for long stretches. Shortly after Mum left he arranged a transfer to the nine-to-five of complaints and discipline.

Complaints and discipline. If an officer was alleged to have transgressed, Dad was supposed to establish the truth of the matter. He used to say that if someone was accused of putting handcuffs on too tight it would take at least three months to investigate, medical reports and all. Anything more serious took a lot longer.

Dad doing the washing. Dad cooking supper. Dad taking me into bed with him when I wasn't well. Mum went to stay with Aunty Gill in Mansfield when I was seven and I never saw my relatives on her side of the family again. For a long time I believed she must have told them something awful about me because they didn't visit any more. I guess I was hurting badly, though I don't suppose I knew what that meant at the time. Instead, I behaved appallingly whenever she came back to take me out, and after a while she stopped visiting too.

Dad used to order panda car rides for me after school on days when he couldn't make it himself. The officers who picked me up should presumably have been doing something more useful. Instead, they would drive me round to his office, where I'd sit drawing with Staedtler pens or playing with pencil sharpeners and paperclips and staplers and the other intriguing things that cluttered his desk. Dad was a full-time parent for the whole six weeks of my summers, which was more holiday than he was allowed, even as an inspector. The day before I left home to go to university, he presented me with a canister of CS spray, bearing the insignia of the North Dakota Police Department, which I wasn't to show anyone but I was to take with me whenever I went out at night. Dad detested policing other officers who bent the rules.

When I was young I used to dream of joining up. Dad kept in touch with his friends from major crime, had them over for drinks a few times a year. I would flit about refilling glasses, offering plates of crisps. Most of them were men, but there were women, too. As I went round I would listen to the conversations: the talk of hard stops and armed response; piling in to help a colleague in trouble. It was exotic, dangerous. They were in a family, with their own loyalties and language and rules. There were plenty of mundane concerns — lack of resources, inept prosecutors — but I never paid attention. I had watched too much TV. As they were reliving some late-night raid, I'd be out there with them, kicking down doors, waving a firearm, one of the team.

Dad loved those evenings. I would catch sight of him standing in a group, red-faced, jabbing a finger, talking excitedly. When the last person had gone, he would flop down with the remains of his drink. I would perch on the arm of his chair, a bit heady at staying up so late, and he would rest his hand on my back. I don't remember us saying much — my mind was too full of law-enforcement fantasies. I never confided them; I was afraid he would laugh at me. And they didn't last. A few years later and whenever Dad couldn't fetch me from school my cheeks would flare at the sight of the panda car waiting. The jeers of the boys stung my ears. Thirteen years old and I was ashamed of him. I stayed like that till well after I left home. No ifs, no buts, say no to Fowler's cuts. At university, with the demonstrations and the sit-ins, having a policeman for a dad was a social embarrassment.

Once, when I was nearing graduation, wondering aloud what to do with my degree, he did mention graduate-entry to the force. But it was a half-hearted suggestion. By then, the organization he'd joined no longer existed. It had become a service and every last thing was regulated by the Police and Criminal Evidence Act. The numbers of complaints had soared. According to Ray Arthur, Inspector, C and D, in an effort to emerge from the deluge of regulation under which it had become buried, the force had managed to crawl up its own arse. Shortly after I got my first job, when I could at last support myself, he put in for a transfer back to major crime. A month later he announced that he was taking early retirement. I asked what had happened, but he changed the subject. I didn't mention it again.

At the inquest the coroner asked me, towards the end of my evidence, if I'd thought my father had been depressed. The question was couched in the hushed tones employed by people who worry they are slandering the dead. It took me a while to work out what to say. As I sat there, becalmed in the witness box, things came back to me. The memory of him during those evenings at our house, animated in conversation with former colleagues. Father and daughter sitting together after the party was through, his hand stroking the small of her back, the remains of a drink balanced on the arm of his chair. Him being there the following after-noon, the VW estate waiting outside the school gates, though not, of course, any longer permitted to be holding a hug in his outstretched arms. I realized that the coroner was waiting for my reply. I looked up and told him I really couldn't answer his question. If my father had been depressed I thought I would probably have been the very last person to know.

★ ★ ★

Our hotel is on a fume-filled dual carriageway called Maid Marian Way. We chose it from twenty-odd hits on an internet search. The address made us laugh.

Holly has her breakfast strapped in a high chair. Paul and I take turns to hurry a pain au chocolat.

'There's a heated pool here,' he tells me. 'Sauna and massage too.'

I grab Holly's hand, preventing her from depositing blueberry and apple on the white tablecloth. 'And?'

'I packed the swimming gear. We could do with being spoiled. Perhaps if the weather turns bad again we could fit some relaxation in here.'

I prise the spoon from Holly's grasp, try to introduce the puree into her mouth instead. Paul is finishing his coffee when I look up.

'I've got things planned.'

'I know. But if it starts raining again, is all I'm saying.'

I call time on Holly's breakfast, start to clean her with a wipe, a move guaranteed to flip her from perfect contentment to raging fury. Amid her escalating cries I catch glances from other residents at nearby tables. At home I find these storms difficult enough, but I feel self-conscious here, find myself shushing and fussing. I unclick the harness and hoick her from the high chair. Pressed against me, her ordeal at an end, calm returns. She leans back in my arms and starts to fiddle with my necklace. But for the tears on her cheeks you wouldn't know anything had happened.

It takes us a while to get going, trying to ensure we've got everything we might conceivably require for the day ahead. Holly and I stay in the room, sorting through the basket of complimentary toiletries, while Paul treks repeatedly to the car. Eventually, food bag, buggy and backpack, changing bag and essential toys all stowed, we're ready. It's obvious, but I can't resist it. I get halfway to the door before pretending to remember Holly. Paul laughs. She stares at him, confused, but once she recognizes amusement in his eyes a smile spreads across her face. I feel a sudden crush of guilt, the full weight of her vulnerability — her delight at a joke she doesn't understand, played at her expense.

At the exit from the car park, Paul revs too hard, tyres squealing as he accelerates rapidly up to traffic speed.

'OK, Batman,' he says, checking his mirror. 'Where to first?'

I think for a moment.

'Lenton,' I tell him. 'Let's go to Lenton.'

Declan

Start your journey in Old Market Square, the centre of this city. It isn't the beginning — I've no idea where that might be — but you don't need one. What you need is a point of departure. You must have been to the square when you came in February, but I want you to look at it with fresh eyes.

To north and south you see great Victorian terraces. Each building is home to a national treasure: Debenhams, Barclays, Next. Most people notice only the storefronts. But look up now, way above your head. Let your gaze drift over the upper storeys, to where balustrades ornament the rooftops. There, do you see them? Tiny grimacing faces, leering at the figures on the pavements below. Some recognizably human, others diabolic hybrids of man and beast, twisted lips, protruding eyes, huge lolling tongues. Gargoyles, stationed at intervals along the gutters. Remember them, imprint their expressions on your mind, the mockery and disgust bequeathed by long-dead stone masons. Such inspiring buildings, such elegant façades, surmounted by the lewd and the grotesque.

What were our forefathers thinking? Perhaps it was nothing more than a bad joke, the masons' critique of their paymasters' wealth. But stop to think. Could they have had something different to say?

Your neck aches, too long craning. Relax, look down, let the cramp subside. It was only a detail, nothing important. Start to walk. Skirt round the Council House, with its magnificent Pauline dome, where the mayor and the city fathers conduct their civic duties. At the end of the Exchange Arcade you'll see Bridlesmith Gate with its boutiques and coffee bars and clubs. All the shit that has made this the place to be. On your left you'll find a passage, Byard Lane. It's narrow, dingy; it doesn't look like there's much up there, but bear with me. Walk up it a way and you will find an unassuming shop, cramped, with just enough room for a couple of clothes rails and a counter. This is where Paul Smith first set up, all those years ago. He still owns it, stocks a limited selection. He's got far bigger places in London, Paris, Milan. He could have any shop he wanted in Nottingham. But he keeps this on, out of a sense of loyalty, perhaps.

Isabel used to buy me things here, shirts and jackets to wear above beat-up jeans. This was the fag-end of the sixties, well before

41

Jessie, well before I met your father. Isabel. Before I say a single word about him, you have to know something of her. I cannot paint a picture of my life without her in the background. Even now, I exist in relation to her: I am divided into the before, the during, and the after. She was my pupil. I coached her in life drawing — portraits, nudes. She was younger than me, spent a couple of years working in a Sheffield gallery before embarking on her foundation. In 1969 she enrolled and within two months she had blown me apart. And it was definitely me falling for her — this was no abuse of a student infatuation. I came in for criticism: the teacher holds ultimate power. What no one asked — none of the people who presumed to judge — was which of us occupied that role.

She was vibrant, amused by things, self-contained, self-assured. Low voice, a soft Yorkshire accent. Hers was the most difficult portrait I have ever made. Her passion was for Renaissance frescos and the Impressionists. Her own art was unrepentantly modern, concerned with the ripples that radiate from us, the effect we have simply by being in the world. She was brilliant — technically, creatively, intellectually — a class apart from her peers. I was astounded by her work, intimidated by it, frightened by the thought of

42

where she could go. Not that I was without ambition. Teaching was a means to an end, a way of existing while I pursued my dreams. I had sold to private collectors in the Midlands, had twice been invited to submit for the Northern Lights. But the best I could hope was to live from my work. Isabel's had the potential to shape her life.

I couldn't believe she would have me but she did. I was so drunk on it I never thought about the risk. The head of faculty called me in and told me to drop it. Drop it, his exact words. Or if I couldn't do that, at least make a bit more bloody effort to be discreet. I didn't listen. All I wanted was to have her, the whole of her, any place, as often as I could, mindless, senseless lust. One minute we'd be talking together, alone in the studio of a weekend, feeling lazy, thinking about working, but tempted to waste the day instead. Then she would get up to go to the loo. As she stood, the stretch of her jumper defined her breasts. I would watch the snag of her T-shirt on her arse as she walked out of the room. While she was gone I'd torment myself, thinking about her sitting there, knickers down, intimate flesh exposed to the air. When she came back she would meet my gaze and somehow she would know: next we'd be kissing, clutching, pulling at each other's clothes. One look could do that, one glance or glimpse or little thing that reminded me.

I couldn't be bothered fiddling about, it would be all right if I withdrew. I was desperate to finish inside her, but it was a small sacrifice. For months it was OK, but I grew blasé. We were young, invincible, the future was a boundless possibility. I allowed myself to lose control. In the end we proved ourselves exactly the same as everyone else; identical physiology to the rest of the human race.

Once or twice I was tempted. Finish it, scoot, do a runner. But I was never going to go through with it. I couldn't imagine a life without her. Once I realized that, I told her we should marry. She didn't respond — didn't say yes, didn't say no. She just looked at me in a certain way. As though by suggesting it I had diminished myself in her eyes.

★   ★   ★

Byard Lane comes out on Fletcher Gate, the outskirts of the Lace Market. There's no need to come directly to High Pavement, take a stroll around. Wool Pack Lane, Weekday Cross, Short Hill. Hollow Stone with its views over Narrow Marsh. Just names to you

44

but they are in my blood, they are my home. On every side you are surrounded by old brick warehouses rising high above your head, cutting the sky into strips. Once they were the manufactories of the great textile firms, the family dynasties of the industrial era. The air would have been hazy with cotton dust, battered by the clattering of the lace looms. Now many of the brick shells have been converted to apartment blocks, others have become nightclubs, restaurants, new colleges. The lanes teem with students, shoppers, young professionals. As you pass them you catch snippets of babble . . . Fantastic area . . . everything on the doorstep . . . can't buy a flat for under a hundred and eighty grand. The more you walk, the more you hear, the more the area seems alive — thriving just as it was a century ago, the last time these warehouses were the hub of this city.

But try to see it with my eyes. When Isabel and I moved here it was derelict, down-at-heel. No one wanted to live in the Lace Market then. The factories and warehouses were abandoned, had been for decades, windows boarded up to give truants somewhere to scrawl graffiti. Here and there some second-division clothing company still plied its trade, a grubby sign above a doorway advertising the commercial life within. Bras, nylon shirts, tights, not a designer in sight. It was a place whose time had been and gone. No one talked urban regeneration in those days. All the first-timers went into boxes crammed together on suburban estates. I asked Isabel once what her motto in life was. She laughed and said, 'Never live in a Barratt home.'

One hundred and eighty thousand. The house didn't even cost us eight hundred, not then. Christ knows what it would go for now. I will never find out. It is full of pictures, moments, fragments of life I can ill afford to lose. We bought it for our home. It was all we could manage. It was all we wanted.

Finish your wander through the Lace Market, make your way here. You'll recognize the house from your previous visit, but put that from your mind. Try to see it as I first saw it, thirty-odd years ago. High Pavement was deserted, the only movement the rippling of a discarded newspaper on the pavement. Ahead was the estate agent who was to show us round, beside me was Isabel. We reached the alley, the agent disappeared, I was about to go after him when Isabel squeezed my hand. Look. I followed her gaze. Yellow, cartoon-cheerful, a ruff of wavy rays. On the wall above the gateway was a sun-face

46

gargoyle. It said something to me about being happy. I guess it said something similar to her.

The house was once a sweat shop. Tucked away at the end of its own cobbled passage, well behind the row of buildings that front on to High Pavement, the light was appalling. But in a booming economy a hundred years ago, gardens and back yards were sold off to build more factories. In the 1930s, when the lace trade had died its death, it became somebody's home. Preamble over, the agent started to lead us around. The boards were grubby and bare, the paint tobacco-stained, the window frames rotten, and the air stale with the smell of piss.

The agent was pessimism made flesh. There had been countless viewings in the year it had been for sale. I was ready to go by the time we'd finished the ground floor, but Isabel wanted to see upstairs. If anything it was worse, but to the south-facing rear the entire first floor was given over to one large workshop, running the length of the building: broad windows, four in all, stretching floor to ceiling, separated by columns of brick. I could practically see the lace makers, crouched over their stocking-frames, working long into the evening according to the season, using every last drop of the sunlight that, amazingly, bathed the upper storey. I saw myself, Isabel too, doing the same — except that our frames would be easels; paint and charcoal our media. I didn't have to say anything, not even look at her. I could tell by the feel of her hand that she had seen it too. This room would be our studio.

That, and its hidden-awayness, and the sun-face gargoyle over the gateway. We made an offer before we left. Something in the agent's eyes suggested he thought a joke was being played, but whether it was on us or on him I had no way of knowing.

We had our work cut out, Isabel and I, racing the countdown. The whole place needed doing and on a budget of fuck-all. She took the brunt of it, tired as she was. I spent my days teaching mediocre students how to draw from life while she painted the walls. Friends of mine, friends of hers, dropped off like flakes of skin. It wasn't simply the illegitimate pregnancy. No one seemed capable of forgetting our roles as pedagogue and pupil. The atmosphere would stiffen whenever I entered the SCR. Her peers drifted away, she was no longer carefree, no longer at liberty. We were out on our own.

I came home as early as I could. Sometimes she looked fabulous, content, her belly filling the material of her overalls. Streaks of emulsion where she'd wiped a hand on her forehead, white flecks where drips had spattered her hair. Other days I would find her sitting on the bottom rung of the stepladder, cigarette in hand, close to tears, done in and had enough of it. Nights like that I would take her down the pub, think fuck the money, get her steaming drunk, myself too, and smoke a pack of fags between us. Usually, after that, it began to feel all right again.

Then one day it was finished. We spent a few Saturdays trawling the second-hand furniture shops on the Alfreton Road, getting up early to have a shot at the decent stuff at Sneinton market on Sundays. Feathering the nest, she said. A two-week lull, the air close, muggy. Waiting for the sky to light up flash-bulb blue, the promise of thunder. A two-week lull then it happened. An ambulance took us to the General — this was years before they built the Queen's Medical. The labour ward was humid, noisy, stressed-out. A sweat shop. It took a long while, I couldn't sit still, I was mad with worry. I had no idea what could be going on in there, hour after hour, day into night into morning. I was certain only that it must have gone badly wrong. Then a midwife found me, asked if it was Mr Lyons. I ignored her assumption, told her yes, how was she, how was Isabel? And the midwife smiled and told me I had a little girl.

It was a fucking joke. A two-week-old child and the head of faculty was telling me the college no longer had need of me. The conversation got ugly. I made accusations, he said it had nothing to do with the affair. They paid me in lieu of notice. I spent the month in overdrive. Isabel was always elsewhere, in another part of the house, coping with the baby, Jessica, Jessie Lyons. Frequently the cries would reach me in the studio, Jessie's or Isabel's or both. I didn't break off, I was working like I never had before. Coffee and whisky were my only food. Sometimes, feeling myself drowning, seeing what talent I had shrinking and blackening like paper on a fire, I stole out and scored some speed. I never told Isabel. I met her sometimes, in the kitchen, in the bedroom. I knew it was her because she looked like the Isabel I had fallen in love with. But her eyes were dull, she had a baby in her arms, and I would stare at her and wonder how it had happened.

I assembled a new collection, touted it round the galleries. No one was interested. These were all dealers who had handled me in the past. I began to suspect a conspiracy. I tried further afield. No, thank you. In the end, Isabel's old boss took pity. I hired a van and installed my work in the basement showroom of his Sheffield city centre gallery. In two weeks I sold one drawing, a nude of Isabel, for thirty pounds. When I went to retrieve the rest I couldn't believe the pictures had come from my hand. A fortnight without seeing them had opened my eyes. The worst of my students would have been ashamed.

The Nottingham art scene was a small world, it still is. One of my former colleagues called round, another life drawing tutor, a guy I had baled out of a debt with a small loan, in the days when I was single, respectable, employed. It was a job he was thinking of jacking in anyway. It had become too difficult to fit round an ever more demanding timetable. The central station was on High Pavement then, just down the road from the house. Blue box-light on a bracket above the double wooden doors. The money is good, he told me, if irregular. He hoped it would help.

There was a bit of shoplifting as a lad, the occasional demo, but nothing to put me on the wrong side. I didn't like the idea, though. The police were best avoided where I grew up. But I had no choice.

My liaison was a superintendent called George Duffield. 'Mostly the work will be property,' he explained. 'What you'll do is sit down with the owners — none of them will have any photographs, otherwise we wouldn't be needing you — and talk them through their rings, necklaces, antiques. You keep sketching until they're happy you've got it right. Some of that stuff will be worth more than you or I'll ever earn, so you'd better not mind dealing with a load of nobs. Anyway, that's your bread and butter. But every now and again we'll get you in on a rape, or a robbery, or an attempted murder. There is Photofit, but no one's using it outside London, and anyway, everyone says it's a pile of shite. We'll take you through those ones to start with — you're going to be dealing with some mighty upset people. You'll have to learn the patter, get good at connecting, help them find memories they don't know they've got. There won't be many, but every few weeks you'll be doing a face. And you keep going with those till you're bloody sure you've got it right.'

As Duffield said, the property was easy. It was the faces that bewildered at first. Confronted by the seriousness of violent crime, I felt completely lost. And CID didn't hold my hand for long. Too soon I was alone with people, women mainly, who did not want to think about what had happened to

52

them. My job was to take them back, try, through an evolution of drawings, to bring to life the men who had brutalized them. At first I'd be surrounded by scattered sketches, no clear progression, not knowing whether the first, the third, or the sixth was the closest likeness. I felt wretched, kept telling myself they deserved better, someone who at least knew what the fuck they were supposed to be doing. A couple of times the victim gave up, refused to engage, saying anything just to bring the session to an end. But after a while I developed my methods, my way of building it up. Start with the hair, that's what frames a face, gives it proportion. Then the eyes, they're what the gaze locks helplessly on to. Only then fill in the mouth, the line of the jaw, leave the middle third to last of all. I will never forget the first time I got it right. A twenty-five-year-old travel agent, jumped in the Arboretum, just an indecent assault, but only because she managed to get away. We did a couple of preliminaries. Then I turned my pad round to show her the next attempt. Her skin went pale, right there in front of me. The rims of her eyes began to glisten. From then on I knew I could do it.

It wasn't often I found out whether it helped. Once my drawings had been handed to the exhibits officer, I would hear no more about the case. Except for every now and again, when George Duffield, or Mike Kidd, or your father would call round and offer to take me down the County, to buy me a drink to celebrate a result.

Inquest

'Would you please give the court your name.'

'Prakash Lal Singh.'

'And you are a sergeant with the Metropolitan Police.'

'That is correct, I am attached to the Area Six Accident Investigation Unit, yes.'

'And I believe you conducted the investigation into the accident which resulted in the death of Raymond Arthur.'

'I did.'

'Would you please summarize your findings for the court.'

'The incident occurred at approximately two thirty in the afternoon of October twenty-third. It was raining, light drizzle really, but visibility was fair, and the ambient temperature was ten degrees Celsius. There was one vehicle involved, a blue Volkswagen Polo 1.3LS, nine years from the date of first registration. The car had been travelling along the westbound carriageway of the A40 when it left the road and collided with the base of the A407 flyover. There was extensive front end damage and, at the time of my

55

examination, evidence of the use of cutting gear to the driver's door. The whole of the westbound carriageway was sealed and I conducted a thorough inspection for tyre marks. None were identified. The vehicle was recovered to the Area Six base where a detailed inspection for mechanical integrity was undertaken. There was no evidence of any mechanical failure. The accident damage was consistent with the collision pattern observed, and there were no paint traces or other bodywork deformity to suggest the involvement of a second vehicle. There was minor damage to the rear off-side wing, but the metal was rusted and I concluded that this represented an older impact.'

'Thank you. Sergeant Singh, were you able to ascertain the speed of the car at the time of the accident?'

'Not with any precision. Ordinarily skid marks will allow an estimate of the vehicle's velocity. As I said, there were no tyre tracks identified. However, from the extent of the damage, together with the fact that the vehicle struck a stationary object, I would suggest that the impact would have been at high speed.'

'Thank you. Mr Forshaw?'

[Mr Forshaw stands.]

'Sergeant Singh, I understand that bridge

56

supports are usually shielded by crash barriers.'

'That is correct, sir, but the barrier on the westbound carriageway had been removed the week before. There was repair work scheduled.'

'Does it not strike you as remarkable that of every bridge the deceased might have driven his car into he should have chosen this one location, where the normal safety apparatus had been dismantled?'

'I cannot say. I mean, surely that depends on whether he *chose* to have an accident.'

'Quite. Thank you, Sergeant Singh, no further questions.'

'Mr Johnson?'

[Mr Johnson stands.]

'Just a couple of things, Sergeant. The absence of skid marks, what does that tell you?'

'Well, simply that the driver did not brake sufficiently hard to cause the wheels to lock.'

'The car was not equipped with ABS?'

'No.'

'And your mechanical inspection, you were able to rule out any defect in the brakes?'

'Absolutely. They were in perfect order.'

'In your experience, if a driver was about to crash at high speed, would you expect them to brake sufficiently hard to skid?'

'Almost certainly, yes, assuming there was time to react.'

'And is that stretch of the A40 fitted with rumble strips?'

'It is.'

'How far from the bridge did the car leave the main carriageway?'

'I was only able to establish this from eyewitness accounts, all of which differed to some degree. The best estimate is probably a distance of some sixty to seventy metres, though there is a wide margin of error.'

'You have said you couldn't calculate the speed of the car. Taking, say, seventy miles per hour, though, how much time would have elapsed between leaving the carriageway and hitting the bridge? Would a driver who had fallen asleep have enough time to wake and attempt to brake his car?'

'I really cannot say. There are too many unknown factors.'

'But it is possible that, if the driver had fallen asleep, it may all have happened too quickly?'

'It is certainly possible, yes.'

'Thank you, that will be all.'

Part Two

Lenton

I know virtually nothing of the few years I lived here, but there is one thing about which I can be certain. Raymond John Arthur was a police officer, Sheila Imelda Arthur was a housewife. I was born on 10 December 1969 in the General Hospital. The address to which my parents brought me after leaving the maternity ward was 16 Devonshire Promenade. It's all there, incontrovertible history, written in the copper-plate script of the registrar of births and deaths for the district of Nottingham.

After a while Maid Marian Way becomes Derby Road, which rises steeply away from the centre of the city. Paul is silent, concentrating on the unfamiliar roads. Holly is patting and chatting to the bee mobile dangling above her car chair. I am lost in the scrolling scene beyond my window. We drive past antique shops, an art gallery, shabby clothing emporia dedicated to the trade in second-hand dinner jackets peculiar to university towns. Cresting the hill, we start down into Lenton. Commercial premises give way to houses that must date from the turn of

61

the last century. Three storeys high, they would once have been magnificent. Now the front gardens are weed patches, house numbers are daubed in white paint on the walls, and platoons of wheelie bins speak of multiple occupation.

What would it have been like when I was young? Dad could tell me if he were here. We go left at some lights, on to Lenton Boulevard, past an Odeon, a pub, some shops. A group of high-rises, set back from the road, towers above the roofs of the terraces. I wonder about him. Whether that was his local, whether he and Mum used to go to that cinema. Such a lot must have changed yet there are bound to be things he would recognize. I imagine the commentary if he were sitting in the back of the car right now. Ah, that's still a chip shop, is it? Hey, Zoe, did I ever tell you about the suicide we had in those flats?

It's Holly behind my seat. He's dead. Even so, for a moment I experience a powerful sense of his presence. Or perhaps I'm imagining it. It's what I half-hoped might happen, confronted by the streets he walked. There's an ancient belief that the spirit returns to where it was happiest. It's the sort of thing I'd have laughed at once, but I am no longer that person. He certainly never got to feeling like a Londoner. Quite something, really, considering how long he lived there. He grew up in the Peak District, moved to Nottingham as soon as he left school, went straight into the force. Worked his way up to detective inspector, by which time he'd married Mum, and they'd had me. So, he'd be bound to have fond memories. Most of the big things in his life happened here.

It never used to take much to get him started. He said Nottingham people were more friendly, the beer better too. I asked him once — after I'd graduated, after he'd taken retirement — whether he ever thought about coming back here to live. 'No', he said, 'why would I want to do that?' He was looking at me steadily, and I was thinking: Because you're always saying how happy you were. But then I thought about how he had no one left, how the friends he had were in London. And I don't know what I said in reply, but I do remember thinking that now that he mentioned it, I could see why he wouldn't want to do that at all.

'That's it there.'

Paul has slowed right down, the indicator ticking. The street looks alien, unfathomable, faintly scuzzy. I can't find anything to give me a sense of what might be special about the place. I feel adrift, like there ought to be significance but there isn't any. I look across to the turning he's spotted. Henry Road. At the end of which lies Devonshire Promenade.

★ ★ ★

'What do you think?'

We're standing outside number sixteen, bodies acclimatizing to the chill. Lulled by the cosiness of the car we've left our coats in the boot. I wrap my arms tighter round Holly. She is wriggling, trying to see what's so interesting. In her world such attention is commanded solely by dogs, cats, horses or other children.

The house is one of a long row of semi-detached: bay-fronted Victorian with an attic window breaking up the slope of the roof. The contents of a disembowelled black sack litter the concrete front yard. A rust-stained bike with a flat front tyre is chained to a bracket on the wall. There's a short flight of steps leading up to an open porch and a collection of empty milk bottles. Devonshire Promenade itself is unadopted, more potholed track than road. There are houses on one side only, facing out over a deserted park, which a sign behind the railings identifies as Lenton Recreation Ground.

'Awful,' I tell Paul my verdict, looking again at number sixteen. 'If I didn't know this was it . . . It must have gone down so much since we were here.'

Paul mms. He appears transfixed and I am thankful for his fascination, real or otherwise. I scan the windows, checking for signs of life, wondering what sort of people live here now, whether they know anything of the history of their home, whether they would even care. I have no actual memories of ever having lived here. I try to picture Dad unlocking that front door, Mum struggling up the steps with a pram, the sound of a crying baby. I feel under threat — something about the house, the road, the whole area. It must have been different then, better cared for, a place for families. The park behind me has swings, roundabouts, slides — two sets of them, no less, on either side of a large grassy playing area. It should have been a good place to raise a child. I'd not long turned three when we moved to London. I wonder whether they believed they'd be here for ever, whether they had once thought of having other children. What they would think to look at it now.

'Are you going to knock?'

It was something I'd said I might do. A few words with the owners, a brief connection with the present. Perhaps, if they were the

65

right kind of people, they'd invite us to look round inside. There are purple curtains drawn in the front room, elsewhere the nets are yellowed and sagging. Students, probably, or DSS. A pair of well-dressed strangers at the door, London accents, the woman with a little girl in her arms and some unconvincing story about her own long-ago childhood.

'No, I don't think so.'

Paul nods, blows into cupped hands. 'Well, have you seen enough?'

'Yes.' I shift Holly to a more comfortable position. She has ceased squirming, seems content to study the recreation ground over my shoulder. 'Shall we give her a go on the swings?'

He shrugs. 'If you like.'

We head for the nearest play area. The wet grass darkens the leather of my shoes. I have a fleeting image of myself, stumbling gait, hand in hand with a towering Dad, rushing towards these very swings as a toddler. Can hear myself breathing hard with excitement, with the effort of keeping pace with his steps. I must have done so, it would only be natural, all this on the doorstep. Back home the closest park is a fifteen-minute drive, or a battle on a bus away. I try to take Holly once a week. For much of her life she's been unable to participate, too weak and wobbly to

66

do more than be helped down the slide. Right from an early age, though, she loved it there. I used to drift around, her suspended on my front in the sling. Seeing another child racing past, or soaring back and forth in a swing, her legs would kick and she would squeak with excitement. It would humble me to think what was going on in her head, aspiring to be like them. Paul used to take her too, on his childcare days. He stopped going after a few visits, though, said it made him feel awkward, a lone male — albeit with a baby — loitering around the mums and children.

We have several goes on the Lenton slide, one of us helping her down, the other waiting at the bottom with open arms and a big grin. Her delight warms me despite the cold, but eventually she grows tired of it and stops responding. We try her on the bucket seat swing, my pushes setting up a gentle momentum. Holly's face has stilled, almost as though she is concentrating on something important. Her hair lifts and ruffles as she swishes to and fro. My heart aches at the serious way her hands grip the bar across her lap. She never wears gloves, always tears them off. Her fingers must be so cold. As she goes back and forth, back and forth, she stares past me into the distance, at nothing so far as I can tell. I get the sense she isn't enjoying herself. But she must be OK, otherwise she'd let us know. Despite that I feel compelled to entertain. She swings towards me again and I roar like a storybook lion, duck down and pretend to bite her feet. She falls away again, back down the parabola, a faint smile on her lips and her eyes on mine. I repeat this several times, try grabbing at her and tickling. Nothing I do breaks through her reserve. Within seconds, a feeling of desperation overwhelms me. I have to make her laugh. I cannot make her laugh. I am close to tears.

Paul steps forward, brushing my shoulder. He takes hold of the seat and slows the swing. 'Let's get her in the car, shall we? It's freezing.'

I stay motionless for a moment, but he's right. I lift her out and she snuggles against me. She's probably just tired. We make our way back to the row of houses where my parents and I once lived.

'Have you brought the camera?'

'Sure.' Paul loops the strap off his wrist. 'What do you want?'

I go and stand in front of number sixteen. In a few strides Paul is over by the railings that bound the park. He turns and takes aim with the Pentax, rotates it through ninety degrees, crouching slightly. I watch all this feeling conspicuous, ridiculous. If anyone's observing from inside. I shift my gaze, eyes watering in the dry wintry air, hold Holly close, her back against my breasts, facing her out towards her dad. The sun is still shining. The swings, the playing field, are empty, not another child in sight.

'Cheese!'

I glance at Paul and hear the shutter click. He straightens up, lowering the camera.

'One more,' I tell him. He frowns, but resumes his position all the same. I am sorry for him, he must be feeling foolish too. It's good of him not to make a fuss.

This time, when the shutter goes, I no longer have my arms wrapped round us. I have switched Holly on to my hip, supporting her with one hand, my other arm dangling loosely by my side.

Back in the car Paul twists the heating control up high. We give Holly a biscuit to keep her going, sit in silence for a while, the engine ticking over, warm air percolating out of the vents. Every now and then Paul clears his throat. It's just gone eleven. The visit lasted no time at all, at this rate I'll be done in a day. I thought there would be so much I would want to see, thought I'd spend ages soaking up the mood and the feel of it all. I'd hoped that by coming here I would feel connected to Dad, yet it's passed in an empty moment. It's as though I've reached out to grasp something, but my fingers have closed around thin air. We've come for the entire weekend — my choice, Paul's neutral acquiescence. I feel stupid; there's nothing here, nothing but shadows and chimeras.

Paul rests his hand on my knee. 'OK?'

I nod and smile weakly. 'Not exactly what I'd expected.'

I don't know what else to say. I imagine getting the prints back, seeing the photo of me and Holly outside that house with its rusty bike and backlog of milk bottles. This half-baked idea of visiting the world where I was born, the chance to see it for myself, to see it for Holly. It had a kind of symmetry, an appealing sense of the loop of time. The possibility of an ending, too.

'Come on,' I say. 'Let's go.'

Paul transfers his hand to the gear stick, starts to reverse back up the track.

'Where now? Rewley?'

I shake my head. 'No, let's nip into town, have some lunch. Rewley can wait till tomorrow, if we go at all.'

'How do you mean?'

'I'm not sure any more.'

He stops the car. 'Not sure about what?'

I stare straight ahead. Holly's feet are thudding repetitively against the back of my seat. She'll have a half-eaten digestive in her hand, gazing absently out the window, unaware of anything in the adult world.

'Seeing this place. It's a let-down, that's all. I'm sorry. Right now all I feel like is going home.'

'What about this bloke you wanted to see?'

'I don't know. Perhaps that's not such a good idea, either.'

'Christ, Zoe.'

'I *know*.'

There's a hot silence.

'Just drive, will you.'

Declan

As you walk along High Pavement you will reach the County Tavern. Make some time. Go through the double doors, over to the bar, order a drink, find yourself a quiet corner. It's a small enough pub, there are no nooks in which things can be hidden. Sit quietly awhile, wait till your arrival is forgotten by the people here. Once they have become reabsorbed in their conversations, their beer, their reheated pub fayre, then you can be more bold. Allow your gaze to rove around the room. No one will give you any bother, not during the day. Try to ease yourself back some thirty years. Imagine it is evening and the night outside is cold and windy. The bare floorboards will be the same, but the taps behind the bar have become pump handles. Instead of the panoply of lagers and bitters they stock only Shipstone's, Burton Ale and Guinness. The Australian lass who served you has changed sex, aged forty years, developed a broad Midlands accent. The optics are festooned with Notts County rosettes. Coal fires blaze in the twin hearths, the air is grey with cigarette smoke, and any music has become nothing more than the muttering of voices, punctuated by the clunk of the cash drawer sliding shut beneath the till.

The door opens. You feel a wash of wintry air. A young man comes in, dressed in jeans and a crew neck sweater. There are no socks beneath his canvas shoes. He pauses for a moment, as though savouring the warmth, then he makes his way, as you yourself did, towards the bar. He swaps a few words with the landlord, stands in silence while his Guinness is poured. Pint paid for, he finds himself an empty table, not far from your own.

You can be forgiven for not recognizing me. I look nothing like you remember. The lines have been smoothed from my skin, the black is back in my hair, which is longer and tousled, as though I have just got up from sleep. You study my face. There are dark sweeps in the hollows beneath my eyes. My jaw is shaded with stubble. You watch as I fumble a cigarette from its pack, break the first match I try to strike. You're not sure but you think the grip I take on my glass is too firm, the tips of my fingers blanching with the pressure they exert.

★ ★ ★

73

An autumn evening, 1971. Isabel finally gets Jessie to sleep around eight, lingering a while on the landing till the breathing becomes nasal and even. I look up from my reading as she joins me downstairs. She pours a drink, finds herself an Embassy, then collapses in the armchair on the other side of the hearth. I close my book, put it to one side, wait while she inhales smoke deeply, sends it out in a sigh, and reaches to the floor for her glass.

'All right?'

'Yes,' she breathes, and curls her legs beneath her.

We sit there, the fire scorching our faces. My eyes are on her; hers study the ribbon spiralling from the end of her cigarette. Eventually I pick up my book and continue to read.

Later, naked, we climb into bed. It is just after nine, but she is so tired. We spend a while lying there, my arm beneath her neck, her head against my shoulder, one leg drawn up and resting on my thigh. Like we used to. When she starts to talk it is not of art, no excited ideas for new work, the media that will create the greatest impact. It is about Jessie. How she discovered Isabel's hair, played with it for ages. How Jessie was so content, then within seconds became incon-solable, serial screams sawing her mother to pieces. How her face became puce with pain or fury or some raw unnamed emotion, not to be pacified by anything, not even the bottle. How it went on and on till Isabel could stand it no more, but had to stand it, paced up and down went in and out of every room upstairs downstairs helpless useless, put her down, left her, closed the door, anything to stop the noise.

As she talks, I stroke the skin of her upper arm, the rhythm of my hand quickening with the acceleration of her speech, her heart. Fuck it, I don't know. Maybe the adrenaline confuses me. Her breast against my ribs, the wiry give of her public hair as she shifts position. I draw my arm more closely around her, no longer hearing what she is saying, feel myself begin to rouse. I rest my other hand on her hip. She edges away, humid air where skin had touched skin. I turn my head towards her. She falls silent, reaching fingers up to touch my lips, then rolls over.

I lie awake for a while, her breath quietly cycling, the bed-clothes rising falling. Three months since the birth. I stroke my cheek with the backs of my fingers. The crackle of stubble beneath my nails is loud in my ear, inaudible anywhere else in the room. After a while I turn on my side and try to sleep. Outside the night is blustering. The wind that gusts along High Pavement plays the entrance to our alley like a first-time flautist, incapable of raising a note.

I slip out of bed, careful not to wake her. It is cold after the heat trapped under the blankets. I drag jeans and a sweater on and cross the hallway in the shadows. A flicked switch lights up the studio, my eyes wince with the glare. I close the door and go to my drawing board, sit down at the stool. If I manage anything it is the curving lines, the sweep of Isabel, naked, desirable, the body that once had me enslaved. At the other end of the long room stands her easel, the canvas roughed out with a grid of ochre wash, exactly as it has been for months on end, no paint ever applied.

My unsold collection leans against the wall, a solid presence, oppressing any attempt I make at fresh work. I can no longer create. Jessie. Give something a name and it becomes a person. But she is not that to me. An intense anger boils inside. She is a black hole, an irresistible demand, selfishness incarnate, devouring every part of Isabel and with her, consuming me. I don't hate her, there is no her to hate. But I do not love her, I do not want her. I crave the chance to go back, back to before, to when it was Isabel and me.

I leave the studio and make my way to

Jessie's room. Downstairs a piece of wood bursts in the dying fire, the *crack!* halting me at the threshold. I remain there, motionless, hyper-attentive as the wind and the hush resume. I have spent the day listening, straining my ears for the first tring from the phone to announce the arrival of work. I've had nothing from the police for a week. Most of what we had is spent. I enter the room, stand over the Moses basket in which my daughter lies face down, blankets tucked tightly across her shoulders. Her head is turned to one side. Even asleep her breathing is fast, the air sucked in, stripped of oxygen, then expelled along with everything else for which she no longer has need. I watch for an eternity. It would take nothing, nothing at all. A pillow, a blanket, a cupped palm. I am so impossibly strong. My hands, artist's hands, hang lead-like at my sides. She whimpers in her sleep, gives a little start, but does not stir. I cannot think what a baby could dream.

I leave her room, the house, its sleeping mother and child, and walk the short distance to the County Tavern. It is freezing out; I haven't picked up a coat. The pub is warm, welcoming, suffused with smoke and firelight. I buy myself a pint, take it to an empty table, strike a match for the cigarette that has found its way to my fingers. As I rest the glass down from my first grateful sup a voice speaks beside me.

★ ★ ★

In the corner of your eye you catch the movement. A man starts towards my table. Confident stride, jacket flapping, tie knotted beneath unbuttoned collar, half-drunk pint in hand. You see his face: handsome, strong, imbued with the glow of success. You must forgive me this. Your breath catches as you recognize your father. I know you will want to jump up, rush to meet him. I know you will want to encircle him with your arms, feel his own around your shoulders, your waist. But you cannot. He is a young man. You are a small child, fast asleep back at home, tucked up in your cot while your mother washes dishes in the kitchen below your room. You must sit and watch. If you approach, you will not be seen. If you call out, your voice will not be heard.

'Declan, isn't it?' He smiles a greeting. 'Ray Arthur.'

I know him from the station. He briefed me on a case shortly after I started — a rare maritime timepiece stolen from a specialist dealer. He's the youngest officer I have dealt with, not much older than me. I felt an

78

imposter beside him, his efficient manner, his air of accomplishment and purpose, his breezy assertion that the theft would turn out to be an insurance fraud. I never knew if he was right; I haven't seen him since.

He sits on the other side of the table.

'How are you settling in?'

'Fine, thanks.'

I don't want to talk to anyone, but I tell him fine. In the silence that follows I look around the bar. Just a scattering of customers. Most in groups, just one solitary drinker — a tart by the looks of her, waiting for trade. I don't know where he's come from, whether there are other people he can rejoin.

He nods at my Guinness.

'Quiet drink, is it?'

'Something like that.'

'Same here — working late. Leastways, that's what I tell Sheila.' He shakes his head. 'How about you? You married?'

'Yeah.'

'Kids?'

'Just the one, three months ago.'

'Ah. It's hard in the beginning, isn't it?'

I nod, like I have any idea. He reaches inside his jacket, brings out a pack of fags. Lights one, takes a brisk drag.

'I tell you. The evenings I was in here,

when mine was that age.'

'Yeah?'

'God, yes. It does get better though. She'll be two come December, Zoe, a real sweetheart. It's much easier when they can walk and talk a bit.'

'You're still in here, though.'

He looks at me quickly, as though noticing me for the first time. For a second I think he's annoyed. Then he laughs. 'Yeah, you're right. I'm still in here.'

There's a lull in which we lower the levels in our respective pints, burn cigarettes closer to their filters. Maybe it's the alcohol, I feel warmer towards him, more inclined to talk.

'So, what happened with that drawing I did?'

'The ship's clock? Yeah, we recovered that. Got a warrant to search his house — the dealer? Silly bugger hadn't even tried to hide it. I don't know what these people think we are.'

'That's what you thought had happened, wasn't it?'

He smirks. 'Didn't take a great detective. Most of what we do is patterns. He'd smashed the glass in the door all wrong, no professional would do it like that. After a while you recognize the signs. Plus he looked guilty as fuck. The only hard bit is proving what you know's gone on. Then again, it's not exactly difficult if they go and leave the goods lying smack in the middle of the coffee table.'

I smile at the idea, think back to the man I'd worked with to get the picture in the first place. I'd been taken in. He'd tied me up for hours, making me try again and again until I'd got every last detail exactly as he remembered. The curve of the instrument glass, the elongated diamonds of the hands, the size of the numerals, the brass pivots suspending it in its case. He'd been fidgety, insistent, determined to get it right. Pedantic in the extreme.

'I thought he was for real. He seemed genuinely upset to have lost it.'

'Yeah, well, you want to watch the ones who try too hard.'

'I'll try and remember.'

'Anyway, it's not your job, is it? You do the pictures, we catch the criminals.'

He raises his near-empty pint, holds it in mock salute. 'Good bit of work, that drawing. You got it pretty much spot on. Made it hard for him to deny it was the thing he'd reported stolen. Which is what he tried once we found it.'

I tilt my own glass. 'Thanks.'

'Keep turning in stuff like that and you'll

do all right.' He stubs out his cigarette, sits back in his chair. 'How are you finding it? Are you enjoying yourself?'

'Sort of, yeah. There's a lot to get to grips with.'

'It was a surprise when Needham left, he'd been doing it for years. You got the job through him, didn't you?'

'Yeah. I used to teach with him at the art school.'

'I expect the extra cash comes in handy, now you've got a kid.'

I am suddenly wary, weighing him up, trying to decide what he knows, how much Pete Needham might have made common currency before taking his leave. 'Actually, it's all I've got at the moment.'

The narrowing of his eyes seems natural enough.

'I got kicked out. Surplus to requirements.'

He nods slowly, as if processing the news. He's trying too hard.

'But you knew that already, didn't you?'

His eyes flick away, then come slowly back to meet mine. 'There's been talk.'

'And what else is the talk about?' My voice is brittle but I don't care. 'That I was screwing a student? That we're living together? That we've got a bastard child?'

'OK, keep your shirt on.' He holds a hand

up, palm out-turned. 'I'm sorry, all right? I was out of line.'

I stare at him, the flash of anger subsiding. It's not that I'm the subject of gossip. It's the way he pretended friendship. The beer, the fags, the fact of fatherhood.

He lifts his glass, drains the dregs of his pint, lands it back on the table and eyes it for too long.

'I'd best be getting back.'

I nod. 'Sure.'

He gets to his feet, picks up his cigarettes and returns them to his jacket pocket. Looks at the floor for a second, then seems to come to a decision.

'My Zoe's keen on babies, you know. Loves them. If you and your lady fancy it, you should come over one Sunday. Sheila'll do lunch.'

★ ★ ★

Your father has left; I didn't ask where he was going. He went straight outside, didn't go back to say goodbye to anyone. I will sit a while longer, eking out a second pint, which will use up what money I have. I am not good company. You should leave the County now, there is nothing more for you here. Like me, you were puzzled as to where he came from,

83

if he was with other people or if he was drinking alone. It's upsetting, I know; you'd think you'd have noticed him before, recognized your own father somewhere in the same small pub as you. But you will have to let it be.

Come back to the here and now, to daylight hours — there are other places you must go. As you walk the streets, on towards your next destination, think on that moment, the point at which Ray and I crossed the line into friendship. It didn't seem like it, not at the time. I don't know how you saw it. But looking back, that was what happened.

You and Jessie used to play together. In the beginning it was one-sided, she was too small and you would simply stand and stare, or gesture repeatedly and state over and over, 'Baby!' But as Jessie grew more aware she would follow you for ever with her eyes, fascinated by the things you could do: walk, talk, jump, dance, run. And you would rise to it, perform for her. I wouldn't call it showing off. You simply revelled in her adoration.

Those occasions, our two families together, are one way I remember your father. I would look on as you ran towards him, hysterical with anticipation, and he would catch you and throw you into the air. His hands always left your body, allowing you to fly completely free for a moment. But you never hit whatever ceiling was above you, and you always fell just a short way before he gathered you again.

I watched and I learned. When Jessie grew a little older, I would try the same. But I was always scared I would drop her, could never let her leave my grip. I felt clumsy, unnatural, my movements stiff. She liked it well enough. Laughed in the way you used to, once she knew what was about to happen. But after a couple of goes she would lose interest, want to do something else. I would stand, unable to think of anything to amuse her. She would trundle off to find Isabel, or occupy herself with some private game. Later on, things would come back to me. Your father pretending to hide, or chasing after you on all-fours. Embarrassing, but you loved it. When I went to find Jessie, to pick up where I had left off, to be the kind of father to her that he was to you, the moment would have passed.

You and Jessie played together, your father and I talked, and Isabel would be paired with your mother. She never liked Sheila, said she found her cold and uninteresting. What would they have in common, the shop girl from Mansfield and the Sheffield artist?

85

Nothing apart from children, and that, I think, was all they ever talked about. But I recognized something in your mother. She existed on the margins, holding herself in, listening, but seldom heard. I didn't know why that was, nor why I should understand her so instinctively. Back home at the end of the day Isabel would protest her boredom, would sometimes poke fun at your mother's awkwardness. I couldn't stand to hear her, it made her ugly, despite her beauty. I told her again and again: If it's that bad, you don't have to come. And she would laugh. And that laugh contained all manner of things. All the answers I would ever need.

★　★　★

The County Tavern is behind you, as it is behind me. Back then it was the closest pub to the central police station. I could go there any time and be guaranteed to meet people I knew, by sight if not by name. These days the police come in vans from the new station at the Bridewell. I hear their sirens sometimes, on weekend nights, not long after the smashing glass and the shouts and screams of the inevitable fight they have come to contain. I no longer go there. When I drink, it is at home.

The money I must have gone though. And it wasn't just money I was pissing away. When I think about all that might have been, I see it swept along the porcelain gutter at my feet in a swirling yellow stream.

Inquest

'Would you please tell the court your full name.'

'Susan Alison Powell.'

'You are a laboratory technician?'

'I am.'

'If you could cast your mind back to the events of the afternoon of the twenty-third of October. In your own words, tell the court what you saw.'

'Well, it all happened so fast. I was driving along the Westway — my son had been taken ill at nursery and I had to leave early to collect him, but this was before I'd picked him up — anyway, I was driving along and this car undertook me on the hard shoulder. I mean, it wasn't busy or anything, but he just shot past me on the inside.'

'By the Westway you mean the A40?'

'I do.'

'And you were heading out of London, in the nearside lane?'

'I was. I mean, sometimes people cut inside if you're stuck in the middle of the road, but he was on the hard shoulder.'

88

'And the car, did you notice what sort of car it was?'

'It was blue. A small car of some sort.'

'And what happened then?'

★ ★ ★

'Take your time, Mrs Powell.'

'Well, like I said, he shot past on the hard shoulder, and I just had time to look over and I think I shouted something like he was a bloody idiot or something, then he hit the . . .'

'I realize these must be difficult memories for you. But if you can continue.'

'He hit the bridge. Went straight into the side of it. I heard the noise, this really loud bang. It was awful. The car flipped up on itself, the roof hit the bridge, then it crashed back down. Something landed in the road in front of me and I thought I was going to hit it, but I didn't have time to steer or anything, so I must have driven right over it.'

'What did you do then?'

'Well, I was so shocked. It took a while to even think. I pulled over as soon as I could and called the ambulance on my mobile.'

'Now, you've told the court that all this happened very quickly, that you were very shocked, which is entirely understandable.

But can I ask: at any point, did you see the driver of this car?'

'That's the thing. When he went past me on the inside I must have caught the movement in the corner of my eye because I looked across. And that was when he was level with me.'

'And can you tell the court anything about the driver?'

'Yes, he was an old man, I don't know how old but his hair was grey.'

'Did he appear to you to be conscious?'

'Oh, yes, definitely. He was sitting right up, looking straight ahead. I only saw his profile.'

'And you're certain about that? Did you see whether his eyes were open?'

'Oh. I don't really know. I think they must have been, otherwise I would have noticed.'

'Did you see anyone else in the car? Were there any passengers?

'No, sir. I'm sure I would have seen them if there were.'

'Thank you, Mrs Powell. If you could remain in the stand for just a moment, it may be that counsel have some further questions for you. Mr Forshaw?'

[Mr Forshaw stands.]

'Just a couple of things, please, Mrs Powell. Can I be absolutely clear about what you are saying. When this man drove past you — on the hard shoulder — you obtained a brief but unobstructed view of his face in profile, is that correct?'

'Yes, sir.'

'And, as far as you are concerned, he was awake and appeared to be in control of his vehicle?'

'That's how it seemed to me.'

'How soon after that did the car crash into the bridge?'

'It can only have been a few seconds.'

'Thank you. No further questions.'

'Mr Johnson?'

[Mr Johnson stands.]

'Yes. Mrs Powell, how fast were you going?'

'I was doing about forty-five, fifty.'

'And the other car, the car that crashed? About the same speed?'

'No, sir. He was going much faster.'

'What? Seventy, eighty, a hundred?'

'I wouldn't like to say. But it was a lot more than I was doing.'

'I see. Now, Mrs Powell, we are all deeply sympathetic to the upset this terrible accident caused you, but are you really telling this court that in the brief glimpse you had as the car passed you, you were able to ascertain that the driver was both awake and in control of his vehicle?'

'That was the impression I got.'

'And this driver, he had grey hair you said. Did he have a beard as well?'

'I don't think so, no.'

'A moustache?'

'I'm not sure.'

'And, what, was he laughing?'

'No, I didn't think so.'

'Singing along to the radio?'

'I can't say.'

'Chewing?'

'No.'

'Yawning? Sneezing? Crying? I mean, honestly Mrs Powell, I don't want to cast — '

'Mr Johnson. I must remind you that this court will not allow adversarial questioning of any kind.'

'I apologize, sir. No further questions.'

[Mr Johnson sits.]

Part Three

Market Square

Despite her McVitie's sugar injection Holly has fallen asleep in the back. We find a space in an NCP and I extract her buggy from the tangle of bags in the boot. Paul lifts her from her seat, shuffling round in the confined space between the cars. She's completely floppy, insensible; as he stoops to lower her into the pushchair her head lolls back. I catch a glimpse of her closed eyes, her pursed lips. Paul rests her down gently, inching his arms from under her once she's in position. He threads her hands, one after the other, through the harness straps. Moments like this take me without warning: how fragile she is, how careful we have to be. I try to capture it, preserve it in my mind along with the hundreds of memories I already hold dear.

We set off, me wheeling the buggy, Paul consulting the map. He takes us along pedestrianized streets towards the square at the centre of the city. I haven't needed to say anything more; he seems to accept we are no longer in any hurry. We lapse into familiar patterns of late, dawdling outside Mothercare, checking out Baby Gap. I feel happier, acting like a window shopper, like a regular tourist. Paul is more relaxed too. We pick up threads from our ordinary lives, on-going musings about schools, a second child. We pass a branch of Savills, pause to browse the properties for sale — elegant town houses, a five-bed farmhouse in an acre of land — none of which is going for a huge amount more than we might expect from the proceeds of Dad's estate, let alone the sale of our London flat on top. The discovery reignites debates that have smouldered since Holly was born: where we should live, the constant juggle of our existence, the dual income necessity of the capital versus a move away, less work, more space, a garden for Holly and her putative sibling. As we talk, we arc along a crescent lined with Georgian shop fronts. Right in the middle of the fairway we find a modern sculpture, a curved granite monolith the entire surface of which shimmers and sparkles with a sheen of running water. We pause to look; the day has grown warmer, I unzip my jacket and pocket my gloves. Down the way a small crowd has gathered round a blues band busking. Paul wants to go and listen, but I worry it will curtail Holly's sleep. And anyway, I tell him, I'm starving.

We lunch at a café called Bank, a high-ceilinged building just up from the square. Drinks are served from teller points along the bar. Paul leaves us at a table and goes to order. Alone for a moment I study Holly, her cheek resting against the horseshoe cushion that supports her head. A loud laugh from across the room causes her to frown. When she wakes it will be in yet another unfamiliar place — this café, or out in the streets of Nottingham. Most places she goes to are new. She may show a passing interest but to her, I imagine, she might as well be anywhere. It's the ubiquitous constants that preoccupy her: soft toys in shops, dogs on leads, brake lights on cars, fire engines wailing. The only fixed place in her life is our flat: its layout of rooms, her cot, our bed, the TV, her toy cupboard, her bookshelf, the bath. Yet if we were to move, to take her to another home, she would soon forget, would quickly learn the new geography. All other things would remain the same.

I look away from her, over to where Paul is waiting. He is leaning against the bar, shoulders hunched, foot on the foot rail. The fingers of one hand tap repeatedly on the wooden counter; his head moves as he tracks the progress of the solitary barman. He works too hard, I know that. Most week nights he gets home after Holly has gone to bed. He tries to take her every Saturday to give me respite but I know he feels dulled by fatigue. It never shows on the outside — to me she is always delighted to see him, to be with him — but he often cites a sense of inadequacy, that he doesn't know the things to do to entertain her, the routines she is in. He had to go to the States twice last August, was out there for a week each time. He said, when he came back, that Holly looked at him as though he was a stranger.

This talk of downshifting. Before, he loved London, we both did. While I was pregnant we carried on the same: eating out or taking away, going to plays, to comedy clubs, getting a video, always going to bed hours after we should have and regretting it the next morning. The only change was I'd given up drinking. Paul did too for a while, out of sympathy, but then it crept back in, a pint here, a glass of wine there. In the final couple of months I became too tired to go out, the smoke in the pubs and bars began to irritate, I craved quiet nights in. There were books I wanted to read, plans I wanted to lay. Paul carried on almost as though nothing were different, hooking up with friends after work, staying out late. I didn't mind — we'd never been ones for doing everything together — but I worried how it would be after she was born. For me the adjustment happened gradually, pregnancy does that. For him it was a rude conversion. He accompanied me faithfully to NCT classes, only missed the one, but the things we learned were for me, not for him. Any time the tutor involved the men he'd retreat behind jokes — about handing out cigars or cutting the cord or how if it was him he'd have every form of pain relief going. There were things he said he was looking forward to, but even then he was flippant — how if it was a boy he'd take him to Highbury from age one, if it was a girl he'd fit a padlock on her bedroom door as soon as she turned fifteen. There was nothing about sleepless nights and colic and nappies and teething and all the grinding love to work out first. I really didn't know how I thought he'd react. It seems stupid now, but I can remember bracing myself for a parting of the ways. I thought. Well, it doesn't matter what I thought. The change in him has been profound.

Finally, he gets served, heads back with a glass of red and an Appletise in hand.

'Sorry,' he says. 'That took for ever.'

His voice, or the scrape of his chair, rouses Holly. She wakes with a start and a dazed cry. He releases her from the buggy, shushing her while she comes to. Catching a telltale smell he lifts her above his head, sniffs at her bum.

'Bad?'

He lowers her again, gives her a kiss. 'Poo positive.'

'Oh, and it's your turn, too.'

The mock horror on his face makes me laugh.

'I'll see if they've got a baby room.'

I trek off to the bar. Nothing doing, according to the man, who looks at me as though I probably shouldn't be out. When I get back to the table the food has arrived, and Holly is riding horsey on Paul's knee.

'Nappy facilities negative.' I hold my hands out. 'I'll take her to the loo.'

'No, fair's fair.'

He stands, hitches her on his forearm, picks up the bag. Watching them disappear inside the gents' I have a moment of gratitude — he does pull his weight whenever he can. I remember Dad admitting, the first time I took Holly to see him, that he'd never changed a nappy in his life. It was meant as a joke, him saying he'd be willing to learn, would even pack in his job if I wanted him to help with child-minding. I was having serious qualms about finishing maternity leave, about entrusting her to a nursery. But it made me realize what a different world Dad had inhabited compared with what fatherhood entails these days.

Once he returns, Paul and I take turns having Holly on our laps. We've brought a jar for her, but she's more interested in our plates. After several samples she settles on Paul's wild mushroom linguini in preference to my lasagne. The meandering chat of our stroll around town gives way to full-on Holly time: jiggling her, feeding her, keeping her hands from causing too much mess, spotting the particular pointing finger that says she wants more water from my glass. Somewhere in amongst it all we both manage to eat.

Paul finishes first. He lays his fork to rest and asks, 'So, what do you want to do this afternoon?'

I haven't considered it. I've managed to block it from my mind since our departure from Lenton.

'I'm not sure.'

What I want to say is that he was right, that the whole idea is daft, that I wish we'd never come away. I can't though. It feels like a betrayal of Dad, of the questions I need answered.

Holly is tugging at her bib, threatening to undo the velcro that's fastened behind her neck. Paul reaches across and restrains her hands.

'Do you still want to see this Declan Barr?'

The effect Lenton had on me, my romantic

notions ridiculed by the tarnished reality. I'm afraid of what Dad's friend might say, even though I need so badly to hear it.

'I better had.'

'Hol-ly!' She's started at her bib again. This time he distracts her with a scrap of linguini left at the side of his plate. 'You could cancel, you know, if you're not sure. We could do something else instead.'

'No, I'll go.'

'OK, so what shall we do in the meantime? Go round town some more?'

Holly's getting restless, leaning forward, stretching out to Paul. He hooks hands around her chest and hauls her across with a pretend groan. I watch as he gathers her to him.

'Would you do me a favour?'

He looks at me, nods once.

'She'd love a dip in the hotel pool. I could do with some space. I can't think.'

He blanks for a second, then switches his gaze to her. 'How about that, tiger?' He hops her up and down on his thighs. 'You and me go for a swim, yeah?'

He grins at her, widens his eyes, then puckers his lips into a cheek-sucking O. Holly laughs at the silly, camp face. I feel my eyes smart.

'Would that be OK?'

'Sure, yeah.' He doesn't look at me.

'You're always saying you want more time with her.'

'It's fine.' He flips her round to face me, lands her bottom on his lap. Meets my gaze, finally, over the top of her head. 'Whatever.'

★ ★ ★

When Paul moved in with me I kept it secret from Dad for months. It wasn't difficult. A couple of years after retiring Dad found himself a security job — said it had been driving him mad, having nothing to do. He worked five nights in seven so it was like we lived in different time zones. He hardly ever visited the flat, it was always me popping over to him when his rest days coincided with a free weekend. I liked going home, dropping out of things for a few hours. I could have kept it up indefinitely, but Paul wasn't happy.

'I don't see why you won't tell him.'

'I don't want to hurt his feelings.'

'Come on. The way things worked out with your mum he's not exactly going to be sold on marriage, is he?'

'That's different.'

'Why?'

'I don't know, it just is.'

'Well, I think it's wrong to deceive him.'

103

'I'm sure he'd be touched by your concern. Anyway, I'm not deceiving him. If he asks, I'll tell him.'

'But he's not likely to, is he? Not if I have to keep up this *pathetic* hiding behind the answer phone every time someone calls, just in case it happens to be him.'

It escalated into a full-scale row. Paul stormed out and went to stay at his mother's. I lay awake continuing the argument in my head, honing the things I would have said if only I'd thought of them at the time. Then I dwelled on how much his mother would have *loved* it, him turning up unannounced with nothing but a toothbrush and a tale of my unreasonableness. I had a crap night.

'I don't see why he can't accept my point of view,' I said to Sarah the following evening.

'Because you're not telling him the truth.'

'Oh. And what's that exactly?'

'You don't want your dad to know you're having sex. While you're living apart there's room for doubt, but once you move in together —'

Sarah reckoned I was caught up in an alpha male situation. Paul wanted to establish his primacy. He was now the man in my life and all that was left for Dad was a lonely limp into the bush to find a quiet place to die. My procrastination over telling him showed I wasn't ready to see him driven from the pride.

Sarah watches every nature programme going. There'd been one about lions the previous week. I said I resented the implication that there was anything sexual between me and my father.

'Not physically,' she said. 'But the emotional transactions are the same.'

'Meaning?'

'Possessiveness, guilt, fidelity, jealousy.'

'Dad isn't like that.'

'I never said he was. It's you I'm talking about.'

Sarah and I had met in a pub in the Strand. Paul was in bed by the time I got home. I could either get in beside him or fold out the sofa-bed in the spare room. He stirred as I lay down.

'How was it?' His voice was drowsy.

'Fine.'

I slid my feet over to his side, felt the heat begin to thaw my toes.

'I've been thinking. I'll go and see him. You're right, he's got to know sometime.'

I waited till Dad was on rest days, when he wouldn't be tired and vulnerable. I rang first, said I needed to come over because I had something to tell him. He answered the door with his habitual smile. I followed him through to the lounge and plunged into small talk. After a few minutes he interrupted me in mid-sentence and asked what it was I wanted to say. I had a dizzy moment, like I was about to step off the edge and abseil.

'It's nothing really. Paul's moving into the flat. I thought you ought to know.'

He stared at me for a second. 'And?'

'And nothing.'

'That's it?'

I nodded.

'I don't understand. He's been there for months, hasn't he?'

My face burned. 'How did you know?'

A smile twitched the corners of his mouth. 'You'll know too, when you've got kids of your own.'

I looked at him, shirt sleeves rolled up over still-strong forearms, thick hair neatly trimmed, twin inroads of scalp over the temples.

'Why didn't you say something?'

'I thought once you were ready you'd let me know.' He put his hands on his knees and pushed himself to standing. 'It's not a big thing, Zoe. People did it in my day too, you know, though it wasn't as common as it is now. As long as it's right for you that's all that matters. Now, do you fancy a brew?'

We trooped through to the kitchen. I sat at

the table while he filled the kettle and flicked it on.

'Actually, I thought you were going to tell me something else.' His back was towards me as he spoke, reaching to get the tea caddy off the shelf. 'Like you were pregnant or something.'

I laughed. 'Dad!'

He glanced over his shoulder, then turned to drop a couple of bags into the mugs. 'I mean, you phone up all serious and come right over. What was I supposed to think?'

'But wouldn't you have known that already, too?'

'Yeah, OK, I asked for that.'

He poured the water, fetched milk from the fridge, brought the tea over to the table and sat himself opposite.

'Anyway,' he looked down at his hands, wrapped either side of his mug. 'Are you?'

'No, I'm not! What is this?'

'Nothing. I'm pleased for you, that's all. He's a nice lad, Paul.' He raised his mug and smiled. 'Here's to you. Congratulations.'

That should have been the end of the matter. We talked some more but it was jokey, teasing. Him saying how he had some put by for a wedding if we ever did decide to marry. Me saying he wasn't getting to give me away that easily. All the time, though, I was distracted. We never talked about personal things. It was always like that; I don't remember ever turning to him as an adolescent. If I'd had a mum, that was the sort of relationship I'd have had with her. Boys and spots and hair. Throughout my teenage years Dad would, from time to time, be too busy to take me shopping and one of my surrogate aunts would be delegated the task. I'd return home with bras and knickers and sanitary towels, as well as a T-shirt or new jeans I could show him and pretend was what I'd bought. I never had a birds-and-bees talk, the way most of my friends did from their mums. Dad had a book called *Everywoman* on the shelves at the top of the stairs. I used to sneak it into my room of an evening, while he was dozing in front of *Nationwide*. It told me everything I needed to know.

I never thought about it at the time. Now, with an adult perspective, I have a better idea of what was going on. Anything to do with being a woman was kept in a separate compartment of my life, one which he never entered. But he was there in the background, pulling the strings, making sure what needed to happen happened. It established a pattern, a set of ground rules that never changed, not even after I'd grown up and moved away. Nothing ever got too personal.

So that day, for him to raise the issue of pregnancy like that was a shock. It was such a rarity, I didn't want it simply to pass. I was twenty-six. Old enough to have an adult conversation with the man who'd raised me — but not with the man who had actually raised me. Maybe it was the prospect of our relationship entering a new phase, becoming something other than it had been. When I was getting ready to go, searching my bag for the car keys, I asked him, 'If I had been pregnant, would that have been good or bad?'

'I don't know, honey. Only you know that.'

'Not for me, for you. Would you have minded, my not being married?'

He put a hand to the back of his neck, massaged the flesh. 'Well, it's not got a fat lot to do with me, has it?'

'I know. But would you have been pleased?'

He stayed silent for a moment, looking at a point on the wall.

'Angry,' he said, eventually. 'Definitely angry. You go and make me a grandad before I turn sixty and I'll have your guts for bloody garters.'

★ ★ ★

Sarah, more shaken than I'd known her in the whole of our first year at university. Sitting on my bed, nursing a cup of coffee and a Hobnob.

'How long?' I asked her.

'Four weeks, not a word. It's fucking awful — if I get him on the phone he just passes me straight across to Mum, doesn't even ask how I am.'

I drew the duvet closer round my shoulders, hugged my knees.

'What does she say?'

'She hasn't mentioned it. Carries on talking about the weather and the shortage of volunteers at the shop and the arthritis in her knees as though nothing is remotely wrong.'

'It'll pass, he won't be able to keep it up for ever.'

'You don't know him.'

She'd been home with her new boyfriend. After some awkward silences round the supper table, Matt had found common ground with her dad in the state of the England team. They discovered they'd both been at Twickenham for a certain Barbarians game a few years before, even sketched tentative plans to see a match together during the coming season. Bedtime came and Sarah and Matt headed off to their respective rooms. Once the house was quiet, Sarah padded back along the landing. She glossed over the details but I could imagine it: the illicit thrill of hitching up her T-shirt, her thigh muscles taut as she lowered herself on to him, the rhythmic creaks from the bed frame as caution got thrown to the wind. And all the while her father, disturbed by the stifled laughter, the knocking of headboard against wall, lying impotent beneath sheet and blankets. She said by the time she got up the following morning he'd gone out and didn't reappear for the entire Sunday, at least not until she and Matt had returned to London.

★ ★ ★

I find a bench by one of the fountains on Market Square. A twenty-foot column of water froths and spumes, a constant roar as it crashes down into the pool. Every now and then a gust of wind sends a fine, cold spray in my direction. The sun is warm on my face. I close my eyes and imagine I am sitting on the deck of a boat, somewhere out at sea.

Paul has long gone with Holly. I am tired of the tugs of war inside. I need some time to myself, to think things through, yet the second I off-load her on Paul I am consumed by guilt. Because it *feels* like I am off-loading, like I do not want her around. She always looks agonized, reaches out when she realizes I'm not coming with her. I hear her crying as I walk away. It's crazy, she won't notice my absence, not after the first few minutes. Paul says she's quickly back to usual form; the staff at her nursery say so too. I ache for a window of freedom yet when I have it I feel so cruel. Sometimes I wonder if I'm abnormal — I've talked to other mums from the NCT and they say they go through the same thing, but it never sounds as bad for them. I tie myself up in knots trying to work out how other people feel. Sarah says it's classic mother stuff, that I'm constantly confronting the pain of being abandoned. I'd give her more credit if she'd had a child of her own.

Paul makes it worse. When we left Bank I said I would walk to the car with them, see them off to the hotel. He told me they'd be fine, that I shouldn't waste any precious head space. The way he said it. This whole trip is an irritation to him. He didn't want to come, but neither did he want to stay in London with Holly. I cannot work him out. A whole weekend with her, he should jump at it. I'd have hated to be apart from her, but I would have if he'd wanted to stay down there. He says he dreams of going freelance, dropping his hours so he's got more time to be a dad. Yet he won't do it when he gets the chance. He says he can't go from one extreme to the other — hardly seeing her all week to having her twenty-four hours a day. The thought scares him, even though I tell him there's nothing to it. In my heart I think it has more to do with where I wanted to go, why I wanted to come here.

Stop beating yourself round the head — he has told me this a hundred times. But I can't. Dad dying, his being no more, the sifting and sorting through the contents of his house, the inquest and the wrangling and the solicitors and everything. I can go hours and hours without thinking about it. When I'm with Holly, getting her dressed, bathed, fed, changed, entertained, comforted, settled for the night. When I'm charging round to nursery, when I'm up to my neck in it at work, when I'm fixing supper, putting washing on, hoovering and cleaning, when Paul and I are slobbed out in front of the telly dying a slow death at the end of every exhausting day. But, at night, when I should fall instantly asleep, and at tiny moments in the bath, on the loo — when the merest chink opens in my day — it swamps me. Dad in the car, driving along that road. Whether or not he intended. Whether or not he saw that bridge and depressed the accelerator to its fullest extent, deliberately steering towards the unforgiving concrete. Paul says I should let it rest: that he's gone, there is nothing more I can do. He doesn't understand. I simply cannot choose to do that. Because it will not let me go. Because I feel I was the cause.

I open my eyes and let them drift across the square. People are criss-crossing the broad space, some idling, others more purposeful. A few teenage skateboarders are trying out tricks directly opposite. On the far side a solitary fairground ride has been set up — one of those ones with cars and motorbikes and horses and buses that the kids sit on and go round and round and up and down. I can just hear the strains of its music. The coloured lights are flashing, there's a huddle of adults looking on. I imagine the pride in their eyes as their precious little people whirl past. That's their child, right there in front of them, riding on a plastic pony. Except that the children are present only in body. They're smiling, hanging on tight, but their eyes are far away, no longer seeing their mum or their dad. Market Square has faded, the piped music plays. In their dream world, somewhere in the future, they're a racing car driver, they're at the wheel of a double decker, they're a top showjumper, a train driver, a California highway patrol.

I didn't make Dad a granddad till he was fifty-nine. He was full of congratulations when we told him I was expecting. Not once did he make any remark about Paul and me getting married, nor did he ever ask if the baby was planned. Paul never gave him credit for that. Holly was two months old before Dad finally met her. He said he realized I had a lot on my plate. He kept his expression carefully controlled throughout the hour of my visit, just the right amount of smiling. He never asked to hold her and I wonder if he knew how I felt whenever someone took her to have in their own arms.

Behind me is a huge neoclassical building, topped by the grey dome I could see from our hotel room this morning. The Nottingham city crest is laid into the piazza in front of it; two enormous stone lions stand sentinel beside its great columns. From inside its clock tower, a bell tolls. Three o'clock. I still have an hour before my appointment with Dad's friend. I don't know exactly where his house is. And I have sat here long enough, getting precisely nowhere. I take the Nottingham map from my bag.

Declan Barr's address is on a note tucked inside the front cover. I scan the index for High Pavement and turn to the city centre pages, to find out where I am supposed to be going.

Declan

Leave the Lace Market now, walk away from my house, past St Mary's church, along to the far end of High Pavement. You will pass the police station where your father was based and where I had my occasional desk in the corner of an office used by scenes of crime. The blue box-light is still above the double wooden doors. But the station, the former courthouse next door, the old Nottingham prison behind them, are all reborn. Red banners flap from flagpoles rising obliquely from the walls. Each bears the logo of the Galleries of Justice. I have been round several times, on days when tedium and solitude rule and I've had too much of drinking. I have studied the exhibits tracing the history of policing since thief-takers and bounty hunters gave way to the Bow Street Runners. Every facet is covered. Yet despite the wealth of detail there is something missing. You will find nothing about the artist. I was a minor player, a footnote in history. I have been replaced by Photofit, E-fit, computer-modelled facial imaging. You will not find me or my kind there.

You may not have time to look round. Museums are not, I guess, what you are interested in. Even the reconstructed trial in the former assizes — waxwork judge, lawyers, defendants and witnesses, their lines taped by actors and relayed over loudspeakers — takes a while to view. The case is from the nineteenth century, when the Corn Law riots destroyed property throughout Nottingham-shire. The three defendants were hung for conspiracy, despite no evidence of their having been ringleaders. It is billed as an early miscarriage of justice — the trial would be laughable were the consequences not so grave. It shows what a long way we've come. When it is finished you are taken through to the prison yard where the gallows were erected. One of the condemned carved his name into the wall during the weeks in which he waited to die. The deeply scored letters are there to this day.

But you want to learn about your father, his life here. Leave the Galleries of Justice unvisited, there will be time enough another day. Walk down High Pavement, on to Lower Parliament Street, up Huntingdon Street. From there, head away from the city centre, out through St Ann's along the thunderous Woodborough Road. As you pass the graffitied precinct, the prefab estates, the road starts to climb, the beginning of its long haul to Mapperley Top. At the steepest part of the hill, where your breath begins to labour, there is a grassy walkway off on the left, set back behind heavy iron gates. Corporation Oaks. If it is spring there will be daffodils beneath the trees that give the avenue its name. Turn up there — you have to be on foot as it's simply a strip of parkland — and go up, up, along the tarmac path with its benches and litter bins and its gentle curves. You can relax now, you needn't look over your shoulder, the noise is diminishing. This is no place for cars.

As you climb, cast your eyes left and right. This whole area is cheapsville, bedsit land; you're on the fringe of the red light district. But on this one, car-free avenue the Victorian houses remain family homes. The paintwork is fresh, the pointing neat, the sash windows preserved. If there were driveways you would see Volkswagens, Volvos, BMWs. You are in the heart of St Ann's, miserable giro-strewn St Ann's, yet for a characterful house, a river of yellow daffodils beyond the front gate and a traffic-free haven for the kids, the middle classes have clung on.

Just when you're thinking you can walk no more, you will top the rise. The path has brought you out on a flat summit, an unexpected open space in the midst of the city. You are high above it all, can see the grey Trent winding around West Bridgford in the distance. And next to you is a huge circular mound, its sloping walls camouflaged with grass. The corporation reservoir. Once, it supplied the back-to-backs of St Ann's, before they were demolished as slums. Now it serves the flimsy boxes that replaced them, which will eventually be condemned as the same, and similarly pulled down.

Circumnavigate, skirting south of the roundel, keeping your eye on the view. At the far side, another broad path leads back downhill to bring you out eventually on the Mansfield Road. As you descend, your legs moving easily now, you might make out the chatter of children. In fine weather, and at certain points of the day, the way ahead will be filled with green uniforms. The nearby girls' school has a small playground, break times see older pupils spilled out on the avenue, a watchful teacher near the gate. If this is so, try for a minute to imagine the path deserted. Try to picture the oaks in autumn, green turned yellow gold brown.

I don't know any of this, my involvement came much later, but these are the pictures I have in my mind — formed, as were all my artist's impressions, from the words spoken to me by true witnesses. Humour me. I want to put you in different shoes. Not for long, but pretend for a while that you are someone else, a young woman called Maggie Mortensen, tracing the route you take to work every day. It is morning — a clear autumn morning thirty years ago — and the Corporation Oaks are shedding their leaves.

Along the path ahead of you walk a man and a girl. Their hands are joined in gloved union. He is tall, an inch or so under six feet, she is two-thirds his size. He is wearing a knee-length coat that dances round his legs as he goes. She has a grey duffel, beneath which pokes the bottom of her dark green skirt. A satchel is looped around her neck.

You can hear the shrieks and shouts of children. The man and the girl draw near to the school. They're thirty yards in front, you see only their backs. Suddenly, the girl tears free, yanking her hand from his grasp. She runs, kicks at a large pile of leaves, sends tobacco flakes flying. They arc, hang suspended, then flutter down, each finding a new place to lie. The man takes hurried strides, catches the girl's arm, renews his grip on her hand. There is a little jostling, she shies away, he bends at the waist, speaks insistently to her. They carry on their way as before.

Before you reach that disturbed mound of leaves, raked by a council worker the previous afternoon, the two strangers have drawn level with the gates. You glance at them again, although you have no idea why. You see their hands disengage, then the girl runs out of sight into the school grounds. The man pauses, for no more than a couple of seconds, watching — you imagine — as she disappears into a cluster of kids gathered for the start of the day. Then he wheels around and starts briskly back up the hill. You are almost upon him, he passes before you have time to register. All you really see is the top of his head — a foreshortened impression of his face, tilted as though studying the ground — and notice that his hair is thick and parted and chestnut brown.

What do you make of it? I watch that scene, again and again, running it through my mind. Nothing about it is extraordinary. The girl breaks free, runs, swings her leg, sends carefully swept leaves into a butterfly whorl. A moment later the man has regained control. He scolds her for her thoughtlessness, though in truth she has done nothing more than will be achieved sometime later by the wind.

It is an ordinary morning. You continue your journey. Arriving on the Mansfield Road you turn left, towards Upper Parliament Street and the branch of the Nottingham Building Society where you work. For a moment you mourn the end of your sojourn amongst the grass and the trees.

Do you give them another thought, the man and the girl? No. Soon you are plunged into the business of the day, the never-ending queue of customers lined up with passbooks and cheques and withdrawal forms and queries. At five in the afternoon you make your escape. It is the same the next day, and the day after. On the fourth day you pop down to Market Square after work to buy yourself some stockings. You feel weary, decide to treat yourself to a bus ride home. On a whim you pick up an *Evening Post* from the vendor on the corner of King Street.

Do you start the paper on the bus? I don't know. Possibly you only get to look at it later, after you have made yourself a reviving cup of tea. Whenever it is, the moment you turn to page three the course of your evening alters. You read the article, read it again. What is it that gives you pause for thought? That's what I would like to know. Is it the swing of that leg, the leaves startled into flight? Or the catch of the arm, the tug of war, the few sharp words from man to child? It is probably something more mundane, the peculiarity of a man taking a child to school, the absence of any wave or parting kiss between them. You remember his abrupt wheel, his sudden galvanization as he heads back up the hill. His ducking past you, face averted. His parted hair, thick and chestnut brown. Once these things have assumed their rightful significance, the rest is easy to reinterpret.

Your phone still shares a party line. It takes endless minutes for your neighbours to finish their call. You consider going round and asking them to hang up. But even now you are not really sure. It is only a hunch, a suspicion, an inkling you are tempted to ignore. When, at last, you press the square button on the telephone and hear the burr of the dialling tone, you suddenly feel committed. Your finger finds the second to last hole and you spin the dial once, twice, three times.

Inquest

'Anthony Martin Jones.'

'And you are a roadside assistance operative with the Automobile Association?'

'That's what they call us these days.'

'I understand you witnessed the fatal accident that is the subject of this inquiry. Would you please tell the court what you saw.'

'Well, it was a complete fluke — seeing it, I mean. I was on a call-out and the member's vehicle had broken down right on the bridge over the A40. I was running some diagnostics when I heard this horn blaring and that's what made me look up. It wasn't just a quick blast, someone was really leaning on it. I looked over the parapet and the first thing I saw was this lorry, headlights flashing. It was him sounding off. I guess the Polo had cut him up but don't take my word for it — I didn't see what happened. He was carving across the road, though.'

'The driver of the Polo?'

'Yes.'

'What do you mean by carving up?'

'Across. Like he'd been cannoning down

the fast lane and he suddenly realized he was about to miss his exit so he veered across the other lanes. That's what it looked like to me, anyway.'

'There was a junction?'

'Sure, yes, the slip road. It comes off a bit before the bridge.'

'And you interpreted the actions of the Polo driver as being an attempt to reach this exit? A slip road he was about to pass?'

'Yes.'

'And what happened next?'

'He never made it. He was going that fast he only just reached the nearside lane by the time he'd overshot. He carried on, onto the hard shoulder, then I lost sight of him. Next thing I knew there was this almighty bang. I could feel it in my feet.'

'Thank you, Mr Jones. If you could remain in the stand. Mr Forshaw?'

[Mr Forshaw stands.]

'Mr Jones. I am trying to make sense of your evidence. You were in the middle of attempting to repair a broken-down vehicle when you heard a horn sounding from the road below. At which point you looked over the wall, is that correct?'

'Yes.'

'Running some diagnostics, I think you said.'

'Yes.'

'It sounds complicated.'

'It is. You can't just check the mechanics these days. You've got to assess the integrity of the on-board computer. The electrics and fuel supply can be fine, but if the engine management system's gone wrong then the whole thing goes kaput.'

'Quite. So, you were in the middle of a complicated technical procedure when your attention was diverted by the blast of a horn. You looked over the side of the bridge and saw the events you have described for us. Tell me, how much time elapsed between your first catching sight of the Polo and it disappearing below?'

'I don't know. A few seconds, maybe.'

'And in this brief interval you were able not only to switch your attention from the demanding task you were performing, but also to size up the motivations of the driver of the car that subsequently crashed into the bridge on which you stood? Is that correct?'

'I'm only saying what I saw.'

'Ah, but you're not, are you? You have told this court — and I quote — He suddenly realized he was about to miss his exit so he veered across the other lanes. That's what it looked like to me, anyway.'

'That *is* what it looked like.'

'And I suppose it couldn't have been a man who had decided to end his life seeing his opportunity and steering his car directly towards his death?'

'Well. I suppose it could, if that's what happened.'

'Thank you, Mr Jones. No further questions.'

[Mr Forshaw sits, Mr Johnson stands.]

'Mr Jones, how long have you been a mechanic with the AA?'

'Thirty years, I went into it as soon as I left school.'

'Your entire professional life has been involved with motoring?'

'One way or another, yes.'

'So you would say you are familiar with drivers and driving behaviour?'

'There's not much I haven't seen.'

'Now, my learned friend Mr Forshaw has suggested that you were over-interpreting the events you witnessed that afternoon. I am more interested in the basis of your interpretation. Could we perhaps take a moment to think carefully about the details of what you actually saw. There was a car, driving obliquely and perhaps recklessly across a three-lane carriageway at high speed. Now, presumably a number of interpretations are possible, anything from a blown tyre to the driver having fallen asleep at the wheel. Yet something made you sure he was deliberately attempting to reach a slip road. What was it?'

'Well, I don't know. I — it was rocking on its suspension. If you're going at high speed and you suddenly turn the wheel the momentum of the car will put tremendous strain on the suspension on that side.'

'I see. But that is hardly specific, is it? Was there anything else?'

'No, that's it. He was rocking pretty hard.'

'Please think carefully, Mr Jones.'

⋆   ⋆   ⋆

'No, hang on. He was indicating. I remember now. He had his indicator on.'

'Can I be clear: the Polo that subsequently crashed into the bridge was *indicating* its intention to cross the carriageway?'

'Yes.'

'Mr Jones, this is very important. Can you recall which indicator was flashing?'

'The nearside one. He was indicating to leave the carriageway, just like you said.'

'Thank you, Mr Jones. I have no further questions.'

Part Four

Weekday Cross

I leave Market Square and retrace the route Paul led me along earlier. High Pavement, where Dad's old friend lives, is away the other side of where we parked the car. I'm not expected for a while. I force my shoulders to drop; make myself walk slowly. It's hard. I am usually in such a rush. The buskers Paul wanted to listen to have gone. The paved street that had been obstructed by their audience is now like every other part, busy with shoppers, no sign that a performance had taken place there a couple of hours before.

Ray Arthur, redirected mail, treat as first class. I try to decide what I want from this encounter. When the Christmas card arrived I was puzzled. I could think of no reason why someone I'd never heard of should send Dad a drawing of an old family photograph. There was nothing to explain it, no accompanying note, nothing but an inscription on the reverse of the picture, 'Rewley Hill Top, September '72.' I had no address, no phone number, just the name of the sender and city of posting. I tried 192.com, but there were no

Declan Barrs listed in Nottingham. I left it. All I wanted was to let him know of Dad's death. It wasn't any more important than that, not then.

Shortly after New Year I got a buyer for Dad's house, a young couple moving to London from York. The man was about to start a new job so they wanted a quick completion. I'd been clearing the place gradually, but I'd concentrated on things that could be turned into entertainment for Holly: boxing up crockery and pans for charity shops, emptying the food cupboards. I'd managed to go alone just the once, to sort through his desk, identifying insurance policies and bank statements the solicitor required to sort out the estate. Suddenly, I needed to get a move on. I started to spend evenings there, once Holly had been bathed and put down. After he'd missed a week's worth of five-a-side Paul got fed up, asked why I couldn't just choose a few mementos and leave the rest to a house-clearance firm. I tried to explain the need to go through everything, to weigh and consider the value of every object, every letter, every note jotted on the back of an envelope. And there was no space in our flat simply to bring it all back there. He shook his head and went back to rubbing dubbin into his boots.

I thought my old room would be the hardest. Dad had preserved it exactly as it was when I left home, down to the LFC duvet on the single bed. There were the posters on the wall, McDermott and Hansen and Dalgleish, George Michael alongside a grinning Andrew Ridgeley. Most of the drawers were empty, but there was still the odd thing I hadn't ever thought to remove — the school shirt signed in black marker pen by every one of my long-forgotten classmates, yellowed now; a collection of hairbands from when I'd had long hair; boxes of exercise books and notes from university I would never look at again. I surprised myself. These things had languished there for a decade or more. I bagged up the surviving remnants of my teenage self and barely kept a thing.

Dad's study was different. Box file after box file of papers, receipts and guarantees; bundles of mail and untidy piles of magazines. I started sifting through, aimlessly, not sure what I was going to do with everything. At the bottom of the very first pile I found a couple of issues of *Club*. I was shocked, spent a while staring at the legs splayed on the front covers, the cheerful smiles on the girls' faces. The image of Dad leafing through them. I almost didn't carry on, was excruciated for him, the thought of how he'd feel if he knew I knew. But I forced myself to continue. Here was the archive of his existence and everything had to be examined. I put the porn mags in the first of several dustbin liners, gradually sorting from the mass of material the stuff of his life I could not let go. There was his marriage certificate, dated 30 June 1969, paperclipped to the decree nisi. And there were hundreds of cuttings from unspecified newspapers, collected in chronological order under lever arches. I skimmed through them. Not all mentioned him by name, but there were a fair few in which he was quoted. Most were from his CID era, when the cases he dealt with made good copy: rapes, assaults, murders, armed robberies in Sneinton, Radford, Forest Fields. There was also the occasional lighter moment: him doing a sponsored three-peaks challenge for cancer research, a picture of him at the launch of a stranger danger campaign in Nottinghamshire schools, a photo with a group of North Dakota officers on an exchange. The most recent file had cuttings from his time with the Met, cases connected with the IRA bombing campaign in the early seventies. There weren't many, though. Three years after he started, Mum returned to Mansfield. There were no articles relating to his eighteen years behind a desk in

136

complaints and discipline.

The photographs on display around the house were almost all of him and me. In his study were the uncensored albums. Many of the black and white prints held no meaning: weddings, christenings, a bunch of gangly national service conscripts. Apart from Dad, and my grandparents, none of the people were known to me. This patchy coverage of his youth proliferated as cameras and film became cheaper. Him and Mum on a beach somewhere, in front of a lifeboat. The pair of them dancing at a party, his hair slicked in a quiff, Mum in a dress that bloomed out from the waist. Then their wedding, a guard of uniformed officers lining the path from the church, him handsome in a morning suit, she beautiful in a way pregnant women are. And me, as a baby, cradled in her arms, cradled in his, then sitting up smiling; toddling in a garden alongside an upended trike; proudly astride a Shetland pony. And the original of that photograph, the only one of her that was allowed on display downstairs, the three of us outside Rewley Hill Top, the farm cottage where Dad had been born.

The last album rattled when I slid it off the shelf. It turned out to be a box, bound in leather-look, the fake front cover acting as a lid. Inside was a collection of tapes, some reel to reel — which I have never yet been able to play — but several cassettes. Each was labelled with my name and a period of time, Zoe Mar — May 1970, Zoe Jun — Aug 1971. It was completely unexpected; the sight of his writing. I took one at random and slotted it in the stereo in the lounge. Long periods of hiss, then a babble of baby nonsense. Or a child's laughter, or a little girl exclaiming distinct words — 'Cat! Daddy! This one! Mummy!' From time to time a clunk suggested a break in recording. There was no narration to tell me what I was listening to. In places I could hear muffled adult voices in the background, the occasional phrase intelligible: 'Go on, darling, who's this?' I sat watching the tiny wheels of the cassette turning steadily, sounds I had no memory of ever having made burbling from the twin speakers either side of the disused hearth.

Over the years familiar childhood photographs would periodically be brought out, mainly to amuse my latest boyfriend. Dad never owned a cine-camera. He never told me he had taped my earliest utterances. The writing on the labels was unmistakably his; I had no way of knowing whether it was him or Mum who had done the recording. I wondered if he'd squirrelled them in that fake album too many years ago, had forgotten they were there. Or if their presence was always in the back of his mind, along with the intention, in the quiet of retirement perhaps, to bring his little girl back to life. I sat in his lounge with the soundtrack of myself as a child of Holly's age. The thought pressed unbearably on my chest.

Those tapes reminded me, hard and brutally, that his own voice was no more. I would never hear it again. I had no recordings, nothing with which to revive the timbre and inflections, the cadence of his diluted Derbyshire accent and his deadpan timing. Even those few months after his death I found it impossible to bring them to being in my mind. I can see pictures in my head — not in front of my eyes but in some other way — but I cannot remember sounds. Paul bought a video camera when Holly was six weeks old. I thought back over the footage we'd taken, film that spanned a whole year of her life. I became quite certain that we had never used it when Dad was around. Plenty of her playing under her activity arch, me cuddling her sleeping form, the first of her being able to sit unaided, a bout of uncontrollable giggles as Paul tickled her with Snuggly Bear, the delighted splashing of bathtime. Nothing of Dad. I felt a cold anger. I had nothing for me, nothing for Holly.

Photographs, yes, but no moving image of him, of her granddad, nothing with the sound of his voice. I tried to think how it could have happened. All that time — she was ten months old when he died. I remembered bringing the camcorder once or twice, on visits I'd made with her to his house. But she'd been too fractious to spend any length of time out of my arms. I'd left it in its padded case. It hadn't mattered. There would always be another time — when she'd be more familiar with him, when she'd be happy to stay on his lap, or when Paul would be there to do the filming and it wouldn't matter if I was unable to relinquish my hold.

The tape was still playing. My babyish babbling seemed suddenly intolerable. I went over and cut the stream of nonsense off in mid-flow. I removed the cassette intending to take it back to his study. In the hallway I passed the telephone, his answer machine next to it. It had never occurred to me. It was off, had been since the day of his death. I plugged it back in and pressed the outgoing message button. There was a click and a brief whirr and then there he was. 'You've reached Ray Arthur, I can't take your call at the moment but leave a message and I'll ring you back as soon as I'm able. Thanks.' A long beep, then the cassette rewound. I played it again and again. Then I flipped the lid up and levered the tape out. In my palm, on fifteen seconds of microcassette, I had him, his voice, for all time.

We have digital voicemail at home, part and parcel of the phone. It wasn't till I borrowed a dictaphone from work that I was able to listen to it again. I did so on an evening when Paul was playing football. Once Holly was asleep I went through to the lounge and rigged up a connection to our stereo's audio-in port. I teed up a standard tape, set it to record, then pressed the play on the microcassette. His voice came from the stereo speakers, the same message, all he would ever now say. There was no beep to mark the end this time, that must have been superimposed by his machine. I let the tape play on for a bit and I sat there soaking up the rumble of nothingness. Suddenly there was a click and an electronic chirp, then my own voice came out at me, bright and cheery. 'Dad, listen, about Sunday, we're not going to make it, I'm afraid. It's Paul's mum's birthday so we've got to go there for the weekend. He did tell me, but I forgot. I'm really sorry, I'll ring you tomorrow. Hope you're well. Bye-ee.'

I was caught unawares. The room seemed to turn. There was another click, another chirp. In a rush I worked it out: I was playing through the part of the tape reserved for incoming messages. Before I could properly take it in another voice started. Female, no name given, asking Dad if he'd be able to do an extra shift on Friday. Click, chirp. The sound of a handset being replaced. Click, chirp. A male voice, distant, disembodied. 'Ray? Yeah, it's Declan. Listen, give me a call, will you?'

★ ★ ★

I pass the estate agent where Paul and I had daydreamed about a different life a few hours ago. I pause outside again, looking back over the houses we saw. The farmhouse is the one that appeals to me most. It's a handsome building, in the middle of nowhere, four miles from Bingham, wherever that might be. To either side there are open fields. I don't want to move up here, neither does Paul, there's nothing for us. But maybe somewhere closer to friends, to work. Four bedrooms, in half an acre of land, space to roam and play, away from London with its failing schools and truancy and Playstations and gangs in the arcades. Holly at nursery three days a week, so I can keep bringing in my share, Paul doing twelve-hour days. It's all right, her nursery, better than some I went to see, empty-eyed kids standing uncertainly around the edges of the rooms. At least the place she goes to feels happy, bustling. She likes it. She cries every morning when I leave her, breaks her heart. She'd hate it growing up in the country, no friends around. I would have. Paul loved Farnham. So maybe there. The price of a decent place in Surrey, though.

All this talk of selling up and getting out. We're tied to London, seduced by her, ensnared. We could never have afforded to move away, not now we've got Holly and all the desires that come ready-packed with her. Dad's will has changed the landscape, but it's thrown out as many new dilemmas as it has the potential to solve. Years ago, he gave me a copy which, superstitiously, I kept sealed in its envelope. A few days after he died I got it out. Paul was there when I opened it. Everything was left to me.

Except that it wasn't. The solicitor had a different will on file, made that summer, about which I had known nothing. There was still a bequest to me, ten thousand pounds, but the rest of the money was placed in trust for Holly. I was named as sole trustee.

I turn away from the estate agent's window and resume my progress up Middle Pavement. Sarah says I should hold off any decision. With the trauma of his dying, the bruising inquest, the legal tussles, the lack of time and space to grieve, the last thing I should be thinking about is moving. She's known me since our first day at university. She says I'll feel differently in time, or at least will be able to see things more clearly. I can find no sign of it yet. Paul keeps pushing, saying we'd be using the money for Holly. We've got to look forwards, not back; that's his watchword. He's right, I realize that, yet I cannot stand to hear him talk that way.

Middle Pavement comes out at a convergence of thoroughfares. A tourist noticeboard tells me this is Weekday Cross. I read some of the history that's written there, but take none of it in. A little further along there's an advertising casement. I glance at the poster behind the shatterproof glass. Eight children's photographs in two rows of four. A slogan: Is two minutes off your journey worth one of these lives? Eight kids, their names and ages printed below their photographs, like children's artwork: Christopher, 9; Naomi, 6; Sanjay, 4; Nicholas, 5; Jamie, 5; Katy, 4; Darren, 8; Jim, 9. Something bites into me, threatens to bring me down. The pictures are family snaps, school photographs, one passport booth shot. There are masses of curls, gappy front teeth, neat blue ties, a port wine birthmark, a soft focus studio haze. The faces grin, wide smiles, happy eyes. The girl, Katy, is beaming. But her chest is puffed up with a held breath, she's looking off to the side at someone, eyes asking, Am I all right? She is so grown up, yet she is so small. Jim's gaze is downcast. His lips are curved into a lopsided half-smile. In his nine years, is this the best they could do? I can't help it, I think of Holly, if we ever had to produce a photograph. We only take pictures when she's looking gorgeous, doing something really sweet. We bin the ones that don't turn out right. I mount them in albums, Paul flicks through them when he gets home, we hold hands and already we're thinking back through the memories. If she gets upset when the camcorder's on he rewinds the tape — her tears will be erased. Every scrap of evidence shows nothing but the happiest of girls, the baby who never cries. I start to walk, past the poster, leaving Jim, Katy and the other dead children behind. I try Paul's mobile, but it's his voicemail. I leave a message, speaking as I walk, asking him to call me as soon as he gets this. Once I've hung up I have to stop to catch my breath. They're fine, she's fine. At this very moment they're splashing around in the pool, she is laughing as he walks backwards, pulling her along in his wake, careful to keep her face above water. His phone, if it rings at all, is buried inside a changing room locker in the depths of the hotel. The thought calms me. I look at my watch. It is four o'clock. They've given me this time, or I have taken it from them. Either way I must use it well. This appointment is the one thing I must see through while I'm here. The man I am about to visit sent Dad a drawing of our family, tucked inside a Christmas card posted months after his death. There was no mention of his existence in any of Dad's papers. His was the last message left for Dad before he died.

Dad's hands clutching the wheel. The Polo crumpling as it ploughs into the base of a concrete bridge. Not knowing if his face was crazed by horror or stilled by a determination to die. Not knowing why.

High Pavement. I know what I want from this encounter. Once this is done, I can start to forget. I can start to forgive myself. I can go home.

Declan

Somehow I must take you back to that morning, to Corporation Oaks, to the girl, whose name you should know was Mary Scanlon. I cannot tell you what happened after she ran inside those school gates — I was not there, I was not witness to events. I was working in my studio, Isabel and Jessie gone out for the morning. Either that or I was locked in session with the aggrieved in some crime, drawing from their descriptions an impression of their assailant. I can only give you my own description, from which you might create a picture in your mind. But you must remember: my words are weightless. They have no substance whatever. They are informed by bits and pieces, fragments as told to me by your father, by other officers, none of whom was there to see these things either, that clear autumnal morning thirty years ago.

Nevertheless, I must find a way to take you back, however artificial. Somehow you must understand.

I am standing on the branch of a tree, one arm curled round the trunk by way of an anchor. Below me, one hundred and forty-five green uniforms form shape-shifting shoals in the playground. The children run dodge link arms, laughing shouting chanting. The girl, Mary Scanlon, is not so different from the couple of dozen others scattered around the perimeter, hugging the railings here, backs pressed against a wall there, a silent sober audience for the many. They look on, they may wish to join in, but they never do. Their principal hope is to avoid attention. Friendless, bereaved, introverted, they are natural targets for the bullies. That Mary has that morning joined them? That is not, necessarily, a crime.

The clanging of a handbell startles me. Mrs McGillivery has emerged from the classroom block. Girls and their silvery breath clouds hurry in for assembly. In go the clever, the keen, the sporty, the plain dumb, jostling at the double doors that lead into the building. Once the last of them has disappeared from view the handbell sounds again, the clapper striking more ponderously, the zing of percussed metal wavering like a mirage. Emerging from the edges come the other girls, halting and slow. I will them to hurry, can't understand their laziness. It takes them for ever to walk a dozen yards. Finally they reach the doors. As they pass

Mrs McGillivery they have to duck beneath her arm, outstretched and holding the door open with patent irony. The teacher clips each straggler on the back of the head with her free hand. The last one is Mary Scanlon. I see Mrs McGillivery hesitate. Then her hand descends the same. As the teacher's fingers connect, the girl flinches. Mrs McGillivery's voice carries to me, Scottish and shrill. 'Mary Scanlon, this is not like you! Get inside and be quick about it!'

Ten minutes into the first lesson. I am perched high in the rafters in Mary's classroom. The walls are decorated with crepe paper montages, coarse crayon artwork, the fruits of an Autumn project which consists, as far as I can tell, of a display of dead flowers and crinkled leaves. Below me twenty young heads are bowed over exercise books. With my exceptional eyesight I can see the hash some of them are making of their Monday morning spelling. I would like to help, but I cannot. Mine is merely to observe. One girl jerks upright, her arm extends, the tips of the fingers point towards me. For a moment I fear I am discovered. But then her agitated motion, her hotching on her chair, these give lie to the true emergency. The teacher sees it too. She strides down the aisle with a bad-tempered sigh. Mary Scanlon is trying

Mrs McGillivery's patience this morning. The girls are eight and nine, there is still the occasional accident, but never Mary. Never Mary. She grasps the girl's hand, half-pulls her from her seat. 'Carry on with your work, *in silence*,' she commands the others. I would love to remain, to see how closely her instructions are followed, but I must away.

The toilets are in a long thin room. I balance precariously on the partition between two stalls. Below me, Mrs McGillivery is stripping Mary of her sodden skirt. The teacher is tight-lipped and I do not blame her. Not a pleasant part of the job. The thick green wool falls to the floor, landing on the white tiles with a soft slap. I am mesmerized by its rumpled folds, the collapse of its shape. When I look back the teacher is stiff, as though gripped by a sudden pain. I follow the line of her sight and my eyes come to rest on Mary Scanlon's pure white tights. The cotton is stained crimson.

Mary Scanlon, Mary Scanlon, she sat down without her pants on.

I am not sure. *Is* nine abnormally young to enter womanhood? Could it be precocity? I think back on my own schooldays, try to remember when the girls began taking bags or pencil cases with them when they went to the loo. We must have been twelve. It was certainly secondary school. I really can't recall, but I know it was older than nine. Nevertheless I have sympathy with the school nurse. How the hell is she supposed to know? She keeps asking Mary: Is it your period? Mary sits silently on the chair, oozing blood on to the towel placed beneath her.

The school secretary appears with Mary's file. A flurry of activity produces a home phone number. I am blessed, or afflicted, with hyperacusis. The call to the Filipino maid is blackly comic. I too am unable to glean more than that the mother is in Paris. I would be prepared to back the nurse in a court of law as to the impossibility of obtaining a work number for Mary's father.

The school doctor arrives. He is a general practitioner, retained by the governors and hardly ever called upon. He is annoyed to have been dragged away from his morning surgery. I myself am tiring of proceedings. My legs are cramped where they are tucked beneath me, such is the narrowness of the space between the top of the cupboard and the sick bay's plaster ceiling. Nevertheless, with the arrival of the doctor comes the prospect of release. A swift check of the pudendum — literally, the shameful part

151

— and all will be resolved.

Oh, stop it! I finally lose patience with Mary. Her hysterical struggling, her shrieks of 'No!', her scrabbling as she tries to keep her thighs together. He's a doctor, for god's sake. I have the suspicion that she's making the most of this, that she's enjoying the attention. Manfully the doctor perseveres. His face has become quite sweaty. At last, aided by the nurse and the secretary, he manages to prise Mary's legs apart. To my untutored eye there is little of any help. The thighs are streaked with red-brown blood, dried on the skin and flaking in places. The vulval mound is hairless and white. I am surprised when the doctor straightens up and tells the nurse, 'You'd better arrange for her to go to hospital.'

'It's not her period, then?' the nurse asks, and despite my own doubts it is all I can do to prevent myself shouting the self same question. It would be so much easier for all concerned.

'No,' he says. 'Not unless girls these days have started menstruating per rectum.'

I decide to remain at the school. It might be my imagination but a sense of foreboding has descended over the buildings. The playground seems uncommonly quiet at midmorning break, the staffroom is hushed.

Around midday a policewoman appears at the gate. White moons at every classroom window observe her progress towards the main entrance. I do not know it then, but up at the hospital opinion was unanimous: no one has ever seen a tear like that from constipation alone. Accidentally or on purpose, something has traumatized that most delicate region. The girl cannot or will not talk, so enquiries have to be made of her classmates. You know how cruel kids can be.

The policewoman gets nowhere. None of the children offers any explanation. Indeed, they look so guilty I believe they must all have been in on it. This despite Mary not being out of my sight since the school day began. The officer leaves, to return to the station and confer with her sergeant.

By lunchtime a new chant is to be heard in the playground. Mary Scanlon, Mary Scanlon, she sat down without her pants on. You know how cruel kids can be.

* * *

Forgive me my games. I wanted you to know how it was for us then. In those days crime was vocal. There had to be an allegation, a victim, a complaint. I was robbed, I was raped, I was assaulted. The only silent crime was murder — and even then a dead body has a powerful eloquence of its own. Mary Scanlon, from the outset, was as quiet as the proverbial tomb.

Inquest

'You are Gordon Robert Findlay?'

'That is correct.'

'Could you explain your relationship to the deceased?'

'Ray and I were neighbours. His house was just up the road. We moved in in the same week, in seventy-two it was. We saw their removal van while we was still unpacking our boxes. Went and said hello and we'd been friends ever since.'

'And it was a close friendship?'

'I should think so. Me and Gay, we used to take his daughter in when he was working — after his wife left, this was. He was out all hours. Our boys were a bit older, but Zoe got on well enough with them. Became part of the family, so to speak. Ray did us favours in return, and over the years we got to know him well. Very well indeed.'

'In the time leading up to his death, did you notice any change in him?'

'It's not easy. He'd been doing this night work for several years — Zoe had left home, see — so we didn't bump into him anything like as much as before. Saying that, we still had him over from time to time, and after Gay died he took a lot of trouble to pop round, check how I was getting on. I'd say he was pretty tired — it's not easy staying up night after night when you're his age. I used to do shift work so I know all about that. You never sleep as well during the day. I used to tell him he should pack it in — '

'Mr Findlay, I'm sorry. If I could ask you just to focus on the question. Thinking back to the weeks or months leading up to Raymond Arthur's death, did you notice any change in him?'

'Well, yes, like I say, he seemed pretty tired. Other than that, no, not really. He was still good old Ray. Always had a moment for everyone.'

'So nothing other than being somewhat tired?'

'No, I should say not.'

'I see. Thank you. Mr Forshaw?'

[Mr Forshaw stands.]

'Mr Findlay, you said in your statement to the coroner's officer that the deceased had struck you as being rather 'down in the dumps'. Do you recall using that phrase?'

'Well, I can't rightly say. That was a good while ago now. My memory's not what it once was, you know.'

'No, quite. But I put it to you that when

you were interviewed immediately after his death you told the coroner's officer that you believed his state of mind had been somewhat low of late. I am happy to accept that you have difficulty in recalling the precise form of words you used, but do you have any recollection of what you meant by this?'

'Well, no. Like I say, he struck me as very tired, that's all.'

'And when you told the coroner's officer you believed there were family problems, what did you mean by that?'

'I can't remember ever saying such a thing.'

'Mr Findlay, I have your statement in my hand, signed by you and dated the twenty sixth of October. That is a little under a month ago. Is it not somewhat remarkable, not to say convenient, that you should have so little recollection of the version you gave at the time?'

'Mr Forshaw, I think you've got to the nub of the matter. Mr Findlay, what counsel is trying to establish is which of your statement or your testimony here today is a true reflection of your impression of Raymond Arthur in the period leading up to his death? I must remind you that you are under oath, and that to give false witness carries the same seriousness in this court as in any other. If it would assist you I can let you have a few minutes to read back through the statement you made to my officer in October.'

'That won't be necessary, sir. I stand by what I say, Ray was his normal cheerful self. I remember that policeman coming round, I didn't get on at all well with him, and I certainly didn't say the things the gentlemen there is saying I did.'

'Mr Forshaw?'

'No, no further questions, thank you.'

[Mr Johnson stands.]

'Mr Findlay, you say Raymond Arthur appeared tired. How did this manifest itself?'

'How do you mean?'

'What did you notice about him that led you to believe he was unduly fatigued?'

'Well, there was the time he and I went for a drink down the Bricklayer's Arms. He'd just finished up a set of nights, it was a little celebration for him. I went to the bar to get the second round, it took me a while to get served, and when I got back to the table he'd fallen asleep.'

'He had fallen asleep in a noisy pub? Sitting upright at the table?'

'Yes, just nodded off like, but he was definitely asleep.'

'And what did he say to you when he woke up?'

'He laughed it off, said he couldn't handle

his booze no more.'

'And when was this?'

'Back end of the summer I should say. August, September time.'

'And you didn't mention this to the coroner's officer when he came to talk to you?'

'I didn't think about it at the time. He'd had a car crash and that was all I knew. I didn't have any idea he'd fallen asleep at the wheel.'

'And that is what you think happened, is it?'

'Must have. I can't believe Ray would have done something like that deliberate.'

'No, Mr Findlay, I'm sure he didn't. No further questions.'

Part Five

Part Five

High Pavement

The road is lined by old houses: low doorways, thick walls, exposed structural timbers. The buildings merge into one another, form a long continuous row, the change from white paint to yellow to cream being the only sign of where one ends and the next begins. My pace is brisk: in all the dawdling I've allowed myself to run late. The light is fading now, the temperature has been falling steadily as the sun sinks from its shallow zenith. I check each front door as I pass: 46, 48, 50.

Look for a yellow sundial, above a gate. It's unsettling when I see it, exactly as he said. I've never set foot in this city, not as an adult anyway, yet with a few instructions I am able to pinpoint one tiny landmark. There's a chain looped through the bars of the gate, a padlock. Both look new, shiny stainless steel against the black of the wrought iron. I have the fleeting worry that something's wrong, that I won't be able to get in, but when I push the gate it opens.

I make my way along a cobbled passage. The further from the street I go, the narrower it becomes. A couple of tiny wooden-framed windows are set in the walls on either side, though how much light they let in is anyone's guess. I keep expecting a quizzical shout, a suspicious can-I-help-you? to come ringing out. There's no sign of a door. I realize I've remembered the sundial and the alley, but not where he said I should go after that. I'm almost at the end before I see that it isn't in fact the end. The passage takes a sharp left, goes another ten yards, then gives on to a small courtyard. I'm at the back of number 54. And there, to my right, facing the rear elevation of the other house, is a separate double-fronted building: white-washed render, a couple of terracotta pots — filled with cracked earth — standing at either side of the entrance. The brass numerals 5 and 2 are mounted on the black door.

I press the bell push set into the brickwork. The door opens almost immediately, as though the man has been waiting right behind it. I'm caught off-guard, deprived of the hiatus in which I'd anticipated preparing myself. I stare at him for a second or two, trying to recover my mental balance. He's looking neutrally at me, pale blue eyes on mine. His hair is short, greying; his face cautious, but not unfriendly. I force my lips into a bright smile.

'Mr Barr?'

He nods, and his features soften.

'Declan, please. And you must be Zoe.' He extends an arm. 'Come in.'

I follow him into the entrance hall and he shows me the stand for my bag and jacket. As I pass him I catch a faint smell of alcohol.

'I thought your family was coming with you?' The door must be swollen from the recent rains — it catches on the sill and he has to shove it hard to get it closed.

'They've gone swimming.' I venture a grin. 'We'd never get a word in edgeways, otherwise.'

He laughs, catarrh catching in his throat. I don't know what I was expecting. Dad was rarely out of cardigans and comfy slacks; he kept Marks and Spencer afloat. Declan Barr, even though he's around the same age, is dressed in faded jeans and a shapeless navy cotton jumper, both garments spattered with paint. His voice is deep and resonant, educated, with a definite trace of Merseyside.

'So, Ray and Sheila's little girl.' He taps a hand against his leg, in the vicinity of his mid thigh. 'Last time I saw you, you were this tall.'

It's a weird thought, that the stranger in front of me knew me as a child, knew our

165

family, events in our lives of which I know nothing.

'I don't remember you at all, I'm afraid.'

'You wouldn't, you were far too young.' He looks away. 'I was sorry to hear about your father. Ray and I were good friends once. It's very sad.'

I study his expression; there's nothing overstated, just a wistful look, the brief stillness of sorrow.

'I'm sorry I couldn't have let you know sooner.'

'You must have had so many things on your mind. I rang him, you know — it can't have been that long afterwards. There was never any reply. I didn't know what had happened.'

'No, well.'

'How's your mother? Is she all right?'

I hesitate, shake my head. 'Didn't you know? She left years ago. We're not in touch any more.'

'Oh, I'm sorry. No, I didn't know that.'

We lapse into silence. I shift my weight from one foot to the other. Suddenly he straightens, holds a hand towards me. 'Look, why don't you come and sit down?'

He leads me back through the house, along a corridor running beside the staircase. As we go he says over his shoulder, 'You were up here for the weekend, you said?'

'Yes, we're staying at a hotel. On Maid Marian Way?'

'OK, yeah.'

'I wanted to see the city Dad lived in. He was always saying how happy he was here.'

We reach a doorway. I catch a glimpse of stripped boards, a huge rug, a scattering of furniture. The room is surprisingly big, given the compactness of the house from the outside. He turns to face me.

'Tea, coffee, something stronger?'

'Tea would be lovely.'

'Good, I won't be a minute. Make yourself at home.'

He reaches round the door frame and switches a light on. As he heads off for the kitchen, I start to do as I am bid. There's a sofa and chairs by the fireplace, but before I get more than a few yards I am arrested by the sight of the walls. They are covered with framed pictures, hung so close together there is barely any space between them. I change course, over to the corner of the room, and start to examine the paintings. They're portraits mostly, watercolours and oils, a few in charcoal, some big, others tiny, dwarfed by their frames. There are numerous subjects, anonymous faces. But as I go round, the same woman crops up again and again. She's beautiful: fine bones, clear skin, dark wavy hair, large green eyes. In one picture she's sitting on a swing, shading herself with a hand. In another she's lying naked on her side on a bed, making no attempt to cover herself. Then she's dressed in black, standing in a doorway, a cigarette and an amused smile on her lips. Again, she appears in profile, perched on a stool in front of an easel in a cluttered studio.

It's obvious they're his own work, but even so — I don't know — it's like I've never seen real paintings before. I have, of course, but only in galleries. You go to anyone's house and all the art work is prints and posters. Dufy, Doisneau, Monet. Here I am in this man's living room and all around me are paintings and drawings done by him. And they're good, too. It's so impressive, to be able to do that and hang it on the wall and think: that's mine. They're so lifelike, so solid, the colours so full. This woman is almost breathing, as if she could walk off the canvas. There's the odd one done much more sketchily, just a collection of curves and lines, but she's still there, definitely. And that's exciting, how a couple of dozen brush strokes can contain the essence of someone. Maybe it's because there are just so many pictures of her, this one face looking out at me from these different scenes and moments in time. As I progress round the perimeter of the room I feel a powerful sense of awe. During our phone conversation some weeks ago he told me he'd known Dad when he worked as a police artist, back in the early seventies. I don't know why, but I never thought that meant he'd be a proper painter.

On the far wall, a child appears. First the woman is standing with a baby in arms — not looking at the infant's face as in the classic pose; she's gazing out into the room, her frank expression echoing that in the nude I saw earlier. Then the little girl, about Holly's age, is pictured alone, viewed from above, sitting on a floor with her arms upstretched. I stare at this one for ages — the perfect subtlety with which she's been captured, her eyes, every nuance of expression saying, *please* pick me up, I want a carry. There are other pictures of her as she grows, turning into a girl, a teenager, a young woman. She's her mother's daughter, no doubt about it, same vivid eyes and lustrous hair. I'm looking at her graduation portrait — her evident embarrassment at the mortar board and gown, the scroll in her hands, almost exactly as I was in the photograph of my own degree ceremony — when his voice comes from behind me.

'That's Jessie. You used to play together.'

I turn to find him standing in the doorway, a steaming mug in either hand. I hadn't heard him come back. I feel guilty, not knowing how long he's been watching me, edging slowly past his paintings.

'I'm sorry.'

He misunderstands my apology. 'Jessie, my daughter. She was a year or two younger than you. She was your biggest fan.'

He comes to join me, hands one of the mugs over. 'Did you want sugar?'

'No, that's fine, thanks.'

'That's you, there,' he says, nodding at another painting. Two toddlers, holding hands, standing barefoot on the grass in front of some sort of waterfall. I'm the taller one, my legs poking out of swirly patterned shorts. It's definitely me, so similar to the skinny girl of Dad's photograph albums. Declan's daughter still has her puppy fat, bow-legged and chubby, dressed only in yellow T-shirt and terry nappy.

'You'd been paddling. That's Chatsworth, Capability Brown's water staircase.'

'I don't know what to say. I mean, they're excellent. I just had no idea I was going to find myself on your wall.'

I take a sip of tea, trying to get my head around the existence of this painting.

Completely unexpected, yet it makes perfect sense. I feel winded. I want to ask if he's got any of Dad. The sight of me as a child has hit like a physical blow. If I'm here, Dad must be. A picture of him I have never seen. I want desperately to know if there is one, yet at the same time it scares me. I'm not sure how I'd react to the sight of his face, rendered true to life by this man's hand.

Before I can decide to ask, he turns away, walks over to the hearth. There's a pile of ash glowing in the grate, almost burned out. I watch as he takes a log from the basket, throws it on, then another, each impact sending sparks shooting. Then he settles into one of the armchairs. I go to join him, leaving the paintings I have yet to see.

'So,' he says, once I've seated myself. 'You were coming yesterday, you said. I thought about you — the weather. I didn't know if you'd make it.'

'It wasn't the best journey ever, but we got here in one piece.'

'And what about your daughter? How old is she?'

'Holly? She's fourteen months. She was fine, she slept all the way.'

He nods slowly, drinks from his tea. I try to think of something to say. I remember the paintings on the wall behind me.

'Do you have any — grandchildren, I mean?'

'No, no. Not yet.' He looks up and smiles. 'I'd like to have met her — Holly, you said? Ray's granddaughter.'

'I'm sorry. It was a spur of the moment thing. I thought it would make things easier.'

He waves a hand. I can't think of a way out of the small talk. There's history here, hanging in the air between us. He must sense it too, I'm sure of it. We talked briefly on the phone, the second time I rang his number. When I told him of Dad's death; when I said I was planning to come to Nottingham; when I asked if I could see him while I was here. He shifts his position on his chair, places his mug on a side table. From somewhere beneath his sweater he produces his cigarettes, casts a glance in my direction. I smile as if to thank him for checking. He lights one, slides the lighter back in the packet with the rest.

'Now then,' he says. 'Flattered as I am that you should want to visit, I imagine there's something you wanted to talk about.'

★ ★ ★

In the days after Dad died, once my letters to the people in his address book were posted, I

172

went on a pilgrimage. There were a few friends of his I simply couldn't notify in writing: the surrogate aunts and uncles of my childhood, neighbours who for years had helped him by looking after me. The Bedfords lived next door but one, the Findlays were at thirty-five, and the Jacksons had the house backing on to ours. Following Mum's departure, those previously casual acquaintances of my parents became integral parts of my life.

There was no discernible pattern. From one morning to the next I was never sure where I would end up having my tea. Best of all would be back home with Dad, his caseload allowing an early departure from work. He never cooked anything resembling a meal, it was always something on toast. Often, though, he'd deposit me elsewhere, escorting me to the door, extracting a promise to be good, then kissing my forehead before ringing the bell. I'd be ushered in by Sue, Gay or Biddy, Dad giving them a hurried word of thanks over my head before returning to the car and driving back to work. I used to steal a last look, the old Variant pulling away from the kerb, Dad's wave a vague movement inside. Then the door would be closed, cutting him off from my sight. I'd be offered a squash and a biscuit, and

173

encouraged to relinquish my coat.

It never occurred to me to wonder about those arrangements. When you're a child, other adults, the things they do, are simply facts of life. You never question why Bob and Gay should be happy to have you. Why it is you go to them and not some other family up the road. It never occurs to you to ask yourself whether they like having you round. You simply accept their presence in your world. They're always nice, always enquire how your day at school was, did you fancy toad-in-the-hole for your supper, would you like to watch *Blue Peter* while they're getting it ready? You notice they speak differently to you; that when they talk to their own kids they use a completely different tone. But you don't know what pity is, and you wouldn't recognize the sound of it even if you did.

I must have been hard work. My life had been set violently churning. Mum was no longer there for me, my house was no longer somewhere I could always go. Dad was busy, invariably in a rush to get somewhere, to get something done. He maintained the same light-hearted chatter as he drove me around, honoured the rituals of bath and book and goodnight kiss once he finally reappeared and took me home. But his sentences would sometimes tail away; or he would lose his place in the story; and he often failed to hear the things I wanted to know.

I can see myself. The thin little girl with the serious face, sitting on the edge of the Findlays' sofa, glass of squash in one hand, untouched Rich Tea in the other, staring at the telly. George and David sprawled on the carpet in front of me, lost in the antics of Val and Pete and John. And Aunty Gay coming in from the kitchen during a break in the cooking, bending down near my ear, saying in a gentle voice, 'Zoe, love, *do* please let me take your coat now. Your dad won't be back for a while longer yet.'

I wasn't like that for ever. I remember being out in their garden on a summer evening, helping the boys while they tinkered with their bikes. Other things: Monopoly by gaslight during the power cuts; Uncle Bob teaching me cribbage while we ate an entire box of mint Matchmakers; the three of us kids doing painting at a newspaper-covered table. By then I was quite happy. But I'm a lot older in those memories. It must have been a long haul for them, the Findlays, the Jacksons, the Bedfords, settling the six-year-old girl from the broken home into their own. It's hard to imagine why they did it. A sense of neighbourliness, I suppose. These days it would be after-school clubs, childminders, nurseries. There are only a few people I would entrust with Holly — Paul's mum, Sarah, a couple of friends from the NCT. But they all live miles away. I can't think of a single person in our road I would dream of asking to take her in. Hurried greetings in the street, periodic moans about the residents' parking, they're not exactly the fabric of community.

I decided to go to see Dad's neighbours in person after he died. I didn't feel up to it for a few days and by then they'd heard the news. It was awkward at first, but once we got past the first exchanges they invited me in, expressed their sympathies, got choked on memories. The conversations rambled, drifting from what-was-I-doing-now into reminiscence. Holly prevented the atmosphere getting too grim, unaware of anything beyond the fact of new people fussing and smiling over her. And when she decided she was bored and started to agitate for a change of scene, it gave me the perfect reason to leave.

Even so I stayed far longer than I intended at the first two houses. I'd left the Findlays till last. By the time I got there it was nearly five and both Holly and I must have been tired. Uncle Bob answered the door. As soon as he saw me he stretched out his arms, as if I were the lost little girl of years ago. I think he'd have hugged me, were it not for Holly perched in the crook of my arm, peering up to see who it was we were visiting now. He stopped short, let his arms fall to his sides.

'Zoe, love, I'm so sorry about your dad. How are you? Are you all right?'

I stepped in after him, followed him to the sitting room where I'd spent many hours as a child. We talked about the accident, the shock of Dad dying, the person he had been. After a while, when it was still just Holly, Bob and me, I asked him, 'Is Gay not around?'

His head jerked back. 'Didn't you know? She passed away in June. Never came home from hospital.'

The instant he said it, I dimly remembered being told. Dad sitting on the other side of the picnic table on his patio, the back garden bathed in sun, a can of Tetley's in his hand. Sometime in summer. Holly, much younger, suckling eagerly. Feeling embarrassed to be doing this in front of him, worrying about her getting sunburned, anxious that the spare breast pads were in the change bag in the hall. Struggling to keep my shirt from flapping open, angry that Paul wasn't here to help. Dad told me then, I was sure of it. You remember Aunty Gay, don't you? She had a stroke a week last Sunday. I could picture him saying it. I couldn't recall what I said in reply; couldn't remember a single other thing about the conversation. What came back was Holly fidgeting as she fed; my preoccupation with keeping her in position.

'Oh, Bob, that's awful. I didn't know. I'm really sorry.'

Despite the lie it was difficult to gloss over. The conversation became filled with stilted exchanges and the silences of loss. A short while later and Holly's patience was exhausted. I made grateful excuses and Bob carried my bag out to the car. Installing Holly in her chair, ensuring the safety harness was clipped snugly around her, I had a few moments to think things through. It explained something that had puzzled me, why David, Bob's son, had been one of the witnesses to Dad's new will. Why Bob's signature wasn't accompanied by that of his wife. I felt mortified by my memory lapse. All I could think was to make a decent exit. I closed the passenger-side door, turned to him and on an impulse planted a kiss on his cheek.

'Sorry to rush away. I'll come again soon.'

It was a couple of weeks before I managed to return. Paul had taken Holly to his mum's for the afternoon so I was on my own and it was a much better visit. By then the insurance companies had written to the solicitor, giving notice that they'd be contesting the claims. Bob and I spent some time discussing it and it made things easier, having something concrete to talk about. He shared my disbelief that someone could think Dad would take his own life. The sense of a common enemy helped us escape the discomfort of our previous meeting. Tea was made and drunk. When he returned with a fresh pot I summoned my courage.

'Bob, I wanted to ask. Dad got you to witness a will, didn't he?'

'He did, love. David came round specially. Back in August it was, if memory serves.'

'Did he talk to you about what was in it?'

'He mentioned a couple of things. Haven't you got a copy?'

'No, I have. It's just. Well, before that, he'd left everything to me. Now it's been put in trust for Holly. I feel embarrassed saying it — it's not the money, I don't care about that. But it hurts. If he'd talked to me about it, it would have been fine — it's so generous, giving her that start in life. It's the fact that he never said. I don't understand. I know it sounds silly, but I feel I must have done something to upset him.'

Bob looked at me for a moment. 'No, I don't think it was anything like that. He made you a trustee, didn't he?'

I nodded.

'Well, then. He wouldn't have done that if he didn't still think the world of you, would he?'

It made sense. It didn't help. 'Did he say anything? Did he explain?'

'No, love, I wouldn't know. I didn't like to ask.'

I'd hoped he could shed some light on Dad's thinking, what was in his mind. The will felt like a rebuke, a rebuff from the grave. I didn't know what I'd done, only that it felt like I deserved it. Sometimes the agitation would well inside, an intolerable desire to have him hold me, tell me I was forgiven. Only he never did. He never could.

Later, at the car, Bob held out his arms, as if remembering the hug he'd wanted to give me when I'd first called round. I accepted his embrace, feeling strange.

'That daughter of yours, where's she off to today?'

The thought of Holly setting out on a trip by herself. 'Her dad's taken her to her grandma's.'

He nodded. 'She's a smashing kid, got her mum's good looks. Ray was very proud of her, you know.'

I managed a smile. 'Thanks.'

180

'And how is he, your fella?'

'Paul? Yes, he's fine.'

'Good, good. Well, Zoe, don't leave it so long, eh? It does this old man the power of good to see you.'

I promised I wouldn't. He stood in the gateway while I got in the car. Then I drove away, leaving him to return to his house alone.

★ ★ ★

'I had a mail redirection on. Any post got sent to me. I wanted to ask you about that picture, the one of us at Rewley. Why did you send it to him?'

This is the first time I've told him that I know about the Christmas card. It wasn't something I wanted to say on the phone. I can sense his indecision. I don't want any of that — what I want is a straight answer.

'Mr Barr?'

'I'm sorry. It was nothing really, it was just my way of . . . Except he never got it. I didn't know about the accident, not till you rang.'

'I don't understand. Your way of what, exactly?'

He's smoked the cigarette right down. He stubs it out and drops the butt in the ashtray.

'You get to a stage in life — I have, anyway

— where you spend your time looking back. You can't understand what you did with it all. The years passed so quickly, it feels like they only lasted a few weeks. Everything was so pressing at the time. Now you're left with a handful of memories, the moments that shaped the course you took. That's what it boils down to in the end. None of the rest of it mattered.'

He runs a hand over his head, brushing the close-cropped grey hair; he briefly meets my gaze. He seems to realize he's making no sense.

'Rewley was a special place for Ray — you know it was where he was born? He used to take us for picnics there, you and Jessie, your mother, Isabel and me. I admired your father. That picture was my way of letting him know. It's difficult to explain. He would have understood. I don't think — '

'Mr Barr. Declan. Please.' I shake my head, trying to clear the confusion. 'Dad is dead, he crashed his car into a motorway bridge. He cannot explain anything any more. I am trying to understand what happened, but every way I look I feel I failed him somehow, I feel it was my fault.'

My laugh sounds edgy. 'I'm really sorry to lay this on you, I don't know you at all, but I need your help. I know Dad spoke to you just before he died. What I don't know is what he said. Then you send him a drawing of that picture, the one that was on his mantelpiece, right by the chair where he always sat, for as long as I can remember. Can you not even *try* to tell me what it means?'

He sits in silence, staring at me. I hear myself swallow. I feel ashamed of my outburst, but I fight the urge to apologize. I must find someone to help me.

He draws a breath. 'I don't know where you got the idea I'd spoken to him.'

It takes me a moment to readjust. I can't believe what I'm hearing. 'I *know* you did. I heard you on his answering machine. I — '

He sits forward abruptly. 'I don't know what you're implying. I haven't heard from Ray in years — all right? I left him a message? So what? I can't possibly remember every last thing I did.'

'Why are you doing this?'

He gets to his feet. The movement is abrupt. I look up at him, get a sudden impression of the power that's there in spite of his age; the breadth of his frame beneath the baggy sweater. My grip tightens around my mug.

'Doing what?'

I try to make my voice sound firm. 'Lying.'

He starts towards me, holding his arms

183

out. 'Look, I realize you're upset — '

Hot tea slops on my hand as I stand.

He stops, seems to check himself. He's a few feet away. I can hear a whisper of wheeze on his breath. His hands fall to his sides, fingers clenched into the palms. I am fascinated by them. Then I force my gaze upwards, meet his eyes, refuse to allow mine to leave them. Finally he breaks contact, looks away.

'I'm sorry, I've got nothing more to say. I think you'd better go.'

★   ★   ★

By my third year at university I had run up a four-figure overdraft. I had my grant, but Dad was earning enough to reduce it by sixty per cent. Student loans had only just come in, a few hundred a year. He always paid his full contribution, plus top-ups whenever I came home. It was never enough. I did feel guilty sometimes, drinking and dancing and eating out and travelling, largely at his expense. But it never made me change my lifestyle. Once I started work I would have the money, I would sort out my finances then. I wasn't the only one thinking like that. Sarah's debts were twice the size of mine.

I had to go and see the bank manager when

I went five hundred into the red. She sat me down next to her and produced a long printout — reams of raw data that represented the activity on my account. Every sum was there, together with the identity of the transaction: TGI Friday, Leicester Square; Next, Camden High Road; ATM, Bishop's Stortford; Taj Mahal, Holloway Road; ATM, Teddington. Even payments and withdrawals made abroad during the previous summer's trip to the States. She said my spending was out of control. I agreed. She authorized a further five hundred pounds and told me to make sure I did well in my finals.

The ease with which my life could be traced stayed with me. The call at the cashpoint in Bishop's Stortford, made during a weekend over at my then boyfriend's home. The curry in Holloway, paid for, but only partly eaten, the end of our relationship. The ATM in Teddington, a retreat back to Dad's to get away from it all. I could take off on a whim, trek out to some random place, not tell anyone where I was going. But the moment I needed money, or paid for something, there would be a record, a sighting, and my secret would be no more.

That evening — the day I borrowed a dictaphone from work — Holly sleeping in her room, Paul out at five-a-side, I let Dad's

185

answer machine tape run on after my message, after that left by Declan Barr. There was a succession of snatches of other calls, a few words from one person cut off by someone else, in turn recorded over. From time to time my own voice recurred, isolated fragments, impossible to tell what I had been trying to say. Messages, layered on top of each other over and over again, the tape constantly rewinding once dad had listened to the collection of calls made during each of a thousand absences from home. Eventually the jumble ended with a man telling Dad the disk drive he needed to repair his Amstrad was no longer made. There was a final electronic chirp then silence.

Mine was one of three messages recorded the last time Dad had used the answer machine. I remembered ringing him, the day before he died. I never called the next day because before I could a policewoman arrived to tell me my father had been involved in a very serious accident. I know he listened to it because when I went round to his house the display on the answer machine said zero. I switched it off and pulled the plug before I left. Which meant that the last message Dad ever received was from the man who later sent him a drawing of a picture of our family outside a derelict Derbyshire farm cottage nearly thirty years before. A man whose number Dad would somehow be expected to know, despite it not being in his address book.

The solicitor had all the documentation in his office for probate purposes. He didn't ask why I wanted the final phone bill. I took it away with me to look at later, when Holly was not commanding the greater part of my attention. I did so in the evening. Paul wanted to know what I was after. I told him I didn't really know.

The bill was itemized for national calls, but not for local, which made things easier. The dialling code for Nottingham is 0115. In the entire quarter Dad had made two calls here, both to the same number. Both were in the week he died. One was short, thirty-six seconds. The other was made on the morning of the day of his death and lasted forty-four minutes.

I didn't call till I was at work the following day. Something about the anonymity of the office. The phone rang three times then an answer machine cut in. The voice, the accent, difficult to place, possibly Liverpool, or Irish, I didn't know. 'This is Declan Barr. All media enquiries please contact Derek Jewell at APS Pictorial. Otherwise, leave a message after the tone.'

★ ★ ★

Dusk on High Pavement. I walk fast, away from the alley, the gate, its padlock and chain, the yellow sundial. My legs are shaky. I'd expected — I certainly didn't expect lies and an abrupt dismissal. I am more confused than ever. For the first time since Dad's death I am also afraid. The lunch things in the kitchen, the pornography left in his study — everything told me Dad had no idea he was about to die. Yet the more I seek answers the more uncertain I am — about the way he died, like that, then.

I could come back with Paul, demand answers. But everything feels unpredictable.

The streets through which I hurry are busy. The presence of others should comfort me. Instead, I'm unsettled. Normal, ordinary people, just like those back home: work over, shopping finished, business done. Yet they are not the same: they inhabit a city I do not know, the geography, the prejudices, the culture of which are alien. I know nobody, cannot know where they have been, where they are going, what they have done or intend or fear they might do. I feel under threat, I wish with my whole being to be back in the hotel with Paul and Holly, those who know and love me. My legs do not feel as though they can possibly carry me there. Ahead, a cab is parked at the kerb. I climb in and state my destination, pull the door firmly shut, sink back and fasten the seat belt around me.

Declan

There is no need for you to remain in Corporation Oaks. Everything you should see here has been seen. It is quite a way to your next destination. Perhaps it's cruel of me, making you travel this journey on foot. But I want you to walk these streets, feel the hardness of the pavements beneath your soles, see the poverty and wealth, the optimism and despair that coexist in this city. As you go let me tell you something first-hand, something concrete after all the intangibility and confabulation.

The first day. Your father comes late in the afternoon, even as the inaudible echoes of a chant are expending themselves against the walls and fences that delimit the deserted playground. Mary Scanlon, Mary Scanlon, she sat down without her pants on. I know nothing of that, not then, not when he strides into the kitchen ahead of me, hooks his jacket over the back of a chair and sits down heavily, drops his cigarettes on the table.

'Isabel around?'

'She's upstairs, bathing Jessie.'

He nods. 'I've got a cracker for you. How's your Tagalog?'

I hold a match to the ring beneath the kettle, turn the gas up high. 'Sorry?'

'Tagalog — the indigenous language of the Philippines.' The way he says it makes it sound like a quotation. 'Don't worry, we'll have an interpreter by tomorrow.'

I sit opposite him, accept his offer of a smoke.

'What a fucking day.' He waits for the nicotine to hit home. 'That prep school on the Oaks? Girl there, nine years old, gets taken to the City Hospital this morning, blood pouring out of her arse. The medics can't explain it, the girl won't say anything, and the uniform boys at Arnold spend till mid-morning *fannying* around trying to get hold of the parents to see if they've got anything to say on the matter. Everyone's hoping it'll be down to constipation or something. It turns out the mother's a singer and she's abroad. And get this, the dad's only Harry Scanlon.'

He taps ash on to a saucer in the middle of the table then checks my face for signs of recognition.

'Brubeck, Scanlon and West?'

I shake my head.

'Lucky you. As soon as the duty inspector

twigs the connection he kicks it straight in the direction of CID. And guess who's picking up referrals today? I tell you, I've had that many roastings from this girl's dad.'

The kettle comes whistling to the boil. I get up to turn it off, spoon some tea in the pot. He continues talking while I'm sorting out milk and sugar.

'We track Scanlon down at the magistrates' court, inform him his daughter's in hospital. He has to get his case adjourned before we can drive him over. He's in a right state. All the way there I'm trying to calm him down, telling him she's not in any danger, that as soon as he gets there she'll likely explain. She's had questions from doctors and policemen all morning, what she needs is her dad. Thanks.'

I set his tea down in front of him and take my seat, wait while he blows across the surface and drinks. 'And?'

'That's just it, at this stage we don't know. She's in a side room so we give Scanlon a bit of time alone with her. I kept telling him to keep his cool, that if she sees he's upset it'll only make things worse. Pete Vardy and I are standing outside the door and it's all quiet for a minute or two. Then we hear the girl crying. The nurse insists on going in, so I bring him out. The daughter's hysterical.'

He's finished his first cigarette, fishes another straight out of the packet. 'Nice one, Harry, I want to say. But I don't know how I'd have handled it, not if it'd been Zoe in there.'

He goes quiet, alternating mouthfuls of tea with lungfuls of smoke.

'And did she say anything, the girl?'

'Nah.'

'So where do the Philippines come in?'

'Yeah, OK. So, we haven't got a clue what's gone on. Arnold have sent a WPC down to the school and she's trying to get somewhere with the other kids. Scanlon's in no fit state to go back to court so we drop him home. I promise to let him know the minute we find out anything. I've not been back half an hour when he rings me. On fire, he is. The girl, Mary, when her mother's away she gets taken to and from school by the maid. Harry's gone and given her the third degree. To start with she says she walked Mary there as normal, but when he presses her — and, believe me, you don't want to be pressed by Harry Scanlon — she admits she and Mary were up by the reservoir that morning and a man approached them. She swears he used Mary's name, that she seemed to know him. The maid's got five words of English but somehow she decides he must be a teacher or a family friend or something, even though she's never seen him before. The next moment the man's flapping his hand like she's to go home. He's well dressed, Mary seems at ease with him, so like the good illegal immigrant she is she does exactly what she's fucking well told.'

He lets a long breath out. 'Scanlon's fucking furious, says his daughter's been buggered right in front of our eyes. I drove straight round, tried to interview the maid myself, but my Tagalog's not exactly up to Harry's standard. There's an interpreter coming from London first thing. I want you to come with me. I'll take her statement then you get this bastard's face. If it was someone the girl knew, Scanlon should be able to identify him straight away.'

★   ★   ★

That much is certainty, fact; you have it straight from the source. But now we must return to the realm of speculation. Imagine it is night. The near-absence of sound roars like a seashell in your ears. You stand motionless beneath a street lamp, the faulty bulb flickering orange on the scene. The road is empty, it is two, three, four in the morning. In front of you the houses are shadowy hulks. What lights are visible are those left on inadvertently by the last to retire, or the bedside lamps of children afraid to sleep in the dark.

A rectangle appears in the wall of the building directly opposite. You focus your attention; someone has woken. The curtains are shut, blocking what would otherwise be a perfect view of an upstairs bedroom. From time to time a human shadow is cast on the fabric. Male, female, one person or more, it is impossible to know. How long do you stand watching? Long enough for someone to pack a case, to pull clothes over cotton pyjamas, to make a final check that what possessions there are have been safely stowed.

The light is extinguished. You remain absolutely still, afraid almost to breathe. In your mind you trace the movements: the soft click as a door is tugged shut, the careful tread along a hallway, the slow descent of a flight of stairs. You have judged it well. Below the blacked-out window another light appears, the perfect circle of the stained glass set in the front door. Which opens. A figure emerges, closes it behind them, starts along the path towards the gate, heading straight towards you. You step swiftly to one side, behind the thick trunk of a plane tree. The footsteps are metronomic in the stillness of night. They grow loud, then begin to recede.

Their owner has walked within ten yards.

Even so, by the time you decide it is safe to reveal yourself the figure is far from distinct. It is a woman, of that much you are certain. She carries a suitcase or some sort of large bag in her hand. As she hurries along the pavement she passes repeatedly beneath the street lamps that stretch in line down the hill. In the pools of light she is clear, but for whole stretches, in the dimness that lies between, she becomes no more than a vague shape. At times you are not even sure she is there. Light, dark, present, absent, the pattern repeats itself, the figure diminishing in size with every apparition.

★ ★ ★

Isabel answers the door. From where I sit in the kitchen I can hear your father's voice, low as he talks to Isabel, the tone and volume changing as he addresses himself to Jessie, held in her mother's arms. I get to my feet, put on the jacket that has waited with me the past hour, and pick up my case with its sketch pads, pastel sticks, charcoal, cotton wool.

When I get to the hallway there's no interpreter; he is alone. He sees me over Isabel's shoulder, breaks off from what he is saying. As I approach I sense something different about him, something changed in his face. It is only when he speaks that I realize it is the absence of the confidence that usually defines him.

'Forget it,' he tells me. 'The maid's gone — sometime over night. Scanlon called this morning in a towering rage. I've been over, there's nothing left, she's cleared her room.' He rolls his eyes. 'I am in such deep shit.'

The following days see a gathering momentum. Every child and teacher is formally interviewed. Doors are knocked along Corporation Oaks and the other roads on Mary's route to school. Doctors, lawyers, dentists, justices, journalists — every male acquaintance, colleague or friend of the family is subjected to questioning without regard to status or affront. Ports and airports are monitored for a trace of the maid. She has vanished, swallowed into the maw of another anonymous city according to your father's best guess. A child psychologist is enlisted, pronounces Mary's condition traumatic amnesia: months of work before they can hope to get anywhere. The laboratory confirms the presence of seminal fluid on the pants she wore that day.

At six or seven every evening your father calls for me. A pint at the County before returning to the incident room. Day two becomes day three becomes day four. I don't know what time he finally goes home, or whether he even does. He is absent from your life for days on end. Every night, once he has left for the station again, I remain in the pub, drinking, leaving Isabel to cope with Jessie as best she can.

On the night of the fourth day he tells me, 'We've gone public in the *Evening Post*. 'Girl Abducted Near Reservoir.' Nothing too specific — we can't identify the family — but it might turn up something.'

We drink and smoke. He says they thought they'd found the maid in Leicester but it was a false sighting. He's distracted, hurries his beer, stubs his cigarette out half-finished.

'Right, I'm heading back. That phone has got to ring.'

I watch as he slips his coat on and leaves the pub, steering people to one side as he carves a way through the crowd. Left alone, I take my time over my pint. When it's finished I buy another. A pair of strangers ask if they can sit at the end of my table. I stay there, eavesdropping on their conversation. The minutes pass, become an hour, longer. I'm marking time so the house will be silent when I return.

'There you are.'

Your father startles me. I look up to find

him standing beside me, his coat still on. He's out of breath, his face shiny with sweat.

'What's the matter?'

'Bingo. Building society clerk, lives up Mapperley way.' He stays standing, ignores the curious looks from the others at the table. 'She cuts through the Oaks every day, saw a man with a girl on the morning in question. Says there was something odd about them, the way they were. I've talked to her on the phone — she got a look at him — not a good one but it might be enough. Can you see her in the morning?'

'Sure,' I tell him. He's buzzing, animated after the leaden air of the past days. He makes no move to sit; seems to expect me to get to my feet. I leave my unfinished pint on the table, follow him to the door, out on to High Pavement where the night sobers me.

'Ray, did you come straight to the County?'

He casts a glance, walking fast. 'No, Isabel said you weren't back yet. I figured you must still be boozing.'

★ ★ ★

At the end of the Oaks you will reach the Mansfield Road. Turn right, walk past the general cemetery, along the side of Forest Fields where every October families flock to

Goose Fair seeking fun and thrills on the rides. Before you know it you will be in Carrington. Any of several side roads will take you into Mapperley Park, where the professional classes huddle in leafy isolation. It doesn't matter which turning you take, all roads lead steeply uphill, all will bring you out eventually in the estates of Mapperley itself, which is where you must go next. But if you should choose to walk up Tavistock Drive, look for the house for sale. There should only be one, properties here are so desirable they rarely make it on to the open market. This house was unsold the last time I was there and it will remain so for some time to come, till memory has faded and it becomes mere bricks and mortar once more. There's no need to dwell — in time I will bring you back. You might want to remember, though, so you will find it easily when you return.

For the time being you must keep going till you reach the Woodborough Road again, a long way further up than when you left it for the Oaks. This is where the hill tops out on Mapperley Plain, where a young building society clerk called Maggie Mortensen lived thirty years ago. Her house was on Breck Hill Road, I cannot remember the number. Go and stand outside five, or fifty, it doesn't matter. Whichever house you pick, let us say that is where she had her home, where I went five days after Mary Scanlon was found bleeding over the varnished wood of her half-size classroom chair.

Maggie Mortensen was twenty-two. She'd be in her fifties now. I wonder if she ever thinks back, whether from time to time she dwells on the memory of the morning when she chanced to see the man with the child. She must do, it was probably the biggest thing in her life. One phone call, made in a spirit of uncertainty, then she was caught in the whirlwind. Your father, quizzing her for three hours, going over her statement again and again, trying to squeeze any detail, however small, that would give them a lead. She seemed bewildered by the time I got to see her. I recognized something in her eyes, the wideness there: part fascination, part horror at what she has allowed herself to become involved with. That was my look too, eighteen months before, in the weeks after I started in the job. The sudden exposure to the filth of what people will do. In time I became habituated, it became routine, as it had done for your father. Except for the occasional case, something that cut raggedly to the core. A nine-year-old girl. A six-foot tall man. Ramming his cock, tortuously veined, again and again into her arse. Pulses of semen slung high into her rectum, later to mingle with her blood and trickle silently on to the pants that should never have ceased to cover her.

Maggie Mortensen was not a good witness. It had been a fleeting look, his face was turned to the ground. I always start with the hair. Chestnut brown. Parted. I drew. Yes, like that. How long? Over his ears? No, I saw his ears, it was shorter than that. OK, what about his eyes, did you see his eyes? No, I'm sorry, he was looking down.

You get what you can. The face is never an exact likeness. People think it is, think my job is to capture true to life. When they see an artist's impression, they assume it must be what the person actually looks like. All it is, is an idea. Something to jog the memory, to prick the conscience, to stir suspicions. If it is anything like him then it might just be the last piece in someone's jigsaw, the confirmation that was all someone required. It could be a wife, lover, mother, colleague, friend. Someone who has noticed unexplained blood, uncharacteristic behaviour, strange comments. It doesn't have to be an exact likeness.

I filled in the missing details. So what if the eyes weren't right? So what if the foreshortening of Maggie Mortensen's view had distorted the proportions of his nose, his chin? I had done this before, not to such a degree, but I had done it. The face only has to be so good.

People cannot tolerate silence with strangers. Even if I am patently occupied with my work they feel they have to fill the void between us. As I finished off my drawing, Maggie Mortensen talked. She didn't really know what it was that had made her look again, what it was about the man, the girl, the way they were together that had jarred. It was awful, everyone taking her so seriously when she herself was full of doubt. It made her feel responsible, like she had to help, like she had to come up with something. She wished she had never made the call.

When I had done, I turned the pad round, showed her what I had drawn. I do not pay attention to what people tell me. I watch the perfusion of their skin, the dilation of their eyes, listen to the rate of their breathing. She remained completely calm. 'Yes,' she said, 'that looks a lot like him.'

Your father was back to his usual form. Now he had something — a witness, a likeness — his faith was restored. I showed the picture to him before handing it into exhibits. As usual, he checked it for immediate recognition — habitual offenders were well known. Even though the features did not suggest a name he remained undaunted. He'd spoken to the editor of the *Evening Post*, secured a promise to run it in the next day's editions. He was confident of success.

'She wasn't good, Ray,' I warned him. 'Didn't really see him at all. Most of that is improvised.'

He laughed, glanced again at the face staring blankly up from his desk. 'You're too hard on yourself, sometimes, Declan. Wait till tomorrow. A pint says we get a call before last orders.'

★ ★ ★

I finished with the police around the time your father took you to London. I had done enough with my own work by then to be able to manage. And I had no one else to support. I still sought regular money — there was something about never knowing how long it would last, what little success I had achieved. I never returned to the school of art and design even though the memory of my affair, the pregnancy, our illegitimate child had faded. Perhaps I should have. Time was moving on, morality changing. There would come a point when what Isabel and I had done would pass without comment. The

204

world would have different things to worry about, other transgressions to deplore. The past can never be judged by the way we live now.

I did find other teaching. Life drawing is popular in evening classes and adult education. I do some to this day, part of the assortment of jobs that keep me going, though the income is nothing to what I earn working the big, newsworthy trials. My students are at a different level from those in the school of art — many of them can hardly draw, they're attracted to the class more by the prospect of naked models than any artistic aspiration. Even those with technical ability rarely manage to reproduce on paper the face and the body displayed before their eyes.

A particular difficulty is outline. It baffles many. The harder you study a person — the more exactly you try to work out the relationships between curve of cheek, line of jaw, slope of neck — the more you are condemned to fail. You simply can't do it, the angles are too subtle. I teach students to look beyond their subject, to concentrate instead on the shapes the model's outline cuts from the wall behind. It's amazing what a difference it makes. All of a sudden you are dealing with triangles, rhomboids, semicircles; other more complex shapes, yes, but still things that are solid, things your eye can perceive. I would go so far as to say that the key to life work rests in learning to look beyond the subject you have determined to draw.

★ ★ ★

It's late. I'm sorry, I have walked you for mile after mile, chasing fleeting moments and imaginings. You must be tired. You simply cannot manage this in a day — I thought you could but I was wrong. It's not your fault: you are strong, willing, you have shouldered everything I've thrown at you. But you will have to return, tomorrow, if you can find yourself somewhere to stay the night here. There is a trip to the peaks of Derbyshire, the splendour of Chatsworth House, a visit to the top of Rewley Hill, a return to Mapperley Park. Memory and association are like that. Coming at random, gatecrashing their way into the mind, fickle and empty-handed yet impossible to be rid of once there. Don't worry, tomorrow you can take taxis, drive your own car if you have it with you. You will fly around, flitting from place to place, pausing just long enough to divine the implication of what you see.

For tonight, though, an end. Force your muscles to make the one final short walk, to the top of Breck Hill Road, past rows of anonymous two-up-two-downs, one of which, Christ knows, is actually where Maggie Mortensen lived those years ago. At the T-junction you will be on Plains Road and a number 50 green 'n' cream will carry you the several miles to the city centre. Alight at the terminus on King Street, you'll recognize Market Square from the beginning of your journey. The best place to find accommodation at short notice is around the station. Cross the square, heading south. It is perhaps six, half-six. The glut of workers has seeped away; the shoppers who thronged these streets are safely home. There are few people around and those who remain are in a hurry to leave. It will be an hour or two before the new tide washes up drinkers and clubbers in search of the frisson of danger that a night on the town can bring.

But Market Square is not quite deserted. Corner of Friar Lane, Market Street, King Street, Exchange Walk, every few hundred yards there is an upright metal box, a flyposter bearing the day's principal headline clamped beneath a criss-cross of metal wire. By now, the stocks will be depleted, but there will still be a pile on top of each stand, heavy stones weighting the stacks of *Evening Posts* against sudden gusts of wind. The city final rolls off the presses in huge numbers, rarely to be sold out, and the men in fingerless gloves have not yet given up trying to part company with a few more copies.

Stand still. Listen. In a succession of echoes their cries come rolling to you from ever increasing distances along the length of the square — E'en Po! E'en Po! — like the alarm calls of birds warning other creatures who fear predation. E'en Po! E'en Po! No two are precisely the same — each vendor has honed his contracted pronunciation over decades. This is their life's work, their reason for being; their haunting cries have hawked the news down the generations.

One more effort of imagination then I promise you can rest. Market Square, the day after I made my drawing from Maggie Mortensen's few remembered details. The news stands bear no headline that evening — instead there is a face, my artist's impression of the man with the child. E'en Po! E'en Po! He stares out from behind the diamond weave of the retaining wires, gazing fixedly at the scissoring legs of passers-by, unblinking, refusing to meet anyone's eye. Such is the vagueness of his features none of the thousands who glance at him feel even a glimmer of recognition. Yet at the same time he is disturbingly familiar. No one who sees him can resist the uneasy sense they must know him. As late afternoon gives way to early evening the cries of the vendors cease one by one, first King Street, next Exchange Walk, then Market Street, until the alarm call issuing from Friar Lane is the only sound to be heard in the vastness of the square. E'en Po! E'en Po! Then he too falls silent. For only the seventh time in its history — and VE Day numbers among them — the city final has sold out.

Go on, now, away with you. Find yourself somewhere to stay for the night. As you fade from sight, no more than a mirage in the future, I am in the County, a brace of empty pint glasses on the table in front of me, waiting for your father to appear with news of the appeal in that day's paper. Nothing important will happen, I assure you. You can retire, you will miss nothing. Yes, he will come, but there will be no progress, not that day. All right, stay if you really want, if you are so desperate to see him again. But do not blame me if you are tired, unrefreshed, come morning.

I am at the bar, buying another pack of Embassy, when Isabel and Jessie arrive. You will not, perhaps, understand. Women are commonplace in pubs, but not so children, especially not in the evening time. There is a falter in the murmur of conversation when they enter.

I am still young. I do not understand what has become of the life I briefly had. There was an infatuation, an insatiable lust, then a dissolution of everything in the birth of a girl. Now she appears before me, borne in the arms of the woman I once loved beyond reason.

'Come home.'

It is not a beseeching. A command. I face up to her, feeling the weight of eyes on me. Jessie smiles coyly from her position straddling her mother's hip, as though I were someone she should be pleased to see.

'I'm waiting for Ray.'

Ray Arthur, who will any minute appear, drink a pint before returning to the incident room, not seeing his daughter, his wife, from one end of the week to the next.

'Come home.'

I shake my head. Raise my Guinness to my lips. She turns, leaves the County, Jessie peering over her mother's shoulder, her smile fading as I shrink in stature with every step Isabel takes. The door opens, closes. They are gone. From one or two places around the bar comes muffled laughter. Mike Kidd, who has been drinking with colleagues, walks over and offers to buy me another pint. I feel queasy. I accept with a cheerful grin. I have no stomach for it.

Nevertheless it is drunk by the time your father eventually arrives. He walks straight to my table, notes the ashtray, the froth dried on the sides of the empty glasses. His expression is more annoyed than anything.

'Pint?'

He has lost his bet. The drink he buys me muddies my mind, loosens my limbs, fills my bladder, dissolving anything I would recognize as myself in a stinking yellow stream.

'Nothing,' he tells me, taking a seat. His tone is bitter. He nods a greeting towards Mike Kidd and the others from CID.

'Nothing at all?' I try to control my tongue, make my speech clear.

'Not a fucking thing.'

★ ★ ★

I said you would miss nothing. There will be calls, plenty of them, but they are in the future. Tonight, there is disappointment, yet also still a guttering optimism. Someone, somewhere, must surely look at my artist's impression and be set wondering. It may take a day or two before they decide to pick up the phone. Tonight that could still happen. Tonight there is room for hope.

I leave the County at half-ten. I have long since lost your father, have no idea where he went. I have seven pints inside me and I am past caring. I trudge, ataxic, through the streets of the Lace Market, the crisply chill night preferable to returning home. The pub door closing, blanking Isabel and Jessie from sight. The muffled laughter from around the bar. I walk, a man without purpose. I stay out for an immeasurable time.

Where are you? Bored by the spectacle, tired of my drunken self-pity, you have drifted away. Had I been in any fit state I would have warned against. Out of my ambit your body has no mass, you are free of gravity, at the mercy of the wind. Gusts blow you this way and that. You become disorientated, lose your sense of time and place. Yet, remarkably, you are not frightened. Instead, you begin to experiment. A single exhalation arrests your momentum. A flick of a hand alters your trajectory. You rejoice as you make each new discovery. Emboldened, you spin on your axis, perform tumble turns like a swimmer, swoop like a swallow through the night. The Lace Market is a toy town beneath you. You dip and weave in and out of buildings, marvelling at the precision with which you can control your flight. Exhilarated, you start to take corners more sharply, zoom directly at roofs, soaring high at the last moment, rough brickwork just inches away as you clear the smokestacks. A narrow alley is an irresistible challenge, you take it in one long dive, emerging from the end in a deafening rush of air.

When you slap against the glass there is neither sound nor pain. Your weightless fingers grasp the wooden frame — an instinct, a protection against injury should you have been liable to fall. Through the window you make out movement in the gloom. The silver light is soft, it takes a moment before you understand that the pale shapes are human flesh, rising and falling gracefully. As your eyes adjust you begin to distinguish male back and buttocks, the female thighs that clasp them. You are faintly amused, at the same time uncomfortable. You are torn between staying and going. Before you can make up your mind, the man's dipping motion takes on an urgency. What was leisured becomes rapid, frantic, absurd. Repulsed now, you make to launch yourself into the magical air. But before you do the man arches his back, rears up on his arms, abandons himself to pleasure. I'm sorry. You should never have had this perspective. For a few seconds your father's shadowy profile is clear. The muscles of your hands cramp. Spent, he rolls to one side, mooning at you one final time. Disjointed limbs coalesce into a woman. Further from the window, at the limit of the vague light, her features are barely discernible. She is slim, though, and her hair is the wrong length and style. She is nothing like your mother.

Your grip fails, you float to the ground like an autumn leaf. You land on the uneven cobbles with a jolt. I'm sorry. I said you should go. I told you to turn in, to get some sleep, to ready yourself for the day ahead. At the time I meant it. There was nothing more to show you of that night, nothing I witnessed or even heard account of from one who was there. What you have just seen has no more substance than your ethereal acrobatics. Yet I have no doubt as to its truth. Perhaps you will eventually share that view. It is no fault of mine if you are unrefreshed come morning.

$\star \quad \star \quad \star$

Isabel is still up when finally I return. I find her in the kitchen, staring vacantly into space from behind the table. She is hunched forward in her chair. I cannot recall what I saw in her, cannot equate the defeated figure

214

before me with the vibrant artist who once had the world at her feet. I am spoiling for a fight. I stand there, leaning against the door jamb, acid burning my heart.

'Don't you ever embarrass me like that again.'

The words sound all wrong. I am so completely pissed, I should turn and go. She sits up, drawing her shoulders back. Stares at me with narrow eyes. Through the mist of alcohol I recognize that I have mistaken her for someone else, for a broken woman who has forgotten how to dream.

'I'm sick of this, Declan, do you hear? I've had enough.'

She's strong, stronger than me. I perceive it — dimly, but I do see it. But the waste of it all, the plans we had, the prison this place has become, the stranglehold on my work, the gridded ochre wash no paint applied not now not ever.

'You've had enough? I've had enough. Why don't you fuck off and leave me alone?'

She's fast to her feet, looming up at me before I realize what she's doing. She's almost past when I lurch to block the doorway. We collide. I knock her sidewards. She staggers but keeps her feet. Starts towards me again.

'Don't you touch me.'

She's not so strong. My hand in her chest sends her reeling back, the sudden movement sets the room rotating round me. I don't see where she comes from, there's an impact against my side then the cold tiles beneath me. A kick thuds against my spine, then another, her voice screaming, 'You fucking *fucking* bastard don't you ever touch me again.'

★ ★ ★

I am not proud, I offer no excuses, I merely record. I am not the same person I was then. What I did not know is there are different kinds of dreams. I have Isabel to thank for the learning of that lesson. I see myself in a cauldron, stewing and sweating and burning my hands on the hot metal as I struggle to haul myself over the side, unaware of the first thing beyond my own pain.

Why did she come to the County that evening, bringing our bastard child with her, telling me to come home? I thought it was because she needed me. It gave me a vicious thrill to repel her. I was punishing her, night by night, for the mess my life had become. Only later did I understand that she had been punishing me too; understand that in

216

her fierce, proud way she had made me an
offer that night, which I repulsed with a blow
to her chest. A blow which sent her reeling
and which set the world spinning for me
also.

Inquest

'You are Doctor Avril Ferguson?'

'Yes.'

'You were Raymond Arthur's general practitioner?'

'I was, yes.'

'For how long?'

'He first registered with the practice twenty-eight years ago.'

'Could you tell the court about the deceased's medical history?'

'Ray Arthur was what we call an infrequent attender. His notes amounted to a few sheets, he didn't consult from one decade to the next. There's nothing unusual in that: unlike women, fit healthy men have little need for doctors till they reach later life.'

'And when did Raymond Arthur last consult you?'

'May I refer to my notes?'

'You may.'

'Well, I saw him twice this year, once on the thirtieth of July, then again on the nineteenth of October.'

'And what did he come to see you about?'

'The July appointment was for difficulty

218

sleeping. I've written: 'Says can't sleep, but NB shift work. Appetite poor, admits to feeling low. Divorced, lives alone. No suicidal ideation. Mentions daughter, granddaughter. Impression: depressed. For amitriptyline, fifty milligrams at night, increasing one hundred and fifty milligrams three weeks, supply one hundred tablets, fifty milligram. See two weeks.''

'You diagnosed depression in July?'

'He had classic symptoms.'

'And the medication you prescribed, that is an antidepressant?'

'Yes.'

'Doctor Ferguson, you will have heard discussion earlier in the course of this hearing as to potential side effects of the drug. Do you have note as to whether it caused any such effects in the deceased?'

'Well, to be honest, I was surprised he was found to have any in his bloodstream at post-mortem. When I saw him in October he told me he hadn't ever taken any.'

'Do you know why this was?'

'Patients are often suspicious of drugs, antidepressants especially. It's probably more common than we think, people not taking the medications we recommend for them.'

'Would his depression have got better without?'

'It might have. It hadn't, though. When he came back in October he was a lot worse.'

'In what way?'

'I wrote: 'Depressed. Won't talk. Denies suicidal ideation, but fleeting thoughts. Plan: encourage amitriptyline (not used). Refer psychiatry. See three days.''

'I'm not clear from that exactly why you thought him to be a lot worse.'

'Well, when I saw him in July, I enquired about self-harm. That's a routine question in anyone with a depressive illness. He hadn't had any thoughts at that time. He talked a bit about his work and family, and I was reassured that he felt he had things to live for. When he came back in October there was still no suggestion of concrete plans, but he did admit to having fleeting thoughts about killing himself.'

'Is that why you referred him to a psychiatrist?'

'Yes, that and the fact he hadn't taken treatment. Older single males are a high risk group, especially if they're experiencing thoughts about violent methods of self-harm. I didn't want to take any chances.'

'You asked him to come back in three days. Did he?'

'No. October the nineteenth was the

last time I saw him.'

'Did you not try to contact him when he didn't keep his appointment, given your level of concern?'

'Well, in an ideal world I suppose I would have. But it's very rare I would do that in practice. There simply isn't time.'

'Thank you. Mr Forshaw?'

[Mr Forshaw stands.]

'Just one thing, Doctor Ferguson. I realize you haven't recorded this in the notes you read out, but do you recall the nature of these 'fleeting thoughts'?'

'I'm not sure I follow you.'

'Well, I think you used the phrase 'violent methods'. What did Mr Arthur say he had thought about doing?'

* * *

'Doctor Ferguson?'

'He said sometimes when he was driving, things would flash into his mind. Pictures of himself dead in a crashed car.'

'Thank you, Doctor Ferguson. No further questions.'

[Mr Forshaw sits. Mr Johnson stands.]

'Doctor Ferguson, if you believed that a patient was going to commit suicide, what would you do?'

'I would have them assessed for compulsory admission to hospital under the mental health act.'

'You didn't do this for Raymond Arthur?'

'No. In my judgement that wasn't warranted when I saw him.'

'And if you were really very worried about someone — not enough to section them, but enough to keep you awake at night — you would chase them up if they failed to keep a follow-up appointment, wouldn't you? Your working life isn't that busy, surely?'

'If you put it like that, I suppose I would, yes.'

'In a nutshell, we can assume — good doctor that you are — that Mr Arthur's momentary ideas about being dead were not sufficiently serious to make you believe he was about to act on them. In your own words, you referred him because you didn't want to take any chances. Is that a fair summary?'

'It is.'

'So, either you were right in your judgement that Ray Arthur did not represent a significant risk, or you were negligent in your management of him. Which is it?'

[Adjournment. Dr Ferguson consults representative of the Medical Defence Union.]

'Now, Doctor, which is it?'

'I am advised to tell you that an assessment can be wrong without that implying any negligence whatsoever on the part of the medical practitioner.'

Part Six

Maid Marian Way

'Mama called the doctor and the doctor said, 'No more monkey business bouncing on the bed!''

I open the door to find Holly, Paul's hands wrapped round her chest, jumping up and down for all she's worth on the hotel kingsize. He's finishing a verse from one of her favourite songs, though which of the five bouncing monkeys has just bumped their head I'm too late to hear. She catches sight of me over his shoulder and breaks out in a beaming smile, flinging an arm in my direction. Her delight is expected, but his pleasure takes me by surprise.

'*There* she is! I told you she wouldn't be long.'

The pair of them are grinning, arch conspirators. The air of excitement infects me, enveloping me after the chill dusk outside.

'Well, someone's been having a great time, haven't they?'

We meet in the middle of the room, Holly reaching out towards me, eager for a cuddle. The feeling as she fits herself snugly in the crook of my elbow, rests a hand on my shoulder, her little body a radiator of heat and energy against my side, I know I've come home.

'Hello, sweetheart,' I say to her. 'Good swim?'

'Brilliant, wasn't it, tiger?'

We both laugh as Holly nods her head vigorously, her expression switching to one of earnest contemplation, as though she's actually giving the matter serious thought.

Paul slides an arm round me, hugs me briefly. 'How are you?'

'Fine, yeah. Glad to be back.'

'Good to have you back.'

He's on a high. I've seen him like it before, when he's spent time on his own with her and it's gone far better than he'd hoped. When he's like this it makes everything feel good. I wish I'd been here too, having fun with them, a family together, instead of out there in a world I do not understand.

'They start dinner at six. I thought we'd take her with us before bed.'

I nod, realizing my hunger. There's barely time to get my coat off before we're heading down in the lift. Paul talks excitedly, telling me about their afternoon, the things he discovered she loved doing in the pool. His evident pride at the basics he's accomplished

228

— the juggling act of simultaneous changing, the constant invention of games — prickles slightly. If he manages a successful few hours it is somehow worthy of congratulation. It never occurs to him that I have to do it all the time. I know he's not trying to run me down, that it has everything to do with how uncertain he feels. Even so, it irritates, threatens to discolour the relief of being back with them after the gathering night of the Nottingham streets.

As we step out into the foyer, Paul starts to tell me about his embarrassment in the changing room afterwards.

'There were a couple of old boys standing full frontal in the shower. She was fascinated, kept pointing. I didn't know where to look. It was too embarrassing.'

I laugh and feel the warmth towards him seep back. She's been like that when I've taken her to the local pool — something about the way bodily appendages oscillate when people lather their hair — but it never seems so bad when it's women she's watching. I've felt awkward myself in front of other mums' sons, sensing their curious eyes on my breasts. There's a sign on the door: Mixed changing only permitted for children under 8 years. The age beyond which these things are deemed no longer to be innocent.

Supper takes a while so we're late getting Holly into her bedtime routine. There's no anti-slip mat in the bath so Paul hops in too, says he could do with rinsing the chlorine off his skin. I sit on the loo seat watching her play. We've bought plastic ducks and her glitter ball but it's the little bottles of shampoo and conditioner she's interested in. She's so unencumbered: standing there, big belly and podgy thighs, chatting in pidgin-Finnish to herself, absorbed in trying to twist the tops off, oblivious to Paul's steadying hand on her waist, his periodic forays with a flannel. Watching them I feel a ripple of sadness. I haven't been in the bath with her since I stopped breast feeding: she used to get so desperate, the sight of me there in front of her. It won't last much longer with Paul, either. Soon she'll get curious about his body, the differences from hers. I've seen her staring. I'm acutely aware of her growing, changing, becoming her own little person. The baby I once held in my arms is already gone.

Once she's clean and has had a bit of downtime, Paul lifts her out to me, warm towel draped over my arms. I wrap her and pat her dry while he has a quick wash. He soaps under his arms, over his chest, down his stomach. My eyes are drawn to his cock,

230

floating just below the surface of the water, slightly engorged. I rest Holly down, kneel over her and get her in nappy and pyjamas. She gets a bit fractious, starts to cry, so I lean on my elbows and nibble at her belly, between times dabbing Sudocrem in her creases. Even as I'm entertaining her, I'm conscious of my bum sticking in the air, half-aware of other times, other places, Paul pushing me apart, his hips slapping against me. Intrusive images of the act that made her, while she herself is lying on her back on the bathroom floor. It's disquieting, forbidden, strangely exciting. I take her to her cot, rush through a couple of stories, feeling unaccountably horny for the first time in ages.

It takes only a few minutes for her to fall asleep. Paul silences the extractor fan in the en suite but leaves the light on and the door ajar. He comes over and slides arms around me from behind, breath hot on the nape of my neck.

'Fancy a drink?'

We raid the mini-bar. I have a sense of misbehaviour. The ring-pulls fizz as we open respective cans; I decant my ready-mixed G&T into a tumbler. We sit in the lounge area of the darkened room, taking a few moments to savour the alcohol and the first unwinding of day-end.

'So, you had a good afternoon?'

'Great, yeah. How about you — how d'you get on? Good head space?'

'Yes,' I smile, rolling my shoulders. 'Thanks.'

'Any further forward?'

'Nooo, not really.'

I sip my gin, look at him over the rim of the glass, his face shadowed in the Holly-level light.

'And this Declan Barr? How did that go?'

'So so.'

I detect the frown in his pause. 'What happened?'

'He admitted sending the picture.'

'And?'

'He wouldn't explain.'

'Perhaps it was personal.'

'Oh, it was personal — he kept going on about moments that shaped his life. But he wouldn't say what a photograph of us had got to do with him.'

'Perhaps because it didn't have anything to do with anything?'

I shake my head. 'No, Paul. He lied about the phone call, you know. Said he hadn't spoken to Dad for years. I told him I knew they'd talked before the accident and all he did was deny it.'

My eyes are adjusting to the gloom. He

shifts position in his chair, contemplates his beer.

'What makes you sure he's lying?'

'Er, it was his number on the phone bill, remember?'

'And? Does he live on his own? Is there anyone else there your Dad might have been talking to? A wife? Have you thought of that?'

As soon as he says it I feel stupid. The woman of the pictures, the mother of his child. The daughter would have left home, but she would be there still. Beautiful when younger, real model material. There was no sign of anybody when I called round, but that didn't mean a thing. Then I remembered; remembered why I'd made the assumption.

'No, it was just his name on the answer phone.'

'You told me, Zo, it was the number for some picture agency? Maybe that's just a business phone.'

I think back to the conversation, my accusations, the offence he'd taken. I shouldn't have jumped to conclusions. Even so, I still can't understand his reticence, his refusal to explain about the Rewley drawing, his sudden desire to be rid of me. But perhaps he, too, wasn't thinking straight. All it would take is a conciliatory word, the offer of Paul's alternative explanation. Perhaps then he would be able to tell me what the picture was about.

'I'll have to go back tomorrow.' I look directly at him. 'Will you come with me?'

He sighs. 'Shouldn't you leave it?'

'No, Paul, I can't. I have to know.'

He shakes his head. 'I don't understand you. We've got enough going on without all this. The first weekend we make it away since Holly was born and where do we go? Your dad's dead, Zoe, nothing you can do will change that. Can't you let it go? You've got your own family now, aren't we the priority?'

'What does that mean — priority? I give you everything. All I want is a single weekend in return. Is that too much to ask?'

'It's not a single weekend, though, is it? You've been moody for months. I don't mind for me, it's Holly I worry about. You're not much fun for her any more.'

'No fun? Christ, Paul, listen to you. I lost my dad, yes? The only proper parent I had. And I'm moody? I'm a bit fucking *moody*?'

He looks pointedly in the direction of the travel cot.

I take a breath, let it out along with the urge to scream. 'I think you'd better apologize.'

He swaps his glass to the other hand, laughs. 'Do you know what I dream about,

Zoe? I dream I'll wake up one morning and everything about your bloody dad will have vanished. No more Ray Arthur, one time copper, admirable all-round good guy. I'm sorry he's dead, I really am, I know he was important to you. But, *please*, for fuck's sake, can we not just move on?'

★ ★ ★

When I found out I was pregnant, everywhere I looked there were mothers with babies. I had never seen them before — I'd only noticed if there'd been a screaming tantrum in Sainsbury's, or if I'd helped a woman carry a buggy up a flight of steps. But after a pair of pink lines on a test stick I was instantly surrounded by evidence I was not alone. It felt like there was some benign conspiracy, a team of new mums drafted in a moment's notice to walk casually past, as if to say: It's OK, it's normal, look at us, we've done it too.

Sarah was the first person I told. I rang her the day of the positive result, asked if I could meet her for lunch. She had a case in court so we made it an after-work drink. It felt like the longest day of my life. I went out at break anyway, just to get some air, to avoid the banter in the canteen. And there they were, the pushchairs and the prams, coming at me from every direction. Far from calming me, it made me slightly paranoid.

'You're in shock, that's all.'

That was Sarah's considered view, after she'd got to grips with the fact of my changed status, after I'd mentioned suddenly seeing children everywhere. 'Have you told Paul?'

'Not yet. It hasn't really sunk in.'

She raised her spritzer, held it somewhere between the table and her lips. 'And? Are you going to keep it?'

She caught me unawares. I'd been struggling with it all day, still didn't really know what I felt. 'Of course.'

'Good girl.'

She propelled her glass forward, clinked it against my mine. 'Congratulations. And commiserations — you'll have to cut out the booze.'

Vocalizing the idea of having a baby, a child, made it much more real. I kept testing it over the coming days, reliving the voltage that shot through me when I broke the news to Sarah, comparing it to the shoddiness of a day off work, the trip to the clinic, the ending of it and the return to my life, which would never be the same. I couldn't decide how Paul would react, couldn't see him there at the head of my bed, encouraging me through labour. But I couldn't see him handing over a cash fee to a white-coated receptionist, either, like he was paying for a weekend in a B&B. In fact, I couldn't see him at all. We'd been together for years. It made me nauseous, realizing how little I really knew him. We'd talked about children from time to time, but it was always abstract, as though the idea belonged to another life we might have. This incarnation we were too busy, thanks: work, conferences, skiing, clubbing, out together, out with friends, tickets to the Arsenal and follow-on comedy at Jongleurs.

I didn't tell Dad before I told Paul, I just wanted to talk to him. Despite my anxiety, my isolation, I kept control, didn't phone and ask to come over specially. I waited till the next Saturday, when I'd already arranged to visit. I didn't let him suspect anything, set myself a minimum of an hour before I would even begin to look for an opportunity.

I engineered the opening. I put my empty mug on the mantelpiece, right by the photograph of him, Mum and me outside Rewley Hill Top. Pretended to look at the picture for a moment. Then I turned to him sitting in his armchair, its cushions moulded and depressed by years of bearing his weight.

'Dad, did you enjoy being a father? Tell me honestly.'

He looked at me for a few seconds till I

broke eye contact, returned to the picture, to Snowy on the stone seat, to Mum's arms wrapped tight around her.

'Of course I did. Still do, as a matter of fact.'

I smiled quietly. 'Never had any regrets?

'No, of course not.'

'Honestly?'

'Oh, all the time, if you really want to know. It was hard, especially after your mother left, but before that too. You never slept much, you know.'

I heard him chuckle. I kept my gaze on the pair of us, sitting on a grassy slope in the Derbyshire of a lifetime before.

'But those kind of regrets don't last. I don't know, Zoe, I can't explain. Things are always changing. I seemed to spend the whole time looking back, mourning things that passed as soon as you'd done them.'

There was a short silence. When I spoke I was talking to the younger him, the him with me perched up there on his knee.

'Would you do it again?'

He laughed. 'Chance would be a fine thing.'

'Seriously. If you had your time over.'

'Seriously? I don't know. It's like falling in love. You want it, but you know it's going to hurt. It's the best and worst feeling, all the time, never letting up. You'd have to have one of your own to know what I'm talking about. But if I knew from the start I was going to have one who turned out like you then I'd say yes, I'd do it again.'

★ ★ ★

'I think we should tell him together.'

Paul stayed staring at his hands. Then the tips of his fingers tapped lightly together.

'OK,' he said.

'Really?'

I was genuinely delighted, I never thought I'd persuade him — or if I did it would be the result of a protracted battle, an arm-wrestle of blackmail and trade-offs. I leant forward, gave him a spontaneous kiss.

'I love you.'

He looked up, smiled.

'I love you, too.'

Driving over, I felt light-hearted for the first time in days. Even Paul's reaction when I finally found the moment to tell him — disbelief followed by idiotic pleasure — went only so far towards quelling my misgivings. I still felt I was tightrope walking, that any second he would turn round and announce it wasn't going to be for him, that he wished me the very best, that he would see to it that I had enough money, but that was all I should expect. Him agreeing to go with me to Dad's — despite the potential for raised voices, blame, angry accusations — said more about his commitment than any amount of frivolous speculation as to names for a boy or a girl. This seemed like a new beginning. I felt, for the first time, that he was definitely going to stick with me, that this was something he actually wanted too.

'Is he going to try and persuade us to get married?'

I changed down to take a rise in the road. 'I don't think so. He was pretty cool about us moving in together. He'll just want us to be happy.'

Paul laughed briefly, put a hand across to rest on my knee. 'I can't wait to see his face when you tell him.'

We arrived. Before getting out of the car I turned to him, looked him in the eye, checking he was all right.

He nodded. 'Let's do it.'

Dad gave me a hug and a kiss, greeted Paul warmly enough, then showed us through to the lounge. Once we'd sat down, there was an awkward pause — Dad appeared to sense there was something out of the ordinary, that now was not the time for chat. I'd thought carefully about how to say it and it seemed I would have to do so straight away.

'We've got some news.'

Raised eyebrows, inviting me to continue. I took Paul's hand.

'We're going to have a baby.'

He sat back in his chair, the one that had borne his weight all these years. I was studying his face, trying to read the reaction there. I saw his eyes flick briefly towards Paul.

'But I know,' he said, looking at me again, his brow puzzled. 'You told me, remember, last time you were here, a couple of weeks back?'

I felt Paul's fingers twitch. I shook my head wordlessly — staring at Dad, his blank expression — thought through the conversation we'd had, me asking *him* if he'd ever regretted becoming a father. I did not tell him, not before I told Paul. All I wanted was to talk to him.

A single 'But' formed in my mind. Paul's hand slipped from mine. My lips closed together, protest unspoken. There was no way to repair it, the damage had been done.

* * *

Holly stirs sometime around one, a startled, frightened cry. I am still awake, furious with Paul, sleeping the sleep of the just at my side.

241

I swing out of bed, bend over her cot, shush softly and reach for her. She can't know where she is. It's all right, I tell her, Mummy's here. I slide a hand beneath her shoulders, raise her gently to sitting, offer her the Tommee Tippee. She sucks water thirstily, breaking off a couple of times to gulp breath before taking more.

The bedroom is limewashed by reflected fluorescence from the en suite. Holly finishes drinking, stays sitting, looking straight ahead, the rising and falling of her shoulders slowing as the remnants of her alarm dissipate. My hand is on her back, but she ignores me, eyes fixed on the end of the travel cot as though puzzled, trying to place it. Her fair hair is turned shimmering platinum in the weird light; tousled, teased, falling over her forehead, strands sweeping in front of her ears, across her cheeks. The twilight does odd things to her eyes, renders her lashes dark, thick with mascara. She looks bizarrely adult, grown up. It's the strangest feeling, a trick of the light, but for an instant my daughter is a miniature of her adult self. She seems bewildered, disorientated, lost in time and place. I do not know who is responsible, who has done this to her. Something constricts, starts to ache. I reach my other arm towards her, gather and lift her from the cot,

242

snuggling her against me where it is warm and safe and secure. I hold her like a baby again till her eyes close. It's an unknown time before I dare to move, dare to return her — as imperceptibly as I can — to lie in her own bed once more.

Declan

Morning, another day begins. Today, I promise, you will complete your journey. I don't know how you slept, whether you found yourself a decent room in which to rest. I gave you no notice, you may have been forced to take what you could find: cash in advance, sagging mattress, ashtrays along the corridors. A bed among the contract labourers, the low-budget reps, the shifting population of men at loose ends far from home. If so, shower yourself down, dress, leave your breakfast uneaten in its film of grease, put it all behind you. You are going on a trip to the country, a drive along the A610, heading for clearer air, fast-flowing brooks, the peaks of Derbyshire. As you go you will see landmarks in transition: the old Players factory, closed now; the Raleigh works, converted to a second campus for the university; mines turned to industrial museums. Cigarettes, cycles and coal. The industries, along with lace, that once made this city.

One destination before you leave — a drive-by, a curiosity in passing. Perry Road, the long artery connecting Radford with

Sherwood, the site of HMP Nottingham. There is no need to stop, to get out of your car, it looks much as you imagine a prison might: grey blocks, high perimeter fences, cameras covering every square yard. As you draw level with the main gate, you may see a handful of people gathered. You will be past them before you've been able to read the slogans on their placards. If you are in the least bit interested, pull over, watch in your mirror for a while. Chances are nothing will happen, but if you've arrived at an opportune moment you may see the small crowd surge forward, hear their shouts of abuse. If so, it will not be long before a line of police officers pushes them back, to prevent them reaching or following the trinity that will soon emerge. While the protesters are penned, three men step out on the pavement, walking hurriedly in the direction of Sherwood and its bus routes and anonymous crowds. They pass within feet of your car — nothing about their clothing gives away which of them are the policemen and which is the paedophile. The jeers and taunts of the citizens of Nottingham follow, penetrating the sealed interior of your car. You are left in no doubt that the residents of our most infamous hotel are unwelcome. Nearby houses, prices depressed by the presence of the prison, have been virtually unsaleable since the sex offenders' hostel was opened in its grounds. No matter that these men have served their sentences, have paid their debt, remain voluntarily incarcerated for their own protection. No matter that they may not leave the prison grounds without a police escort. Men such as these are not wanted, not here, not anywhere.

Put your indicator on. Pull away, leave the eternal arguments behind you. You can no more say what should be done than I. They are inhuman, beneath our contempt, the scourge of society. Perhaps the expense of the hostel is worthwhile — a few pence on the council tax to ensure we can sleep soundly, our children tucked up safely in the next-door rooms. How little we have learned. Drive. Accelerate. Pass them, the plain-clothes policemen walking their child-molesting charge. As you do, spare one glance. I don't know, I cannot say. Perhaps in the fleeting glimpse, the confusion of heads and limbs and bodies, you will form the unshakeable impression that one of these men has thick, chestnut brown hair.

★ ★ ★

Chatsworth House, multimillion pound tourist attraction, seat of the Duke and Duchess of Devonshire. They're rich enough already, there's no need to swell the coffers unduly, admission to the grounds will do. The ornate rooms, the fine art collection, the extraordinary antiques, the intricate plaster work and towering shelves of leather-bound Greek classics, these do not concern you. Go round the house if you want, if you can afford — it can be refreshing to immerse the spirit in the highest achievements of civilization. But when you are done, go out through the Orangery, up the slopes of the Arboretum, till you find yourself on the clearings that flank Capability Brown's water cascade.

Sit on the grass awhile, enjoy what sun there may be — it's unlikely you'll arrive when the pumps are active. If your night was restless, perhaps you will doze. It's a tranquil place, it's easy to be lulled. Snooze awhile. In time, your ears will detect a new sound above the distant conversations of picnicking families dotted around the lawns — a low rumble, more vibration than anything. You sit up, look around, try to place it. Then something catches your eye. At the very top of the broad stone staircase set into the hillside you see the first sparkle and froth as a hundred thousand gallons begin their descent.

The water is magnetic, the pied piper would be cowed. Children hurry. Indulgent parents strip them, tuck socks into empty shoes, roll trousers above dimpled knees, lift sons and daughters into the crystal stream. Soon the cascade is teeming with young life. Some stand motionless, awed by the cold, heads lowered while eyes study the eddies their bare feet cause in the flow. Others squat, reflecting on the patterns numb fingers make while playing in the little water-falls that tumble over the edge of each step. Those more fond of action trudge side to side, climb up and down, paddling and exploring, from time to time throwing arms wide to regain balance lost on the slime that coats the stone under-foot.

Can you see yourself? You're a tiny figure at this distance, marching determinedly towards the staircase, just a few weeks past your third birthday. You are holding hands with Jessie, my daughter, not long walking, but keen to wet her feet along with you. She relies on you to steady her and you are infallible in your task — in any case, the water is shallow, a couple of inches deep at most. I have no concerns for her safety, none at all, I am enjoying the peace the sudden eruption of the pumps has brought. But Isabel is different.

'I'll go with them,' she says suddenly, standing, brushing the grass cuttings from her trousers as she starts across the lawn.

'I'll come too.' Sheila gets to her feet, hurries the few yards to catch up with her. I watch as the two women walk away.

Your father shakes his head. 'Mother hens.'

He lies back on the rug, shades his eyes with a hand, following their progress as they pursue their daughters. 'You're a lucky man, Declan.'

I look at Isabel's retreating form, the swerve of her hips below her waist, the maddening perfection of her arse. The bruises her kicks made on my back have faded. There is a truce of sorts between us. I say nothing. I feel nothing. I take another bite of sandwich and concentrate on chewing, the bread dry and coarse on my tongue.

'I was going to come and see you tomorrow.'

Today is the first day he's had off in the three weeks since my drawing was reproduced in the *Evening Post*. I know it has been a desperate time. After the initial silence, the incident room phone has not stopped ringing. There are always people who think it funny to go to a telephone box and call with false leads. One person named the sitting MP, another identified a senior church figure. Someone got it into their head to pass an anonymous tip-off that the perpetrator was Ray Arthur, the policeman in charge of the case. These distractions your father dealt with swiftly, but other hoaxes proved more serious. A sheep and beef farmer in the Vale of Belvoir; an academic at the University; a newsagent in Arnold; a local TV weatherman; a paediatrician from the City Hospital. They've tied up hundreds of man-hours: checking movements, previous records, alibis, backgrounds, connections — of which there proved to be none — with the Scanlon family. Far from advancing the inquiry, the picture I drew from Maggie Mortensen's recollections has set it back weeks. Weeks in which, again and again, the papers have published the face of the man with the child, each new appeal generating dozens of blind alleys, sucking more men and resources into the fray. Weeks in which the colourless, odourless gas of suspicion has descended, heavier than air, to choke the city streets. Weeks in which girls and boys on bikes have become an endangered species, parks have been deserted, daily papers left undelivered, cross-country runs become a thing of the past. Weeks which have seen parents bundle children into cars, those without transport banding together to shepherd whole groups to school, every passing stranger shunned. The *Evening Post*, cooperative at the outset, has become critical, editorials castigating the police in general, your father by name, for their failure to apprehend someone for this base crime. The talk now is of vigilantes, of parents' patrols. At least one man has had his cheekbone splintered for loitering near a set of swings. People are saying that whoever this girl was — her whose name cannot be revealed — she is charmed. Brady and Hindley are fresh in the mind. She was lucky not to have been found in the canal, or a ditch, or buried under two feet of sod in a field. The pressure has worn your father down, sapped his energy and his belief in himself. There have been meetings with the chief constable, the appointment of a DCI to oversee the inquiry, talk of crisis in the incident room, the numbers of cardexes becoming unmanageable.

I glance at him. Only then do I see it — I've been too wrapped up in my own concerns. Taking a day off in the midst of it, looking far more relaxed, more like his real self, than I have seen him for some time. I prop myself higher up on my elbow.

'Have you had a call?'

'Not from your picture.' There's no humour in his laugh. 'Nothing but time wasters there.'

'A new witness?'

'No.'

251

He rolls on his side.

'Do you know that brothel on Redcliffe Road?'

I shake my head, momentarily confused.

'Specializes in schoolgirl stuff. Uniforms, shaved twats, hair in bunches, the works. The madam's a friend of mine. She called a few days ago — thought I ought to know there's been a new man in town. Likes his girls to take it up the arse.'

His delivery is conspicuously casual. I have a sudden appreciation of the world in which he moves, does deals, the contacts he cultivates among the hookers and the fences and the petty criminals. I look past him. Isabel and Sheila have overhauled you and Jessie, have taken charge. Mothers and daughters walking line abreast, hand in hand. I watch while Sheila helps you into the crystal stream, Isabel doing likewise with Jessie.

'Name of Vincent Hunter. I've had him checked out — he's on bail from Worksop, indecent exposure. South Yorks have got his blood group on file from an indecent assault on a minor a few years back — it matches the spunk on the Scanlon girl's pants. This is the guy, Declan, I'm sure of it.'

I shake my head slowly. 'That's fantastic news.'

'It would be, if it weren't for that building society clerk. Hunter looks nothing like the impression you did.'

'Can't you ignore it? I told you — she didn't get a good look.'

'It's too late. The day we went public with the face we stuffed ourselves.'

'What about a line-up? If she picked him out of a parade?'

'We're going to have to risk it. But if she fucks that up, too . . . '

I'm distracted. I can no longer see the children. I spot your mother and Isabel, standing a little way from the staircase now. They are face to face, arms gesticulating, both of them talking at the same time. As I watch, Isabel's hand chops the air.

'Mary Scanlon would be better, but the psychologist says she's not capable.'

Isabel starts back towards us, Sheila following a short way behind. I have no idea what they could have been arguing about. Your father looks at me, squinting, even though the sun is behind him.

'You all right, Declan?'

I nod. 'Yeah, sorry. That's great, Ray, really terrific.'

★   ★   ★

Away from Chatsworth now. Don't look back as you leave its carefully kept lawns, its state rooms and hidden passages that have hosted so many intrigues down the centuries. The affairs, the betrayals, the political backstabbings; the lives sullied by the actions of those above the law. You must drive the few miles to Rewley. To the place your father was born.

As you wend through the lanes, the hedges high on either side, let your body do the steering, the clutch work, the gear changes for you. Loosen your mind, send it streaming in a trail of spangled ether, bound neither by space nor time. Come to rest in a small darkened room, somewhere in the Nottingham of then. You are not alone — like you, I am a ghostly presence. And there are others with us, a man and woman who stare through the two-way mirror that fills the greater part of one wall.

The room beyond the mirror looks cosy, inviting. It is wallpapered, furnished like a regular living room, carpeted, a cupboard full of toys. There's a coffee table in the corner, cluttered with the remains of lunch — paper cups, a jug with some orange juice, a few uneaten sandwiches with the crusts removed. In front of the sofa there's a dolls' house, the doors open to reveal the innards of a pretend family home.

A girl and a woman are playing on the floor. From time to time we see their lips moving, on one occasion the woman laughs. But even though we are supernatural, although we respect no physical laws, we cannot hear a sound. Our companions in the viewing room have cumbersome headphones clamped over their ears. Only they are privileged to bear witness. We must manage with four senses.

Pay attention to the game. It does not take long to observe that the woman, whom you should know is a psychologist named Gabrielle Sinclair, takes no active part. Her role, so far as we can tell, is to prompt, suggest, encourage. The only one handling the dolls, the one who is actually playing, is a nine-year-old girl called Mary Scanlon.

How does she seem to you? Look at her awhile. Her posture is open, she is absorbed in the cloth figures in her hands, moving them in and out of the dolls' house, feeding them plastic food, putting them to bed, getting them up, walking them across the carpet, swapping one figure for another, bringing their faces together, making them jump up, lie down. Perhaps your own daughter is now old enough for you to have seen her lost in the world of make believe. Mary Scanlon is like any other child, at ease, engrossed in the game she is playing. It hasn't always been so. A fortnight ago, her first session in the play suite, she sat motionless for four hours, arms wrapped round knees tucked into chest. The scene you see is the result of patient persistence, trust-building, gradual engagement, a process that is about to bear first fruit.

Watch a while longer. Mary has a doll in either hand, one a girl in a school uniform, the other a man in suit and tie. They have straw-coloured string for hair; their cornflower blue eyes and fixed red smiles are embroidered into the pale pink cotton that represents their skin. Truth be told, they are rather crude, homemade, you can't imagine anyone selling toys like these in the shops. Mary seems happy enough — it's amazing the allowances made by the imagination. She circles the dolls round, bouncing them off each other, running them hither and thither as though engaged in a kiss chase. It goes on for ever. You grow bored, unable to discern meaning in the intricate dance being played out before you. On and on, round and round. Then, seemingly at random, Mary puts the male doll down. You narrow your eyes, wondering if this is significant, or if it is merely an end to the game. Mary begins to undress the girl, pulling her green uniform over her head. Skirt, blazer, blouse come off as one.

Listen — this is what I mean. Can you sense it? The change in breathing, the hint of sweat in the air. The man and woman watching from beneath clumsy headphones — their reaction tells you this is important. You glance at them, see the renewed intensity with which they stare through the mirror. You look back to Mary and the naked doll, smooth pink cotton skin. The little girl in her hand, the cloth effigy. In the hairless triangle between her legs someone has carefully embroidered exaggerated female genitalia.

Gabrielle Sinclair is entirely still. Then her lips move. Mary puts the schoolgirl doll on the floor, picks up the man. His clothes come off with similar ease: a strip of Velcro at the back — you convince yourself you can hear the rrrrip — then suit, shirt, tie fall away. His body too is featureless pink, but your eyes are drawn to his crotch. From between his legs juts a sausage of material, surrounded by an untidy mass of black cotton threads.

Who are they, the woman and man watching through the two-way mirror? You could be forgiven for assuming they must be Helena and Harry Scanlon. Their daughter

257

has been defiled; day after day she comes to the play suite where Gabrielle Sinclair attempts to gain access, however oblique, to the events of that day. She deserves their support, their involvement. You would think they'd be insatiable in their desire to know. But they are busy people, the Scanlons. There is an unrelenting caseload at the courts to occupy Mary's father. And her mother had to cancel four performances just to fly back to England to organize a replacement for the absconded maid. Helena Scanlon's voice is widely acclaimed as that of an angel. The world of opera is at her feet. Still, there are ranks of aspirant sopranos eager to step into her shoes. In her profession, you are only as good as your last aria.

Cloth-girl is face down on the floor. Her stuffing is constructed in such a way that her legs are forever parted. Mary brings cloth-man's hand repeatedly to land on her buttocks. Gabrielle Sinclair's lips move, almost imperceptibly. Mary stops, is still. You can sense the pulses beating in the necks, the wrists, the groins of our fellow observers. Then Mary raises cloth-man, repositions him, brings his sausage cock to lie between cloth-girl's buttocks, next to the knot of needlework that is meant to be her arsehole.

The man beside us turns to his companion, taps her shoulder. She removes the headphones, flicks her hair back into place. His voice, when he speaks, is unnaturally loud. 'You'd better get straight on to Ray.'

Inquest

'I now call Zoe Jane Arthur.'

[She takes the stand.]

'Ms Arthur, the evidence you gave prior to the adjournment of this inquiry was concerned solely with the identification of your father's body. I do now have to ask a number of questions that touch more generally on the circumstances surrounding his death. Before I begin, please be assured this court has every sympathy with your loss. If at any point you wish to have a short break from testifying then the court is more than willing to allow this.'

'Thank you, I'm sure I'll be fine.'

'Can I ask you first of all: relationships between parents and children vary so much. Do you consider yourself to have been close to your father?'

'Yes, extremely. He raised me single-handedly from when I was six.'

'When your mother left home?'

'Yes.'

'And would you say he was prone to depression, to low mood?'

'Not at all. Quite the opposite. I think it

must have been hard for him. He kept working all the way through, plus he managed to give me a decent family life somehow. That went on for years. I never remember him complaining. I can only think of a handful of times when he lost his temper. He always seemed happy.'

'And more recently, in the months leading up to his death, did you notice any change in him?'

'No. I hear these people saying he meant to kill himself, that he was depressed, but I think they're talking about a different person. He had his low moments, everyone does, but he always bounced back. He really enjoyed life.'

'Were you aware that he had consulted his general practitioner? That she had prescribed antidepressant medication for him?'

'No, of course not. If I'd thought he was ill . . . He seemed fine to me.'

'You have heard testimony to the effect that your father was chronically tired, which, it's been suggested, was linked to his shift work. Did you see any evidence of that yourself?'

'I think that's true. He used to do five nights on, two off. He was always pretty exhausted at the end of a stretch.'

'And the day of his death? Had he been working the night before?'

'No, that's the thing. He was on a week's — '

★ ★ ★

'Please, take your time.'

'He was on a week's leave. I can't think he'd have been that tired.'

'And were you aware of any particular problems — financial worries, for example?'

'No, he had a good pension, plus what he earned at work. He was always comfortable.'

'What about personal matters? Had he been in a relationship?'

'No, he never met anyone after Mum. He always said there'd never been time.'

'Do you think he was lonely?'

'I don't know. He was the sort of person who liked company — he enjoyed being part of things. I don't think he was all that good on his own. But he didn't need to be — everyone liked him, there was always someone he could go and see.'

'Do you know where he was going on the day of the accident?'

'No, I'm sorry.'

'Did that stretch of the A40 form part of any regular route of his?'

'Not that I'm aware of, no.'

'Had he said anything to you about plans

262

to visit anyone, any meetings or engagements that day?'

'No.'

'And he didn't keep a diary?'

'No.'

'You went to his house shortly after he died?'

'Yes, to get his address book. That's what I mean, there were so many friends I had to inform.'

'Did you find anything there that might have indicated where he'd been going?'

'No, not at all. If anything, it looked like he'd just popped out.'

'What gave you that impression?'

'It was all so ordinary. I don't know — the light was on in the loo, he hadn't washed up after lunch. It was as though he'd just nipped round the corner. I kept expecting him to come back — '

★ ★ ★

'Would you like to take a short break?'

'No, I'm fine. I'm sorry.'

'Now, I do have to ask. When you were at his house, did you discover anything that might have constituted a last message or declaration of any sort?'

'If you mean a suicide note, no. I had to

263

look everywhere for his address book. If there'd been anything, I would have seen it.'

'Thank you, Ms Arthur, that's all I need from you. Please remain in the stand. I'm sure counsel will have further questions. Mr Forshaw?'

[Mr Forshaw stands.]

'Ms Arthur, you say your father brought you up after your mother left home, when you were aged six.'

'That's right.'

'It's rather unusual, is it not, for custody to be awarded to the father — one with a full-time occupation at that?'

'I wouldn't know. That's how it was for us.'

'There was presumably something of a battle between them, though — your mother and father — over who should have you?'

'I don't think so, no. She just packed her bags and disappeared, left me with him.'

'Why would she do something like that?'

'You'd have to ask her.'

'Was there someone else?'

'I really don't know.'

'Has she never tried to explain herself?'

'I haven't seen her since I was eight. I don't even know where she lives now.'

'Well, was she depressed, alcoholic, in some other way unfit?'

'Mr Forshaw, I must say I fail to see where

this line of inquiry is leading you. We are talking about events a long way in the past. This inquest is concerned with Ms Arthur's father. I'm not sure I understand where the mother's failings or otherwise come into it.'

'I'm sorry, sir. I am merely trying to establish what would lead a woman to relinquish custody of her child. It strikes me as unusual. I am interested to know whether it tells us something about the mother, or, perhaps, whether it reveals more about the character of the deceased.'

'Very well, you may continue.'

'Thank you. Ms Arthur, as I was saying, are you aware of any reason why your mother might not have been considered fit to look after you?'

'No, but I didn't know her very well.'

'And what about your father? Presumably he explained his side of the story to you at some point?'

'He always said she didn't like London. He had his work, but I think she never settled in. They'd moved down from Nottingham when I was three and she left all her family and friends behind. His job meant he was often away for long periods of time.'

'And that was sufficient cause for her to abandon you?'

'I don't know about 'sufficient cause', but

265

that's what she did.'

'Very well, we'll leave it there. Ms Arthur, thinking about more recent events, how long before he died did you last see your father?'

'A few weeks.'

'A few weeks. Is that three, four, five, six?'

'I'm not sure. I never thought I had to keep count.'

'I'm not suggesting you did. What I am suggesting, however, is that when you told the court that you saw no change in him in the period leading up to his death, what you really meant was that you weren't in any position to see such a change, were you?'

'We spoke on the phone at least once a week.'

'You spoke on the phone. I see. Ms Arthur, where did your father work?'

'As a security guard.'

'That wasn't what I asked. Where did he work?'

'At a distribution depot, over in Teddington, he used to man the barrier — '

'What was the name of the company?'

'I can't remember.'

'How long had he worked there?'

'Several years. Four or five.'

'Six. Your father worked for the one firm for six years and you don't recall the name of the company?'

'It really wasn't important.'

'Do you know how much he earned?'

'No.'

'Nine thousand four hundred pounds per annum. Ms Arthur, what did your father do before he became a nightwatchman?'

'He wasn't a nightwatchman, he was a security guard.'

'What did he do beforehand?'

'He was in the police.'

'What rank did he achieve before retiring?'

'He was an inspector.'

'Yes, that's correct. Your father was an inspector, he retired on what you rightly say was a good pension, then he took his thirty years' experience as a senior police officer and used it to secure a position as a night car park attendant at a Londis food distribution centre. I am genuinely puzzled. Could you give us the first idea what on earth led him to stretch himself in this fashion?'

'Mr Forshaw, I must remind you that I expect a respectful manner of questioning in this court. Furthermore, I find myself once more at a loss to know where this line of inquiry is leading us, other than to cause the witness distress.'

'I do apologize. I was merely — I withdraw the question.'

'Very well. Ms Arthur, are you able to carry on?'

'Yes, thank you. I'm fine.'

[Examination continues.]

Part Seven

Part Seven

Rewley Hill Top

The road climbs steeply for a couple of miles, snaking round tight bends, before levelling out on a gorse-covered plateau. We haven't passed a single house since leaving Rewley, and the way ahead is pure moorland.

'Sorry,' I say. 'Wrong again.'

I turn in seven points — Holly is amused by the flurry of arm movements. Once we're facing back the way we've come I smile at her, tell her she's a sweetheart. She loves it when she's up in front — better view, plus a parent next to her for handing pens and sunglasses and mobile phones to play with. She swings her legs and laughs, as though the driving and turning, driving and turning, is a game for her benefit. I won't get away with it much longer. I admit defeat, decide to ask for directions when we're back in the village. I should have done so the first time I went wrong, could have saved us all this hassle. But I wanted this to work out fine, just so I could tell Paul we didn't need him anyway.

We drive back down towards Rewley. I'm chatty, light-hearted, singing along to Holly's jungle tunes tape, for all the world as though everything's OK. As far as I can tell she's taken in. This is an ordinary day, her and Mummy out in the car, heading off to do something interesting. Daddy's so rarely around, there's nothing unusual in his absence. She did catch the mood this morning, was playing up over breakfast — something about the painstaking politeness of the short exchanges between Paul and me. Now we're on our own I am better able to pretend, to put a brave face on it for her sake. She's back to her normal self, seems excited at what the day might bring.

Paul said he'd spend the morning in the pool and spa. I bet he's taken a Sunday paper back to bed. I really don't care what he's up to. I've got the essentials of Holly's kit, I've half a mind to drive straight to London from here, leave him to make his own way back. It would be outrageous, unacceptable, but he more than deserves it. I know I won't — it wouldn't be worth the fall-out. But the thought gives me a righteous pleasure.

'Ne-ver smile at a croc-odile, no you don't get friendly with a croc-odile . . .'

As I sing along to the tape there's a part of my brain churning through things again. The uncalled-for comment about Dad, the absence of an apology this morning, the way, when I announced I'd decided to go to

Rewley after all, Paul simply said he'd stay at the hotel. As if that was a perfectly natural thing to do. I'm so angry with him — not just for this, for his whole attitude. It's not as if his mother is particularly easy to get along with, always telling me I should do this with Holly, or I shouldn't do that. But I act the dutiful daughter-in-law, smile sweetly and thank her for the advice. She treats me as if I'm clueless, as if she was the last word in child-rearing. The few times I've mentioned it to Paul — just wanting a bit of solidarity — he's accused *me* of being over-sensitive, saying she means no harm, that she's only trying to help.

We come into Rewley again and I pull up outside the pub, contemplate the whole business of getting Holly out, her inevitable protests when she realizes she's got to go straight back in, the arched back and rigid legs as she struggles against the car seat straps. I glance along the street, its stone cottages and early daffodils, the elderly couple turning into the churchyard. I leave the tape playing, turn to her and speak over the music.

'You hang on here, poppet. I'm just going to get some directions.'

I plip the central locking behind me. At the door to the pub I look back to see her watching me through the grey gauze of her cat-face sun-screen. I give an exaggerated wave, grin at her like I'm about to play Where's Mummy? Her arms flail excitedly. Then I disappear inside, to see if anyone can tell me the way to Rewley Hill Top.

★ ★ ★

'So, what, the court of appeal got it wrong?'

It was excruciating. Only the third time I'd taken Paul to meet Dad and the two of them got into an argument.

'Do you think we could leave this now, talk about something else?'

Paul waved a hand. 'Just a minute, Zoe, I'm interested. That's what you're saying, Ray, isn't it? The appeal court judges made a mistake?'

'All I'm saying is, there's no smoke without fire. You don't know the first thing about that world. What goes on in a courtroom is all lawyers' games and technicalities. It's got nothing to do with what actually happened.'

'So we should forget trial by jury, should we, the innocent-till-proven-guilty thing? Just leave it to the police to decide?'

'Well, maybe. The number of times we *knew* who'd done something, then watched them pull the wool over some jury's eyes.'

'You're not saying it was right of those guys to fabricate statements, tell that bloke the only way he wasn't going down was if he implicated the others?'

I can't remember which particular miscarriage had got them going, which Four, Six, Three or Two was in the headlines. Paul had been SU president at college, had lost little of his antipathy towards the establishment since graduating. I wished one of them would have the grace to drop it.

'You've no idea what it's like — when you *know* what's gone on, but it's hard to prove. Sometimes you have to make sure a jury gets the truth.'

'I can't believe you're saying that. It's OK to fake evidence if you get the verdict you want?'

'You should see what defence barristers get up to. There's nothing straight about how they play it.'

'Christ. Forgive me if I'm missing something here, but what if they're actually not guilty?'

'They wouldn't be, though, would they? No one would tart up evidence if they weren't a hundred per cent sure.'

Paul laughed, long and exaggeratedly. 'You're not seriously suggesting — I mean, that's exactly what happened here, wasn't it?

Conviction quashed, unsafe and unsound?'

Dad spread his hands, smiled faintly. 'Like I say, lawyers' games.'

We left as soon as lunch was over, the atmosphere irreparably soured. Paul drove in silence till the end of the road.

'Prat.'

'What?'

'No, I'm sorry, Zo, I know he's your dad, but I've never heard such a load of absolute bollocks in my life.'

'He was winding you up, Paul.'

He shook his head, swung the car sharply on to the High Street. 'He meant every word.'

'He isn't like that, I don't think there's a more decent bloke. He was playing with you — and you swallowed every last line. It'd be funny if it wasn't so sad.'

'Yeah? And you thought it would be fun to let him take the piss?'

'Of course not. I did try and change the subject.' I waved a hand at him. *'Just a minute, Zoe, I'm interested.* I bet he couldn't believe his luck.'

We drove on, Paul staring fixedly ahead. After a mile or two he jabbed the radio on. Kiss FM, straining the speakers. I sank lower in my chair, put my feet up on the glove compartment. I remember thinking then that it wasn't going to work, that he was too sulky,

276

too self-important. I should have finished it, it wouldn't have been a drama, we'd only been going out six or seven months. But I didn't. It got glossed over the next day and we went back to living our own lives, separately and together. Even though visits with him to Dad's were always edgy afterwards, I wasn't exactly fond of his mother either. It seemed a fair trade.

★   ★   ★

I turn off the road and park on a large gravel apron, leave the rattlesnake band to finish off their number on the stereo while I contemplate the grey stone house in front of us. It's clearly occupied: roof retiled, ornaments on the windowsills, freshly dug soil in the flowerbeds. I retrieve my handbag from the passenger foot-well, find the card-backed envelope with the drawing in. Holly makes urgent noises, holds a hand out to be given whatever it is I've got. I fob her off with a lipstick and slide the picture out.

I'm sure it's the cottage, the front door is in the same position, at the L formed by two perpendicular walls. Other things are different, though. There's no grassy bank, but that could easily have been levelled to take the gravel on which we're parked. There is a stone mushroom, the same as the one Snowy's sitting on, but it's further up the hill. The windows are different too, their arrangement at odds with that in the drawing. And the house in front of me looks longer somehow.

I go round to fetch Holly. She's managed to get the top off the lipstick and the tip of an investigative forefinger is coated in sticky red cosmetic. I find a tissue and repair the damage — there's a smudge on one cheek, but otherwise I've caught her in time. She protests at the removal of this interesting toy, but once I've liberated her from the chair she quietens, starts to look for what I've brought her to see.

I don't know if this is it. There's no name on the wall, no slate with the words Hill Top Cottage. Holly on hip, I knock at the door. A simple confirmation will do, they've no need to go to any trouble. But the house is quiet. There are no other cars, I realize. I'm sure this is it. I can't convince myself, though. It seems important to know for sure.

Fifty yards uphill a pair of stone pillars flanks the entrance to a large farmhouse. We make slow progress, Holly deciding now is the perfect time to practise her walking. I follow immediately behind, stooped slightly, her upstretched hands in mine, taking her weight while her legs rehearse their eventual role. By the time we shuffle through the gateway into a large yard, my back is aching. Holly halts, wants to inspect some plant growing between the flagstones. I'm bent double, holding her chest to prevent her toppling over, when the voice comes.

'Can I help you?'

There's a woman at an open door. She's aproned, stooped, ancient. Her hands are white with flour.

'Yes, I'm sorry. I was trying to find Hill Top Farm.'

'This is it. What do you want?'

'Nothing. It's a silly . . . My father, he was born in the cottage. We were in the area, I just had the idea. I wanted to see it for myself.'

She comes over — sparse grey hairs on her chin, crackle glaze skin. 'Well, this is the farm, the cottage is down the hill a way. What's the name?'

'Arthur. My dad was Ray, his parents were Kate and Philip.'

'Arthur? Now then.' She looks thoughtful, shakes her head. 'No, I don't remember any Arthurs.'

'It would have been a long time ago — he was born during the war.'

'Well, the Maddoxes had it then, I'm sure. Their sons, both of them, went away and never came back. I don't think there've been any Arthurs in the cottage, not in my lifetime, anyway.'

She's rubbing her hands together as though washing them, fingers winding round fingers. I lift Holly up, hold her against my chest. 'But that's Rewley Hill Top — the cottage with the gravel outside?'

'It is, yes. It was the Maddoxes, though. They had it twenty-odd years, then the Vickers, they weren't there that long, mind — '

'Well, thank you. I'm sorry to have bothered you. We'll go back down.'

She's still mumbling a litany of names, hasn't heard me. A thin string of dribble is dangling from her lip. I start to move away.

'Thank you,' I say again, more loudly.

She looks at me, at Holly, her eyes narrowed. 'No, I'm sorry, dear, I don't think there was ever any Arthurs.'

★   ★   ★

It will do. It will have to do. For all I know the woman is demented, was probably talking about the First, not the Second World War. I sit on the steps leading to the cottage, Holly on my knee, looking over the roof of the Peugeot at the scene below. Wooded fells rise

280

either side of green pastureland on the valley floor, a couple of matchbox cars make their way along the grey ribbon of road. We're above it all, detached from the real world. It's the kind of place I imagine you could hold in your heart. There is sun again today, weak through wisps of cloud. Up here the wind would blow unbroken yet it's completely still, calm. It's perfectly peaceful, sporadic birdsong the only sound. It's also perfectly boring for Holly — far too young to see anything in a view. She tries to lever herself off my lap, eager for more walking. I don't want to end this yet, I'm trying to feel something, some connection with Dad, with the photograph he kept on his mantelpiece. I search for something to interest her, hoping to keep sitting here long enough to understand the importance of the place.

I point at some white blobs on the hillside opposite. 'Look, darling, sheep!' She stops struggling, suddenly motionless, no doubt trying to equate anything in her field of vision with the mental construct formed from her books at home. In the lull, the cessation of her movement, while I look in vain for the next thing to show her, it occurs to me that were Paul here I would have him photograph us. Holly would be entertained, watching her daddy hiding behind the camera, waiting for him to reappear with a smile and a 'Boo!' And I realize I have never asked myself, if Dad and Mum were both in the picture, who had taken the photo from which the drawing in my handbag was made?

Declan

You steer your way through the heart of Rewley village, with its olde worlde charm, its summer tourist trade, its weekend cottages, its phone lines burrowing through the earth, linking people to the offices they have left behind. Turn right by the pub, drive past the churchyard with its three hundred and fourteen marked graves, on up the hill towards the cottage where your father was born. Your movements are mechanical, automatic — your mind is elsewhere, a trail of spangled ether stretching over both land and time to a darkened viewing room somewhere in the Nottingham of then. For every minute that passes, your body, trapped in the steel shell of your car, moves another quarter of a mile closer to your destination. But your mind is fixed in a single point of space. As a result, it suffers outlandish, Einsteinian distortions of time. Whole days pass in the blink of your eye.

You are still here, staring through the two-way mirror at the game Mary Scanlon continues to play. Only, you are alone in your supernatural state. I have long since coalesced, solidified, become the me of thirty years ago. I am young, my own art is beginning to go well again, I have a partner and a beautiful daughter. I could even say I am still on course. On course for what? Yeah, right. All the hopes and dreams, the stuff that never, in the end, came true. The stuff that flaked and crumbled and blew to the ground on the wind.

Look at me. I have a sketch pad supported on a drawing board which in turn is balanced on my thighs. It is far from ideal, but none of us would be in this situation given the choice. Despite my padded headphones, you recognize my profile as the man you saw coming into the County, crew neck sweater and jeans, no socks beneath the canvas shoes on his feet. Now I am different. I am focused, I am working, I am doing a face. It is the last face I will ever do in the cause of justice and this one will take days, and a complete fresh start, before finally I get it right.

You see my stick of charcoal move, scratching the surface of the paper, see the lines it leaves in its wake, the hasty rub of cotton wool as I revise an outline. You cannot hear what I hear. In my ears are the voices of Gabrielle Sinclair and Mary Scanlon.

Whole days have passed in a few blinks of your eye. Days in which Vincent Hunter's every movement has been shadowed by even more intangible presences than you. He has been sighted across the road from a youth club in Beeston; photographed leaning on the railings while children feed ducks in Arnold Park; spotted watching a pack of girl guides in a hall in Burton Joyce; at various times logged loitering outside each primary school in a four mile radius of his bail hostel. His every act, his every movement is observed by spectral figures in doorways across a hundred different roads — your father, Pete Vardy, Mike Kidd, George Duffield. They are incredulous, these hard-bitten men, of the single-minded depravity of the world they have stumbled upon. Hunter's every act causes waves of anxiety, his every movement seems designed to taunt: I am death, I am danger, I am the living embodiment of your fear. How long dare they wait? It can only be a matter of time before another child is seized. Perhaps, caught red-handed, the case will be snapped shut. But what if he slips away — a terrible mix-up, an appalling misunderstanding — and there's another one buggered and bleeding over a varnished half-size chair. Or dumped lifeless in a back garden, a skip, the canal?

It's too much, the risks are too great. Your father has seen enough. He takes Pete Vardy with him to arrest Hunter at five o'clock one hoar-frosted morning, hauling him bodily from beneath the blankets that cover the semen-stained mattress of his bail hostel bed. Somewhere between arrest and arrival at the custody suite he sustains a fractured rib, a broken finger, and bleeding from a kidney which turns his urine dark red. Have no pity for him, shed no tear.

Your eye blinks. The hopeless Maggie Mortensen picks a man, any man, out of an identity parade. He is the owner of an angling shop on Castle Boulevard, doing his civic duty to assist the police in their quest to apprehend the man with the child. The next day, Vincent Hunter walks free on police bail. He does not walk alone. Your father is with him, a plain-clothed angel, shadowing from a hundred yards as he goes in, comes out of adult shops and brothels. Yet now he strays nowhere near any school, parks are anathema to him, and he will cross a street to avoid an oncoming child.

Mary Scanlon holds cloth-man — cornflower blue eyes, pink cotton sausage jutting out between his thighs. I hear Gabrielle Sinclair articulate the same question she has asked, at careful intervals, for two days. What colour is cloth-man's hair? It is yellow, as any fool can see. In the heart-straining silence I glance up once more from my sketch pad, through the two-way mirror to where Mary Scanlon squats on the carpet in front of the dolls' house, her thighs open in a V, her arse hovering a few inches above the floor. Mary Scanlon Mary Scanlon she sat down without her pants on. I have never thought this will work, this is desperate, she has never said a word about what happened that day. Gabrielle Sinclair insists we will get somewhere, has told your father repeatedly it is the only way. That to show her a half-dozen photographs, one of which is the face of Vincent Hunter, would be to traumatize her beyond hope of repair.

'Brown.'

I stare at her, the enormity of the single word sucking my insides into a vortex. I have an unbidden vision: this snub-nosed child, her angular body folded over, hair curtaining her head, bare buttocks gripped in meaty fists as a faceless, brown-haired man humps against her. My pulse pumps urgently. My mindless, shameful cock stirs beneath the drawing board.

Gabrielle Sinclair is as cool as they come. 'Dark brown like chocolate, or light brown like bread?'

Mary twists cloth-man in her hands, doesn't look up. 'Brown like yours.'

Gabrielle Sinclair's chestnut hair is cut in a shoulder-length bob.

'Longer or shorter?'

'I don't know.'

'Try to think, Mary. I know it hurts, but try to think.'

'No! I don't want to.'

Impasse. Your eyes blink. A girl loses her mother on Market Square. She stands, bewildered among the bustling crowd. She starts to cry. A rates assessor for the city council, making his way home after an early finish, stops to ask what's the matter. Between her sobs he understands her predicament. Taking her hand, he coaxes her back towards the Council House, to where she can be looked after in warmth and safety while attempts are made to locate a responsible adult. A man, pulling a tearful child by a reluctant arm. His hair is as black as coal, he looks nothing like my artist's impression. A crowd gathers. Words are exchanged. A citizen's arrest is made. He is lucky to escape with a split lip and throbbing balls.

'Shorter.'

'Was it over his ears?'

'He's got sticky-out ears.'

'Cloth-man has, Mary. What about the man?'

'The man has too.'

'And what about a parting, did his hair have a parting?'

'I don't know.'

'OK, Mary, you've done really well, let's leave it for today.'

And my charcoal moves, scratching, shading, darkening the blank whiteness of the paper.

You blink again. A male primary school teacher is suspended on full pay, his crime to put his arms around a girl in junior 2 whose rabbit has died. City-wide, public baths advertise women-only sessions for mothers to bring their children to swim in peace and security. Assistants in photo-processing labs are briefed by management to be alert to the mere suggestion of prepubescent nudity.

'Tell me about his eyes, Mary. Cloth-man's eyes are blue, blue like the summer sky. What were the man's eyes like?'

'They're green.'

'Green like grass, or green like the walls?'

'Green like her school uniform.'

'Cloth-girl's uniform is grey, Mary.'

'Green like my uniform at school.'

You blink again. The *Evening Post* rolls off the presses, leader columns demanding an end to the terror: Mr Arthur, for the love of God, give us the man with the child. It's an overwhelming burden, pressing on your father's shoulders, driving him down till in the end he can do nothing but walk on his knees.

This is how I picture him: painful gait, impossibly slow, his arms his shoulders swinging to maintain his momentum, trousers worn through, shoes ruined by the constant scuffing on the pavement. The skin of his knees is a bloody mess. I picture Vincent Hunter, pallid face, lank brown hair tied back in a miniature pony tail, emerging like a sprite from a brothel on Redcliffe Road, an establishment specializing in gymslips, shaved cunts, girls who will take it up the arse. It's night, too dark for the camera. Hunter hurries away, his head sunk between hunched shoulders. As he does, a dwarf-like figure, a double amputee, leaves the safety of a driveway opposite: your father, shuffling after him in the orange street-light.

'Cloth-man's eyes are big, aren't they? Look how big they are. Were the man's eyes that big or were they smaller?'

'I don't know.'

'Try to think, Mary.'

'Smaller.'

'Close together or far apart?'

'I don't know I don't know I don't know.'

'OK, OK, well done, you're a good girl, a

really good girl. Would you like some juice?'

The frantic scratching of charcoal on 150 gram paper. The sweat on my palm. The repellent arousal.

Blink. This is pure conjecture. This is a rotten fairy tale. A man walks down Redcliffe Road. He passes Vincent Hunter, their shoulders within a foot of each other. The man's hair is thick, that much is clear. Were it not for the artificial light from the street lamps it would also be apparent it is chestnut brown. Down the hill, your father hesitates, seems for a split second to be riven with indecision, then he obeys the instincts that have made him what he is. Does he shuffle by, head turned to the side, continue his painful pursuit of the man every parent warns their children about? Or does he turn on his knees, leaving smudges of his blood on the paving stones, scrabble back to the shelter of the rhododendron-lined driveway where he has already spent the best part of his evening, there to observe where this other man's brisk pace is taking him? Or does he know already? Has he seen him there countless times before? Only Ray Arthur can say. And Ray Arthur is dead, he crashed his car into a bridge and he cannot explain anything any more.

Day after day my ears are squashed beneath the headphones, insensible to the noise and nuances of the world outside. Day after day I pounce on scraps and morsels which Gabrielle Sinclair is able to encourage from the walled-off depths of Mary Scanlon's memory. It is the messiest face I have ever drawn — the paper turned grey by the obliteration of a thousand unwanted lines. Ordinarily I would do draft after draft, showing each version to victim or witness, observing their reactions, assimilating their comments before beginning again. This time it is different. I am never to show my drawing to my informant, a nine-year-old girl who hasn't the first idea I am here, behind a two-way mirror, listening to her every word like some seedy voyeur.

When the face is finished, when every detail has been interpreted, drafted, incorporated, it has a certain authenticity. I would dearly love her to look at it, for me to be on the other side of that mirror observing her skin, eyes, breathing, sweat, the manifestations of fear, which would tell me I have got it more right than wrong. But Gabrielle Sinclair is adamant. We take what we can get, do with it what we will, but the girl is never to be shown.

★ ★ ★

Your father hasn't been seen for the best part of a week, George Duffield tells me. As far as the department is concerned his every waking moment has been spent trailing Vincent Hunter round the streets. I tuck my portfolio tighter beneath my arm and turn, about to leave his office.

'Declan,' Duffield calls.

When I look back he has risen, is standing behind the expanse of his desk. His fingers are twiddling a pencil round and round.

'Is everything all right? With you and — what's her name?'

'Isabel.'

I think of the interminable skirting around each other, the hostile silence that reigns whenever Jessie is in bed.

'Yes, fine. Why?'

'No reason. I'm glad to hear it. This case has put a strain on us all.'

I nod.

'I don't suppose you've had much time at home lately.'

'No.'

He laughs. 'My wife is threatening divorce.'

I smile. There's something about Duffield sharing this intimacy, the habitual aloofness of the superintendent forgotten for a moment.

'Well,' I say, 'I hope she doesn't.'

He waves a hand. 'I get to know a lot of what goes on around here, Declan, all sorts of things people don't think I see.' He pauses, as though thinking through what he is saying. 'Your work is much appreciated. Not just by me, by everyone.'

'Thank you.'

I leave his office, pulling the door shut behind me. Down the stairs, just along the corridor from the exhibits officer's counter, I take a final look at the face I have drawn, the blank stare and dispassionate expression. Then I take a few more steps and hand the man with the child over to the safe keeping of the forces of law and order.

★　★　★

It's been good money, five days in the pay of the police, but I'm relieved to get back to my own work. I shut myself in the studio, spend the whole of the next day trying to rediscover what I was doing. I'm absorbed in it, oblivious to everything else, when Isabel's head appears round the door late in the afternoon.

'It's Ray.'

I lay my brush on the easel ledge, go down to the kitchen, am surprised to find it empty. In the sitting room, Isabel is alone with Jessie, helping her play at feeding her dolly.

'Where is he?'

She looks at me. 'On the *phone*.'

I can't remember the last time your father didn't come in person, he always took the chance for a cup of tea and a brace of fags away from the cauldron of CID. Bunking off, he called it, though the work never went away, was always waiting for him. The receiver is lying on the table in the hall. I pick it up. There's another conversation going on in the background.

'Ray?'

'Hold on a minute, will you?' Your father's voice, distant. Then he comes loud in my ear. 'Declan, how are you?'

'Yeah, I'm fine. Everything all right?'

'Good, yeah. Listen, what are you doing tomorrow?'

'Nothing, really. I was going to work here. Why?'

'Do you fancy an outing? I'm thinking of taking Sheila and Zoe to Rewley, get out of Nottingham for the day.'

'Sure, yeah.'

'If it's fine we could picnic, otherwise the pub's good for lunch.'

'That'd be great. Things going well?'

'Sort of.'

There's a pause. I can't understand the conversation.

'Did you see the drawing? I handed it in to exhibits yesterday. You were out, I tried to find you.'

'Yeah, I had a look this morning. It's good, Declan, really good. I'll pick you up at eleven, will I?'

'Eleven's fine. See you then.'

'Yeah, see you.'

I go through to the sitting room, to where mother and daughter are playing. I watch for a few seconds, the pointless transfer of spoon from empty bowl to immobile plastic lips. Isabel either doesn't hear, or chooses to ignore, my arrival.

'He wanted to know if we'd like to go to Rewley tomorrow.'

She looks up, Jessie does too, smiling at the figure of her father in the doorway.

'We've got something on.'

'I told him we'd go.'

'Fine. You go, then. Jess and I have got other things to do.'

★   ★   ★

296

You are finally here. You bring your car to a stand-still just below the summit, hand reflexively grasping the handbrake. It is high time your mind hurtled back along the ethereal trail, scintillating as it accelerates towards you. Reunited, you can function once more as a sentient human, grounded on the earth, operating according to natural law, deprived of every special power with which you have been endowed.

I don't know what you will find at the top of Rewley Hill. Last time I was here, the cottage was in disrepair, a home for rats and mice and non-migrating birds. That was the day your father took me, you, your mother on the last trip we made together. He seemed unsurprised when he collected me, when neither Isabel nor Jessie appeared. And if you were disappointed at the absence of your young playmate, you didn't show it. Permanence was an unknown quality to you, the child.

We drove out of Nottingham on the A610, wending our way along a route we had travelled a half-dozen times before. I sat next to your father; your mother and you were in the back. Little was said by us adults, but you kept up a commentary of the scenes through which we passed. It was a fine, late autumn day, almost an Indian summer, and your mother had brought a basket of food. We passed the pub, the church, the graveyard, the Variant ploughing onwards up the hill, an oblong box of sky-blue in the greens and browns of the Derbyshire peaks. Eventually we arrived where you yourself are now. Get out, stretch your legs, spend a moment savouring the view over the land your father cherished. When you are quite ready, sit yourself on the grassy slope in front of the cottage, somewhere near the spot where we all sat those thirty years ago, and listen to the shimmer of the breeze in the ash and elm and oak that have populated this hillside since before any of us came into being.

Your father balances you on his knee. Your mother sits off to the side. Your eternal companion, a white rabbit, rests on a stone seat. I look at you all, a happy family. I am reminded of the last time we were here, a day when Isabel and Jessie came too. A day when we debated, long and hard, the respective merits of the camera and the artist's eye. When I sketched the three of you, sitting much as you are sitting now, pencil on paper torn from your father's pocketbook. And when, taking the opposing case, Isabel photographed you with your father's Kodak Instamatic.

Inquest

'Now, Ms Arthur, if I could turn to the subject of your father's estate. He has, of course, named you in his will?'

'Yes.'

'Would you please tell us how much you stand to benefit from his death?'

[Mr Johnson stands.] 'Objection.'

'Mr Forshaw, I hope I need not remind you again.'

'I apologize. If I could rephrase the question. Ms Arthur, are you aware of any factors which could have a significant effect on the eventual size of your father's estate?'

'His house is a large part of it. I've no idea how much that might eventually sell for.'

'I am thinking more of the insurance policies he held at the time of his death. You are aware, are you, that the sums assured are subject to certain exclusion clauses?'

'I am, yes.'

'And that one of these clauses covers intentional self-inflicted injury?'

'My father didn't kill himself.'

'That is not what I asked. Are you aware of this clause?'

'Yes, I am.'

'Thank you. Now, Ms Arthur, you were present during the evidence given by Gordon Findlay earlier in the course of this hearing.'

'I was.'

'Mr Findlay being better known to you as Uncle Bob?'

'When I was younger, yes.'

'Because he and his wife helped look after you on the frequent occasions your father was away from home?'

'Yes.'

'So Mr Findlay was a close friend of the family?'

'He was.'

'Could you explain what was meant when he alluded to problems within the family?'

[Mr Johnson stands.] 'No evidence to that effect has been admitted.'

'Mr Forshaw?'

'Very well. Perhaps I could ask you directly. Were there any problems between you and your father, or indeed within the wider family?'

'No.'

'None at all?'

'No.'

'But you didn't see him that often. You live, what, some five miles away and you last saw him six *weeks* before his death?'

300

'I loved my father. You've no right to go twisting things to make them sound the way you want.'

'It is not my intention to twist anything. How many times did you see him this year, for example?'

[Mr Johnson stands.] 'Counsel is badgering the witness.'

'Mr Forshaw?'

'All I am attempting to do, sir, is establish the basis of the relationship between the witness and the deceased.'

'To what end?'

'Ms Arthur, as we have heard, states consistently that her father could not have committed suicide. I would submit that it is material in weighing such evidence to consider the foundations of that opinion.'

'Very well, you may continue.'

'Thank you. Ms Arthur? How many times did you see him this year?'

'I don't remember.'

'Was it once, twice?'

'More than that.'

'How much more? Three times, four times? Did you visit your father five miles across west London four times in the year before he died?'

'Something like that, yes. But he was always working, and I — '

'And how long did you stay, on these three or four occasions when you paid him a visit?'

'Several hours. We'd usually go for lunch.'

'And how often did he come to see you?'

'He didn't. I always went to him.'

'Your father never came to see you?'

'No. That's just the way it was. I liked going home, there's nothing wrong with that.'

'No, indeed. Why did your father never visit you, Ms Arthur?'

'As I said, I liked going home.'

'You are married, are you?'

'I have a partner.'

'And you have children, is that right?'

'One, a little girl. That's why I didn't see him so often. Things are so hectic — '

'You, your partner, your child, you all had to get in your car, in the midst of this hectic life of yours, and drive to your father's house every time you wished to see him and it never occurred to any of you that it would be easier if he came to you instead?'

'Look, you're making something out of nothing. You don't understand.'

'Ms Arthur, I have to agree with you, I do not understand. What I would suggest, however, is that spending a few hours in your father's company every three months or so does not best place you to pronounce on his state of mind or indeed the likelihood or otherwise of his having committed suicide. Would that seem a fair conclusion to you?'

'I told you — we spoke on the phone at least once a week.'

'Ah, yes, the phone calls. Thank you, Ms Arthur, that will be all.'

[Mr Forshaw sits.]

'Would you like a break before taking questions from Mr Johnson?'

'Thank you, yes.'

[Adjourned.]

Part Eight

Galleries Of Justice

Lunch inside her, Holly falls asleep on the way back to Nottingham. I switch off the tape and drive in silence, my mind alive with fresh insight. I could phone Paul on his mobile, tell him I'm going to be late, but there's no way of doing it without losing face. He's the one who is in the wrong, it shouldn't be me calling first. Besides, he himself resolved my confusion the previous evening — at what I thought were lies on Declan Barr's part, at the stand-off between us — with his smug assertion that Dad must have spoken to someone other than the man whose name was on the answer phone. I have to speak to Declan Barr again — about the phone call, the photograph — and it has to be face to face.

I suspend all thought throughout the confusion of lanes and one-way roads around the city centre. Finally I pick up signs for the Lace Market, then recognize a few buildings, realize I'm just along from Weekday Cross. I take a right and find myself at the far end of High Pavement. There's nowhere to park — double yellows all the way — but it's

Sunday so I chance it and leave the car outside the Galleries of Justice, a museum just along from the sundial that marks the alleyway to his house. Holly's had barely half an hour, but there's the journey to London to sleep through later so I lift her gently from the car and let her wake in my arms as I walk down the street.

The gate remains unlocked. I carry her along the passage, talking rubbish, telling her how we'll go back and see Daddy soon, how he'll be so pleased to see her, how she'll get to have another bounce on the bed before we set off, how we're going home soon, darling. Daddy, home, daddy, home. She listens to my voice, seems to be weighing every word, her eyes looking at my chest, her face sober as she jolts with the rhythm of my strides.

Everything can become a game. I let her try pushing the bell, but it's stiffer than the one at home and I have to help. We stand in front of the house, waiting for a response, the seconds accumulating till it seems there can be no one there. We ring again and this time Holly manages it by herself. She's more awake now, goes into a sudden jig in my arms, excited at the noise she's managed to create. It won't be Daddy, I tell her hurriedly, in case she's got the wrong idea, in case she thinks that any moment Paul will appear, feigning surprise at the sight of his little visitor, which is what he always does on those occasions when we return to him at the flat.

Declan Barr opens the door. He looks at me, then at Holly, then back at me.

★ ★ ★

Eight days since Dad died. It was cold and raining. I'd arranged a service at a local C of E church, even though he was not much of a believer. I wanted something dignified and it is still the church which supplies that.

Paul took Holly to his mum's. He was right: she'd be disturbed if I got distraught, and in any case, she'd never have made it through without getting bored, needing bright, cheery entertainment, completely inappropriate to the occasion. I wanted Paul, though, but he thought he ought to stay with her in Farnham. I was not alone in the chapel, Bob Findlay was in the pew by my side. Behind me, Bill and Sue Jackson kept Biddy Bedford company — her husband was laid up with flu. A manager from the food distribution depot had come, as had another man I recognized as a colleague from Dad's days in complaints and discipline. At home, a pile of condolence cards spoke of Dad's popularity and the affection in which he was held. But it was short notice, a weekday, and I realized then that my form letter must have seemed impersonal, not at all inviting. I was still hoping for other mourners to appear, to swell this miserable scattering, when the organist struck up. The coffin was borne into the church by four professionally sombre pallbearers from the Coop.

* ★ ★

'So, this is Ray's granddaughter.' His speech is slower than I remember, more ponderous.

'Mr Barr,' I tell him, 'I'm sorry to call unannounced. I wanted to apologize for yesterday. I was wrong to speak to you like that.'

He stands inside the threshold, gazing at Holly with a steady stare. I think he might be drunk. After a few seconds' silence I hitch Holly up on my hip.

'It's just that, I had Dad's final phone bill. He made a call to your number the day he died, spent three-quarters of an hour on the phone. I'm sorry, I'd assumed it was you. It didn't occur to me there might have been someone else here he spoke to.'

I see him frown, as if trying to understand what I'm saying. I realize I'm disjointed, that I'm announcing the result of deliberations that have been going round my head for hours. I'm waiting for him to say something, anything. To say: Oh, yes, I see what you mean, that would have been my wife, my daughter, I'll have to ask them. Or else to say: I'm terribly sorry, I lied to you, yes your father and I talked at length that day and all he repeated over and over again was how good you were, how you had such a lot on your plate, how none of it was your fault, how he would miss you so very very much when he was gone.

★ ★ ★

My breasts had budded, small mounds of flesh beneath the skin. I lay in the bath, soapy hands running over nipples darker than they had ever been before. I was becoming a woman, it was daunting, exciting. I stood, the tepid water lapping round my shins. Lifted a foot, clear of the enamelled side, shifted my weight forward to land a sole on the fluff of the mat. My other foot slipped on the scooped bottom of the bath, I dropped precipitously, a scuffing blow to the top of my thigh before I toppled, an involuntary cry leaving my lips. I was face down, dazed, leg still trailing over the side of the bath, when Dad burst through the unlocked door.

311

I felt his hands on my shoulders, beneath my arms, as he lifted me.

'Are you all right?'

Gathered me against him. Put his arms round me, wet as I was.

There were no tears to comfort. I was shocked, I was shrivelled with embarrassment.

'I'm OK,' I managed, finding it difficult to suck air into my chest. 'Please, go.'

He stood me on the floor, had turned away even before I had finished wrapping a towel around myself. His check-shirted back disappeared as the solid wood closed behind him. I sat on the chair and felt the throbbing in my thigh, could see the faint impression of a bruise beginning in the smooth skin.

★ ★ ★

'Mr Barr?'

He seems suddenly to remember himself, to remember Holly and me on his doorstep.

'I'm sorry.'

He looks momentarily undecided and I wonder if he will ask us inside after all.

'I see what you're saying, but you're wrong. There's no one else here. Isabel left me a long time ago, I haven't seen her or Jessie for thirty years. If your father spoke to anyone it would have been me.'

'You admit you spoke, then? The day he died?'

'We may have done. I really can't remember.'

I hug Holly a fraction tighter into my side. 'Surely you'd remember if he'd phoned? I'm not out to make trouble, I just want to know what he said, what was going through his mind. It's desperately important to me. The inquest recorded a verdict of accidental death. Did I tell you? It's what I wanted at the time. But I just don't know if it's true.'

'She's beautiful, your daughter, she takes after you. I can see your mother in you both.'

I am getting nowhere. I have to find some way round his reticence.

'You took that photo, didn't you, the one of us at Rewley? I've been out there today — I'd never thought about it before, but someone had to have taken the picture. That's how you had a copy, isn't it? How you did that drawing?'

He shakes his head slowly, his eyes remaining on Holly, who is looking back at him with all the unabashed curiosity of her age.

'No,' he says. 'I'm an artist — the camera's no friend of mine. I've never taken a photograph in my entire life.'

'Who took it, then?'

He draws a breath in through his nose. 'That photograph, my drawing, they were two sides of a bet.'

Holly starts the faint moans of boredom, of what-are-we-doing standing outside this house talking to a strange man?

'What do you mean, a bet?'

'Nothing, really. It was all a long time ago. It's best forgotten.'

'*Why* won't you talk to me?'

He moves a hand to hold the edge of the door. 'I'm sorry.'

I feel utterly defeated. The only way I can express my frustration is to refuse to say goodbye. I have turned away, am heading back towards the alley, when a thought strikes me, a sudden, startling realization.

'Hold on,' I call, my voice stopping the front door inches from closure. 'You said you've not seen your daughter for thirty years?'

'Yes.'

'But I've seen those pictures. The ones of her graduating, skiing, at school. The paintings, in that room. How have you done those if you've not seen her?'

He shakes his head, starts to close the door again. The latch engages with a solid clunk.

Without a further word he shuts me out, leaves me staring at the black paint and the numerals 5 and 2. I think about ringing the bell, keeping my finger on it for as long as it takes to get him to come back. But there's Holly, writhing now with impatience. Plus I think I could lean on the doorbell for an hour and it would make not the slightest bit of difference. I am locked in a never-ending pursuit, the thing I'm chasing forever beyond my grasp.

★ ★ ★

Towards the end of January I cleared the last of the boxes from Dad's house. All the rubbish had gone to the tip, all the unwanted clothes and appliances had been taken to charity shops. What remained was the stuff I could not afford to let slip away. I took it back to the flat and piled it in the spare room till I could decide what I was going to do with it. Paul fussed, said we were pushed for space as it was. I told him I wasn't going to be forced into anything I might regret.

A couple of days later the solicitor called with the news that we had completed. The proceeds, less the legal costs, would be transferred to Holly's trust fund to join the rest. Dad had been canny, he told me. What with the insurance payouts, his estate had gone above the threshold for inheritance tax. Had he left it all to me, the treasury would have got their hands on a substantial proportion. I thanked him for all his help. He said he'd be sending my bequest within the week.

Holly was having her lunchtime nap. I continued my rummage through the boxes, till at last I found the framed photo I was looking for. The three of us outside Rewley Hill Top. It was the first occasion I'd had both it and the drawing sent to Dad at Christmas in the same room. Only when I compared them directly did the deficiencies of the artist's version come to light. There were the inevitable shortcomings in detail — trees rendered sketchily, whereas the camera had depicted every leaf. But there were more substantial flaws. In the drawing, I am smiling; in the photograph I am more serious, puzzled by something I appear to be able to see. And Mum. In the pencil sketch she is no more than a couple of feet from dad and me, her arms crossed loosely. The photograph has her far further to the side, and the way her arms are wrapped around her would make anyone think she was freezing cold.

Declan

Go a little way up the hill until you reach the gates of Hill Top Farm. These days I cannot say, but back then there were half a dozen horses stabled around the flagstone court-yard. It was a tradition: you and Jessie would go there every time we visited Rewley, mothers in tow so you could be lifted up to stroke the velvety noses, to feel the warm whinnies of breath. Your father and I would be left sprawled on the grassy bank, overlooking the Derbyshire Dales, granted anything up to half an hour of uninterrupted adult time.

Today, the last time I will ever come here, Jessie is off somewhere with Isabel, I don't know where. Sheila says she'll take you to the stables. Ray and I remain with the picnic things, drinking beer and watching you go. I wouldn't know what passes between your mother and you — perhaps she holds you that little bit more closely as she brings you face to equine face, perhaps she indulges your ever-changing whims with a degree more patience than usual.

'The Mortensen woman fucked up.'

I expected Ray to quiz me as soon as you were out of earshot, to ask what is wrong. Not a word has been said about Isabel and Jessie's absence, no questions asked, no explanation given. I have none to give, anyway, and I refuse to lie for appearances' sake.

'What happened?'

'She picked some random fisherman out of the line. Hunter walked out with a grin all over his fucking face.'

I shrug. 'I always thought she was making more of it than she should — I don't know if she even saw anything.'

Your father leans in towards me.

'I *told* her his number, Declan. She only had to say it and we'd be home dry.' He throws his head back, looks skywards. 'We're fucked, not a scrap to go to court on. The stupid fucking cow.'

I look at him, the stretch of his neck, the slope up to his jawbone, the solid hoop of the underside of his mandible.

'What about the semen? That matched Hunter's blood group.'

'Yeah, along with fifteen per cent of the rest of the population. I need to place him at the scene, something to narrow the odds. Without that, the bastard's untouchable.'

'What about my picture? The girl gave a lot

318

of detail, in the end.'

Your father shakes his head. 'It was asking too much. It's nothing like him. Gaby Sinclair says it's all we're going to get — she doesn't think there's any other way in.'

We are silent for a moment. I think back to the countless revisions, the remodelling of nose, of lips, of hair, every feature described in comparison to something else — the colours of the everyday world, the faces of TV presenters, of showjumpers, of characters in *Swallows and Amazons, The Railway Children*. I never really believed it would be possible to do a face like that.

Your father reaches behind him to where he's laid an attache case. He removes a manilla envelope.

'Would you want that within a hundred miles of Jess?'

A Land Rover grinds along the road below us, wrestling with the steepness of the incline. As its engine note draws level, begins to recede, I slide out the contents, three 10 x 8 black and white prints on fine-grade Ilford paper. I study the photos. The top one has water in the foreground, a group of children standing on a tree-lined bank, a flotilla of ducks on the lake in front of them. Only when I look at the next picture do I realize what I missed. Taken at higher power, it has just a couple of the kids at its very edge, bits of bread discernible in their hands — one of them is caught in the act of throwing. The skew away from the composition of the first is deliberate: in the centre of this photo is a line of railings along the path beside the lake. The figure of a man leans against them. He is alone. The third print is the highest magnification of all, the graininess suggesting darkroom enlargement rather than shorter focal length. The man's features are blurred, but he can be made out, as can the direction of his gaze, fixed where I estimate the unaccompanied children to be. The narrow chin, the pinched cheeks, the blade of the nose, the deep-set eyes, the straight hair hanging limply either side of his out-jutting ears. He looks nothing like my initial impression, formed from Maggie Mortensen's obliging fictions. And aside from one or two characteristics, he looks nothing like the face Mary Scanlon has had me draw.

'I tell you, Declan, the stuff we've seen. The best we'll get is a breach of bail — Worksop magistrates put an exclusion from schools and parks on his conditions. He'll disappear somewhere else and start all over.'

'The maid? Surely she'll turn up?'

'Not a sniff in over a month.'

I'm still staring at him, at the man with the

child, at the face I've spent five days in a darkened observation room trying to capture. Still trying to picture him, to see those features grimacing as he spurts hot spunk high into the arse of the girl I have watched playing in the land of make believe. Still trying to see her, out in the open air by the reservoir that feeds the slums of St Ann's, bent double, school skirt flung up over her back, pants and tights looped around one ankle, skinny legs goosebumped and splayed.

'Daddy!'

You are running full pelt towards us, your mother following some way behind. Something exciting has happened — a horse has eaten a piece of apple from your palm, I don't know — you are flushed with the excitement of everything life has to offer. Your three-year-old body is in full flight, racing across the uneven ground, the hillocks of grass, the depressions of abandoned rabbit burrows. I start to slide the photos back in the envelope — there's something obscene in the idea that you might catch sight of them.

'Daddy!'

Your father levers himself to his feet, a smile starting on his face, his attention completely diverted by the reappearance of you, his daughter.

I'm looking at your mother, walking in the

background — her hand shoots towards her mouth. I switch my gaze to see you sprawling, your sprained ankle trailing. You hit the ground with a thud we can hear at forty feet. Your father is running, I have never seen anyone move so fast. He has you, he lifts you, he holds you. You are screaming, sobbing, you are struggling for breath. He brings you back, Sheila catching you as he reaches me. There are tears on your face, snot on his jacket, your knees are green with chlorophyll and red with blood. You are hurt, physically. You are hurt at the abrupt loss of all that had been wonderful to you.

There is a time of calming, of convincing you that you are safe, that you are protected, that you are all right after all. I watch your father, his absorption in your distress. I am helpless: do not know where my child is, nor if I could ever be this to her.

The picnic is abandoned, the need now is to get you home and bathe your raw flesh. Once you are over the worst, Sheila carries you to the car while your father and I bundle things together, piling plates and knives, leaving half-eaten sandwiches for the birds. With the absence of mother and child once more, a change, a reversion takes place in him. A shift from indulgent father to jaundiced detective.

322

'Eddie Ault, the exhibits officer? He lost your picture, you know.'

I stop what I'm doing, look at him as he slings undrunk drink on to the treacherous grass.

'You said you'd seen it.'

He glances up. 'Yeah, and now the clumsy bastard has gone and mislaid it. It's a major fuck-up. I told him, I'm seeing Declan tomorrow, maybe he can help you out.'

I hear the wind rustling the trees, blowing leaves to the ground. The solid clunk of a car door shutting, your mother having settled you inside.

'That drawing is unique.'

'You can't remember it, have another go?'

It's laughable, he can't have any idea what went into the creation of that face. 'No way, Ray, it simply can't be done.'

He shakes his head, slips one empty glass inside the other. 'Ah, well, never mind. Like I said, it wasn't much good to us.'

He gathers the blanket, drapes it over an arm, collects his attache case. The only thing left on the grass is the manilla envelope. We look at it, both of us, almost as if we have no idea what to do with it. Then he reaches down, picks it up. Passes it to me.

'Tell you what, why don't you try, at least. Eddie's up shit creek. If you manage anything, let me have it first thing. I can probably slip it in the file before anyone else notices the original has gone.'

★   ★   ★

It is time you left Derbyshire, returned to the city. Perhaps you are on your own in the car, perhaps your husband and daughter are with you. As you drive back, as you enter the outskirts of Nottingham, try to imagine how it was for me. I am in the front passenger seat of your father's car. Behind us, you and your mother are singing songs, playing I Spy, anything to entertain during the journey home. In my hands is the envelope containing the photographs of the man with the child. Your father is silent — he has already said all he needs to say. He seems content to let me listen to the sounds of a happy family, to imagine the enormity of anything that might rip it asunder. The house on High Pavement is empty when I return, no sign of Isabel and Jessie. I take whisky to the studio and sit drinking. Only when I am drunk enough not to care do I set about drawing my final face.

And while I am working? While I am struggling with the task your father has set me? I don't know. Perhaps he is back home with you, with Sheila, finishing the day as a family man should. Or perhaps he has gone into work, proclaiming the gravity of the inquiry, and even now is drinking in the County, or out prowling the Nottingham streets, a lone hunter in the night, afraid of what lurks within his own breast.

This is the me of now, the me who has seen it all unfold. Tonight I would snap my charcoal in two, fling it to the studio floor. Tonight I would grab a jacket and leave my half-finished portrait and my abandoned home and pursue him through the back streets and the darkened alleys seeking him in every late-night drinking den and blind-eyed brothel till eventually I find him somewhere in the shadowy no-man's land between right and wrong and good and evil which is, after all, his domain. And when I recognize him I will touch his shoulder and turn him round and ask him straight out: who was the man of my impression, whose was the face Mary Scanlon had me draw, who was he, the man with the child?

★ ★ ★

The last job I did for the police was the artwork for a stranger danger campaign. They wanted a flip-pad made to look like a children's book — *Sally Likes Sweets* or some such crap. I can't remember much about the story: Sally's mum won't give her any pocket money because she always blows it on chocolate and she's already got a mouthful of fillings and she's only nine. She's moping round the park and a car pulls up and it's got this guy inside and he says what's the matter? And Sally tells him and he says I'll buy you something, what's your favourite, why don't you hop in? Blah blah blah. It's all right — she doesn't get buggered and strangled and dumped in the river. She just gets driven round and keeps saying I want to go home now and the guy won't let her and she gets pretty scared and starts crying but then her mum sees the car and grabs the door while it's stopped at some lights and Sally's really happy because she's back with those who love her. She never gets her sweets, though — wrong message, if she'd been taken straight down to the newsagents to make it all better.

The brief from the writer was unimaginative. Sally was to be a pretty little girl with bunches, her mum should look harassed but caring, and the man in the car was to have long hair and a beard. I followed my instructions faithfully and the first version was accepted without revisions.

Your father launched the campaign a

couple of days before the Hunter case came to trial. The *Evening Post* was covering it, plus a camera crew from regional news. I watched it that evening — your father standing at the front of the classroom, turning the pages, the kids fidgety and giggling at the idea of being on TV. The end shot shows them getting their little duffel coats and trooping out of the door, heading for the gates where the teacher's waiting to hold them up till they're matched with their mums, thence to be carted off home. Every one of them safe now that they would know how to recognize a stranger if they ever saw one.

★ ★ ★

The prosecution barrister leads me through the evidence in chief. The circumstances of the picture, the degree of consistency in Mary Scanlon's replies, the extent of my liaison with Dr Sinclair. Then he asks permission of the judge to introduce an exhibit. I am shown a copy of the face, asked if this is the result of my five days sitting in a darkened observation room. It is, I confirm. Further reproductions are distributed to judge, defence, the twelve members of the jury. I have done my job well. It is by no means an exact likeness — these things never are. Yet it is plain to anyone in the court that the face I have drawn is that of the accused.

Defence counsel could eat me alive, I am well aware. I quickly realize he is going through the motions. Unlike the jurors, he is privy to Hunter's previous record: his convictions for knob-waving, for fingering the fanny of a five-year-old girl. The barrister has, moreover, had more than one instruction from Harry Scanlon in the past. He is as indifferent to his client's fate as it is possible to be without being mistaken for a member of the prosecution.

Leaving the courtroom, your father is waiting for me.

'How did it go?'

'Fine,' I tell him. 'Better than fine.'

He claps me on the back. 'Good on you. Fancy a drink?'

In those days the courts were next to the central police station; they now form part of the Galleries of Justice. We stroll along High Pavement till we reach the County Tavern. Your father stands the first round, brings it over to me at the table, where I am already midway through my second cigarette.

'Ray,' I say, after accepting my pint, 'I'm resigning. I thought you should know.'

He looks at me carefully for a moment.

'Nothing I've done, I hope?'

I shake my head. 'I need to concentrate on my own work.'

'That's a shame, Declan. You'll be missed, I mean that. You've done well.' He takes a drink from his bitter. 'You've not been put off by this business?'

'No. Not at all.'

'What does Isabel say?'

'She doesn't know yet. I've only just decided.'

'What about the money? You'll miss that, surely?'

'I'll find something else.'

We sup from our pints. Your father takes a light from me.

'What about the trial?' I ask. 'Which way is it going to go?'

'Fifty-fifty, I'd say. All depends whether his brief puts him on the stand. If he does, we're home and dry, he's such trash. If not — well, who knows.'

We leave the County, your father turning down a second, wanting to return to the double doors leading to court number one, where he will peer through the windows and read the runes in the protagonists' expressions. We reach the pavement outside the Crown Court and I prepare to take my leave. A pair of suited men trot down the steps, bundles of pink-ribboned documents beneath their arms. Both murmur greetings to your father. I have only a glimpse, just enough to fail to recognize either of them. Just enough to be bothered by the sense that I have seen one of them before.

'Who was that?' I ask your father, once they have passed twenty feet along High Pavement.

He smiles. 'You've got to hand it to him. Bloke who buggered his daughter's on trial and he carries on as if fuck all is happening.'

★ ★ ★

George Duffield calls me in two days later, after he has received my resignation. I stand in his office while he re-reads the letter.

'Sit down.' He flicks my handwritten note. 'Has this got anything to do with Ray?'

I am instantly on my guard — no one else should know, there was an unspoken understanding. 'No. Personal reasons, pure and simple.'

'It's just that if it has, he's about to be seconded to London. I realize it would be difficult for you to keep working with him, but you wouldn't have to. He'd be out of your hair in a month.'

My mouth dries, I feel appallingly exposed,

wonder how much your father has confessed, who else apart from Duffield knows what we have done. 'It's got nothing to do with him.'

He fixes me with a stare. 'You'll be hard to replace, you know that, don't you?'

'You'll find someone.'

'You've made up your mind?'

I nod.

He lowers his eyes, gets to his feet, walks round the desk to show me out. 'Well, all I can say is, I'm truly sorry. You didn't deserve to be treated like that.'

I feel his hand on my back.

'If it's any consolation, you weren't the first, and I doubt you'll be the last. There's been more than one bust-up in the department over his behaviour.'

We walk to the door, him shaking his head.

'He's a bloody good copper, you know. A bloody good copper and a fine detective. He just can't keep his trousers on. Still, that'll be the Met's problem now.'

The door is open, I am through it before I realize what is happening.

'By the way,' Duffield is suddenly brighter. 'Have you heard? The jury returned a guilty verdict on the Hunter case this morning. You did really well for us there, Declan. You couldn't finish on a better note.'

He takes my hand, finds it limp and lifeless,

shakes it with firmness and vigour nevertheless.

'If by any chance you reconsider, please, let
me know.'

★   ★   ★

I go straight to the kitchen, find Jessie playing
with some wooden spoons on the floor by the
table. Hearing the door she looks up, beams
at the sight of me, levers herself laboriously to
her feet, toddles across with her arms held
high. I pick her up, stare at the back of
Isabel's head, watch her pretending to be
busy.

'I've just been to see George Duffield.'

She half-turns, throws a glance at me.

'He tried to persuade me to stay on.'

She holds my gaze for a second. 'And?'

'I said no.'

She nods, once, then turns back to the
stove.

'He told me Ray's about to be moved to
London.'

'Oh?'

'He'll be gone in a month, apparently.'

I'm looking at her hair, ignoring Jessie's
hand, which is groping and exploring my lips,
my ear, the stubbly flesh of my cheek.

'You'll miss him, won't you?'

She doesn't reply, carries on stirring whatever is in her pot.

'Ray,' I say. 'You'll miss him when he's gone.'

'Not really,' she says. 'He's your friend, not mine.'

I can feel my heart beneath my ribs, right where I am holding Jessie. 'When did you find the time?'

She lays her spoon down, rests a hand against the work surface either side of the cooker, sighs. 'It wasn't difficult. You spend every evening down the pub.'

Jessie is pulling at my sideburn, her nails digging into my skin.

'So, what, you're fucking him while she's asleep upstairs. Is that it?'

She wheels around, glares at me. 'We'll talk about this later.'

'No, we'll talk about it now. What the fuck do you think you're doing, screwing my friend behind my back?'

'I wasn't screwing him — he was screwing me. Your friend? You're all the same, none of you think further than your next fuck.'

Jessie starts to cry. I hold her away from me, see her face crumpling, her lips down-turning. Look back at Isabel, the infuriating haughtiness giving way to a look of alarm.

'Give her to me.'

I wrench her from Isabel's outstretched hands, lock her against my chest with my arms. Jessie screams.

'Declan!'

Isabel scrabbles, ripping at my hands trying to prise them apart. Her sudden panic, the smell of her fear, I am too strong for her; she cannot wrest the child from my arms. I twist and duck, Jessie's shrieks piercing my ears. I am all-powerful, she dare not hit me lest she strikes her baby, Declan Declan Declan she's shouting, her voice as hysterical as her daughter's naked cries. You bitch, her nails gouge my hands. I tighten my grip, the scrap of flesh and bone in my arms so infinitely fragile. Let her go let her *go!* I can do what I will and I will hurt her, I will pay her back for what she has done, teeth now sinking through skin. I am roaring with fury, all the people who knew, who were laughing. And she grips a finger and bends it back with a primitive force. And it is not her, not the loss of her, but the loss of my pride. And a bone in my artist's hand gives with a *crack!* and a blinding white-hot pain.

Inquest

'Mr Johnson?'

[Mr Johnson stands.]

'Ms Arthur, I do not propose to waste time correcting the erroneous impressions my learned friend has been trying to create. I merely ask one question of you. You do not believe your father could deliberately have caused this accident. Might I enquire your reasons for this view?'

'Well, he was — I'm not sure I can explain this. My father devoted his life to protecting the innocent. Although he'd retired he was still a police officer at heart. There is simply no way, even if he had been intending to end his life, he would have done so in a way which might have endangered others.'

'Ms Arthur, we have heard testimony to the effect that this accident occurred on a busy stretch of a major A road, that at least one driver almost came to grief as a result of a collision with wreckage from the crash. You are saying, are you, that if your father had intended to commit suicide, this would have been the very last method which would have occurred to him?'

'I am, yes. He simply wouldn't have done something like that deliberately.'

'No, I'm sure he wouldn't. Tell me, you have a young child, do you not?'

'Yes, a daughter. She was ten months old when he died.'

'And he was a good grandfather, was he, your father?'

'Yes, he doted on her. When she was born he opened a savings account for her, paid fifty pounds a month into it. He even changed his will so the majority of his estate was held in trust for her.'

'She gave him something new to live for?'

'Yes, I think so. I mean, we didn't get to see him as often as I'd have liked, but it always cheered him up, spending time with her.'

'You didn't get to see him because of the pressures in your lives?'

'That's right. He always said he knew I had a lot on my plate. He never minded, said there'd be plenty of time to get to know her when things were less hectic.'

'And, in fact, he himself was busy, too, was he not? You've described the demanding shift work he did.'

'Yes.'

'But he was looking forward? Anticipating a time when both you and he would be less committed? When he might become a significant presence in the life of his new grandchild?'

'Yes. I believe so, yes.'

'As well as a significant presence in your own?'

'Yes.'

'Hardly the attitude of someone about to kill themselves, would you say?'

★　★　★

'Ms Arthur?'

★　★　★

'Ms Arthur, I think counsel is asking whether you believed your father to have been depressed at all?'

'Yes, I'm sorry. I didn't think he was.'

'You didn't think, or you knew not?'

'I'm not sure.'

'Ms Arthur, in earlier testimony you stated that you did not believe that your father was depressed. Now you say you're not sure. Which is it to be?'

'I'm sorry. It's just — well, the more I think about it, the more I realize that if he had been, I would probably have been the last person to know.'

[Testimony ends.]

Part Nine

Part Nine

Home

'Did you find it then?'

We're past Leicester Forest East services before Paul speaks. Neither of us has said a word since the functional exchanges that saw us checked out and loaded up and finally on the road back to London.

'I think so. It's changed since the photo was taken but I'm pretty sure it was the cottage.'

'And?'

'Yes. It was good. I'm glad I went.'

I see him nodding in the corner of my eye. I check my rear view, indicate, pull out to overtake a line of lorries, their lights glowing fiercely in the night.

'At least something went according to plan, then.'

'What do you mean by that?'

'Well, it's not been a conspicuous success has it, this great pilgrimage? Or has it? Did you get anything out of it?'

'I'm not talking to you if you're going to be like that.'

'Like what? I'm genuinely interested, Zoe. I'd love to know whether coming here, seeing

341

your old home, meeting that friend of your dad's, going out to Rewley — whether any of it has made the slightest difference to anything.'

I reach the head of the convoy, duck back to the inside lane again, plough on for a while in silence. It's going to be a long journey home. I feel like pulling up on the hard shoulder, telling him to get out, driving the rest of the way just me and the sleeping Holly. I wish now I'd had the guts to leave without him as I'd fantasized.

'Only I'm looking forward to things getting back to normal now, to us being able to get on with the rest of our lives.'

The overhead signs are flashing a fifty mile an hour speed restriction. A few miles ahead I can see a condensation of tail lights, the hazy glow of slow moving traffic.

'I'll tell you one thing I have sorted out — Holly's money is staying untouched.'

'Sorry?'

'I've decided — we're not using it to fund a move. Dad didn't want it used like that. If he had, he wouldn't have put it in trust.'

'You heard what the solicitor said. That was a tax-saving measure.'

I shake my head. 'No, he wanted it to be used for Holly.'

Paul sighs. 'And a bigger house, a garden,

you and me not slogging our guts out to keep going — that's not in her best interests?'

'I'm not going to argue about it, Paul. It's what I've decided. End of story.'

His turn to fall silent. I can sense the sulkiness seeping out of his pores. When he speaks, his tone is moderated.

'Look, I know it's been a difficult weekend for you. I'm sorry if I've been out of sorts, but it's been difficult for me too.'

'How, exactly?'

I can practically hear him thinking, can imagine the thoughts whirling round his head. The things he'd like to say, the stuff he'd like to get off his chest, the irritation he let slip last night being just the tip of the iceberg. Only he won't, not while Dad's money remains up for grabs. He's pathetic. No time for him while he was alive, his umbrage at what he claimed was my disloyalty. All that has been quietly buried since he's understood what a difference the money could make to his — to our — lives. Bitter laughter wells inside me, I force myself to keep it under control. He was always so indifferent, so ready to consign Dad to the difficult in-law bin. And Dad wasn't easy; I admit that. But how clever he was, how clever he has been.

'Look, Zoe, let's not make any hasty

decisions, OK? Let's take a bit more time. You're still upset, there's a lot of guilt floating around. Maybe we should put the idea of a move on hold, come back to it later in the year.'

'No, Paul, that's the one thing this weekend has helped me see. We're staying put — the flat is Holly's home, mine too, whatever else is wrong with it.'

We approach the back of the jam and I allow the car gradually to decelerate. We're still moving, only about forty, but at least the road ahead is not completely blocked. I stay in the nearside lane and actually it's the fastest moving. We cruise along, inching past vehicles on the right hand side. From time to time I glance across, see drivers illuminated by the confusion of artificial lights, caught in profile, staring ahead, some composed, others beating time on the tops of their steering wheels; some talking on mobiles, one or two miming bizarrely to whatever music is on their stereos. Paul remains quiet and I am content to let it stay that way, to let him confront his own dilemmas, come to his own decisions as to what the future holds. I have Holly in the back and a trust fund in the bank and I know we will be all right whichever way the wind blows.

After a couple of miles we reach the cause

of the hold-up. Blue lights pulse dazzlingly in the night, portable halogen lamps bathe the scene, a recovery vehicle is winching an upturned car from the embankment. Groups of police and fire crew stand watching, hands on hips, ranged behind the protective cones. The tableau imprints itself on my retina — I can still see it as I look forward again, the traffic speeding up, lungeing ahead, suddenly unfettered, free to move at limitless speed once more. I get a flash of memory, a sheet being pulled back from Dad's face, a dressing over his forehead, his eyes closed in sleep, wanting to shake him to wake him to have him sit up and see me and smile. I press my foot against the accelerator, feel the Peugeot's engine respond, gather momentum to take us the rest of the hundred or so miles back home.

Declan

'Enough of the past, leave it behind where it belongs. What was done was done, and cannot now be changed. You have seen the world we inhabited, perhaps you will understand. Drive back, away from Rewley, away from the place your father was born. This is to be your last leg, the final destination. To reach it you must weave through Hucknall, the urban wastelands of Bestwood Park, down the never-ending hill that undulates through Daybrook, Arnold, Sherwood, till once more you are in Carrington, where roads to your left lead up into Mapperley Park with its professional classes huddled in leafy isolation.

Your journey takes you through the northern reaches of our city — it takes you thirty years, three decades, half a lifetime to complete. As you drive, as the tachometer on your dashboard marks off every passing mile, babies are born, people die, governments rise and fall. Huge shifts in culture occur from one set of traffic lights to the next. Doctors write learned papers, new terms appear in dictionaries, newsprint spools by the yard,

346

knowledge is learned and old orthodoxies forgotten. Old men beget new men, whose every action is subject to suspicion, open to interpretation, tainted with the sins of the father.

Make your way towards Tavistock Drive. As you progress through the streets, as the litter swirls, as the decades churn, I must let you travel alone. You leave me behind in the Nottingham of then, standing once more on the branch of a tree, arm curled round the trunk by way of an anchor. Below me, a single green uniform traces unseen paths on an early morning lawn, round and round, up and down, buckled shoes flattening the wet grass. A sudden outburst startles me, a babble of unknown tongue. The words are incomprehensible; their tone is universal — exasperation, anger. I look up to see a squat, olive-skinned woman emerge through a set of French doors, her nose flattened into her pockmarked face, her long black hair tied in a single bunch, which extends down her back to her waist. If the green-uniformed girl below me understands what is being shouted, she chooses not to. She continues her introspective, baffling, pointless game as if the woman were not there — as if she were far away instead, waking, hungover, next to a stranger after a first night party in an anonymous Parisian hotel.

Another voice, deep, booming, all too clear to comprehend. Mary! Come inside this instant! Do you hear me?

Harry Scanlon, sober navy pinstripe, briefcase in hand, greatcoat dangling limply by his calves. His face is livid. The girl flinches at the verbal assault, hesitates, then continues her intricate tracery.

Mary Scanlon!

Round and round, up and down, dark trails in the dew.

Her father looks at his watch, thrusts his case into the arms of the maid. He is quick across the garden, I have seldom seen anyone move so fast. The blow he lands on the side of his daughter's head sends a dull thud which threatens to displace me. I cling on, tightening my grip around the trunk of the tree.

I will not tell you again! Come inside!

A hesitation. Up and down, and round and.

Her feet gouge tramlines in the glistening lawn.

The maid sits herself on a white-painted metal chair, placed to catch the evening sun during the summer months. She uses her apron to wipe the matching table before resting her employer's briefcase down.

You have arrived on Tavistock Drive, you park outside the house with the For Sale sign. On the pavement, your car safely locked behind you, you are struck by a sense of *déjà vu*. You have been here before, in the dead of night, the near-absence of sound roaring like a seashell in your ears. You stood motionless beneath a street lamp, the faulty bulb flickering orange on the scene. The road was empty then, it was two, three, four in the morning. What lights were visible were those left on inadvertently by the last to retire, or the bedside lamps of children afraid to sleep in the dark. A light appeared in the building directly opposite, the perfect circle of the stained glass set in the front door. Which opened. A figure emerged, closed it behind them, started along the path towards the gate. You stepped swiftly to one side, behind the thick trunk of a plane tree. The footsteps were metronomic in the stillness of night. They grew loud, then began to recede. The Filipino maid walked within ten yards of you.

By the time you revealed yourself, she was far from distinct. She carried a suitcase or some sort of large bag in her hand. As she hurried along the pavement she passed repeatedly beneath the street lamps that line the hill. In the pools of light she was clear, but for whole stretches, in the dimness that lies between, she became no more than a vague shape. At times you were not even sure she was there. Light, dark, present, absent, the pattern repeated itself, the figure diminishing in size with every apparition.

From my vantage point, high in a tree which has grown substantially with the passing of thirty years, I can just see through the French doors into a reception room. Mercifully, no sound carries. I see Mary Scanlon, kicking and flailing, face-down across her father's knees. His arm rises, falls, rises, falls, each descent a blur of motion which brings his hand into muffled contact with the seat of her green skirt. She wriggles and writhes, squirming against his thighs his hips his crotch with every one of her attempts to escape.

The maid shifts position on her chair, turns her back on the house, folds her arms across her bosom. She stares out across the immaculate garden, her eyes looking directly at me. For a moment I fear I am discovered. But if she sees me she pretends not to. She knows better than to question the circumstances of the world on which she depends.

I look back, see the skirt already flicked up, see the father yank tights pants down to mid-thigh. His arm rises, falls, rises, falls, each descent a blur of motion that brings his hand into stinging contact with the bare flesh of the daughter's arse. She continues to struggle, wriggling and writhing, squirming against his thighs his hips his hardening crotch, her buttocks quivering with every blow, clenching with every one of her attempts to escape.

This house has been for sale for some time. You search its façade for cracks, for subsidence, scrutinize the window frames for signs of rot. It will be a long while yet before it becomes mere bricks and mortar, before an outsider, someone new to the area, unaware of the totem it has become, makes a purchase. Perhaps they will be lawyers, doctors, accountants, musicians. They will certainly be well-off to think of living here. They will feel secure, the surrounding Victorian properties home to people just like them. No matter that they are but a short walk from the hookers on Forest Fields, that five minutes would see them outside the brothels of Redcliffe Road. As they drive through the city each morning, as they pass the drug-addled chaos of Radford, the Meadows, St Ann's, they will suppress a shiver, thankful that they don't have to live in it. Their new neighbours will be pleased, it will be good to have the house occupied again. A nice normal family, please God

— friendly folk with kids whose laughter can erase the crying of a child that the more fanciful insist can still be discerned on wind-riven nights.

A blur of green breaks free, struggles away somehow from the fevered punishment being meted upon her. She gets but a couple of yards before the fetters of tights, pants, yanked down around her thighs, topple her. The father catches her, picks her bodily from the floor, flings her on to the sofa. Pulls at his belt, ripping it from the hoops around his waist. I try to move, try to leap the thirty feet to reach the trimly cut lawn. I cannot. I am decades too late. Mine is helplessly to observe, to bear witness to the scene that repeats itself down the years.

He stands over her, face-down on the sofa, her arms covering her head, protecting it from what she knows will come. To what she has resigned herself. He is so very strong, something inside has told her to submit, to propitiate his colossal rage. The belt flicks, fast as a viper, down on the pale flesh of her naked buttocks. She lies there, head buried in the cushions, exposed to the next blow she knows will come. Does she hear the belt fall to the floor, the zip being undone? Is there a moment she senses the gravity of the danger she is in? There must be: she jumps up, tries once more to reach the French doors, the wide-open spaces of the garden, the possibility of being heard by unsuspecting neighbours. Now he too is hampered by clothing, his trousers, his pants dropped down around his ankles. Theirs is a sack race, an egg and spoon. All too briefly she is the winner.

The maid twists round at the sound of the French doors flying open. Lurches to her feet, catches the girl in outflung arms. Hugs her into her breasts. Releases her at the few harsh words of Tagalog from the father, who grips Mary's arms, pulls her back inside, closes the French doors, locks them, puts the key in the pocket of his greatcoat which still dangles around his calves.

The maid is impassive. She takes her seat again. Possibly she is thinking of the money she sends home for her children each month. If she noticed her employer's erect penis, thick as a girl's wrist, tortuously veined; if she saw his trousers his pants lying in a heap on the floor, she pretends not to. She knows better than to question the world on which she depends.

The father emerges on to the verandah, pulling his belt tight around his waist again. His greatcoat flaps as he walks towards the maid. In the room behind him I can make out a sprawl of green on the sofa. He approaches the table, the garden chairs; the Filipino maid gets to her feet. With one hand he takes the handle of his briefcase, with the other he waves in her general direction. A gesture that seems to be telling her to go home.

★   ★   ★

Pick up a paper, start a story, any story you like. I guarantee: you'll read a bit, then you won't be able to help yourself. Your eyes will stray a few inches to the side. It's never enough to read. We want pictures. We stare at the images, arrays of dots, black and white and grey. Our eyes drink them in. Our view of people doesn't come purely from words, we have to have the face. We *know* we can do it, read the language of a million years. Gut instinct, first impressions, I didn't like the look. You can't define it, you can't reduce it, it's instinctive — a visceral thing. Newspaper editors know it. They give over space, they could use it for something else — more stories, advertising. But they have to have a picture.

Where in this world can a camera not go?

The reverberations spread no further than the East Midlands. Perhaps it was always going to be that way. It was, after all, a parochial matter. The daughter of a former mayor seeking an injunction to prohibit him from access to her children. It was something for local tongues to wag over. Wonderment at the humiliations our city dignitaries should endure at the hands of their offspring. Speculation as to what could have caused such a deep rift in a family.

Yet, as the case unfolded, it became one the nationals should have devoured. My earnings should have been swelled by syndication fees. But at the time there were riots in Portsmouth, marches on estates from north-east to south-west, fuelled by the denunciations of a Sunday tabloid. Paint was being daubed, windows smashed, innocent men attacked, all because they bore a passing resemblance to the published likenesses of registered paedophiles. This, then, was the news.

For most of the trial I was sketching so hard my muscles threatened to cramp. Pastels giving simplified voice to the colours of flesh, eye, hair, clothes. Only when she entered the courtroom did my hand fall still. I hadn't set eyes on her for three decades. Somehow I'd expected the same nine-year-old girl, snub-nosed and uncertain, to walk through the doors. The woman who came in her place was palpably frightened, but her fear seemed underscored with resolve.

Before she was allowed to speak there was a protracted legal argument. There had been a conviction. Some of the matters she sought to raise were spent. In the end, the magistrates allowed her testimony, citing differing burdens of proof.

Prosecution counsel led her through the evidence-in-chief. The first assault, the bewilderment of doctors, police officers, nurses, firing questions at her from left from right from centre. The dreadful apprehension that she had done something terrible, something appallingly wrong. The appearance of the father, who should have gathered her, raised her aloft, held her till the hurt the pain subsided. The threats that, should she speak, she would be taken from her family for ever. The year of grace — the only help the authorities granted. Then the recommencement, the escalation, the descent into perdition.

Harry Scanlon, our esteemed ex-mayor, representing himself in this his most important case. He rose behind defence counsel's bench, the space he had occupied throughout his legal career. Even now, his skin lined, his flesh looser and flabby, I could feel his power, his rage, his absolute conviction. He spent an interminable time simply staring at her, a slight figure holding determinedly to the sides of the witness box. The blood pulsed in my throat. When he began, his voice came out thick with fury, shredding the hush that had settled on the courtroom. False memory, the spite of the ungrateful daughter, the revenge of the unhinged child. He tore on; it was as though there were just the two of them in the room. There had been a conviction, she was rewriting history, her motives were malign. Mary Scanlon tried to deflect it, a terrible tremor in her voice, yet most of her replies were cut short by a fresh tirade issuing from her father's mouth. The pallor of her cheeks; the high colour in his own. I sketched the faces, then those of the magistrates and wondered who among them would refuse to believe. Who among them was shrinking with shame. At last, the stipendiary intervened. He had to bang his gavel several times before Scanlon's cross-examination could be halted. I looked at the daughter, standing alone in the witness box. She turned to go. As she did so, her eyes connected briefly with mine. The vacancy of shock. For a moment she was nine years old again. There was no two-way mirror between us. I burned with my own mortification.

What led her to break her silence? That there were precedents, new orthodoxies, the chance her story would finally be credible? The years of watching her father — Rotarian, hospital trustee, city councillor — admired and respected by all? Or simply that she was now Mary O'Neill, that she had given birth to a daughter of her own, who was approaching the age she was then?

Three fifty-five, afternoon adjournment. I raced outside, first to leave the court after the bench rose. Found the camera crew, taped up the best sketch, they took their shots of the picture, rushed off to file them and suddenly it was over. Later, on *Midlands Today*, in the *Evening Post*, thousands of people looked at my drawing, the face of Scanlon as I had represented him, scrutinized his expression for signs of arrogance, contrition, innocence, capability, culpability. Guilt. The most difficult thing is to draw what you see. Not to let prejudices, preconceptions, on to the paper.

Even allowing for the passing of the years, he looked only vaguely like the face I remembered drawing in that darkened observation room in the Nottingham of thirty years ago. But, in truth, I can barely recall that amalgam of erased and revised outlines. How close my original impression was, only one man can say. And he crashed his car into a bridge and he cannot explain anything any more.

That evening I sat in my studio and tried yet again to paint what my own daughter has become. I was a fuck-up, a failure. I didn't deserve to have her. I have no idea what she might look like. The last I heard she was in Canada, where her mother has been making waves with her art, concerned with the ripples we create simply by being in the world. The Jessie I paint is more Isabel than me — all her in fact. I cannot see myself in her at all.

I telephoned your father. His number was hard to come by, obtained only with the help of George Duffield, long-retired but still with contacts. Ray and I spoke about the trial, the implications for what we had done. He told me to keep my nerve. There was evidence still to come, character witnesses on behalf of the father, people who had known him for years. For all we knew, what Mary Scanlon was now saying might be a pack of lies. Even if not, Hunter might be dead, there might be nothing more to come of it. We turned it over and over. Wait for the verdict, he told me. Do nothing till then. We spoke of nothing more.

I tried to call him again once the trial was over, once the bench had reached its decision. Tried to tell him that the injunction had been granted. That, as a result, the magistrates had announced they would refer Hunter's long-spent conviction to the court of appeal. I tried to call, but I got no answer. The phone simply rang and rang.

I would like to say he was stricken with guilt over the fate to which he condemned the girl, Mary Scanlon. I would like to think that was true. Yet all I recall from the last conversation we had was his revulsion at the thought that Vincent Hunter might win. Might, in the end, be absolved of the crime for which your father had him convicted. Ray never once asked about Isabel, what had happened to her, nor of Jessie and what she now had become.

I couldn't tell you, not when you came. Even now I am uncertain whether you will ever hear these words. I have been summonsed to give evidence at Hunter's appeal. The last time I spoke to George Duffield he told me that Eddie Ault, the exhibits officer to whom I handed the man with the child some thirty years ago, has also been called to appear. While I am in the stand, a London court artist will sketch my face. I will appear in every national newspaper alongside reports of my testimony. With Ray Arthur dead, I alone know what we did. No one can contradict me, I have free rein. I can, if I wish, find a way to acquit myself, even though he will carry all the blame. Christ knows, I am sorely tempted. Perhaps this was his legacy to me. His way of atoning for Isabel, Jessie.

Whatever I testify under oath, the truth is contained here. I hope you will forgive me what ultimately I might say.

★   ★   ★

You are floating high, our city becoming smaller beneath you. The air is rarefied, hard to breathe. You are in no mood for tumble turns, for swooping like a swallow. You see houses, streets, districts, diminishing with every moment. Much further and you risk collision with the jets that ply the route between Heathrow and New York. You are beginning to succumb, flashes of light in your vision, your mind muzzy with lack of oxygen.

Tilt your head — a modern British city like a toy town beneath your dangling legs — and listen. Attune your ears, discover the hyperacusis with which I was once afflicted. You hear laughter, babbling, the nonsense of children as they go about their lives. In amongst it, beneath the welter rising up to meet you on the thermals, you will be able to make out a counterpoint. Unbroken voices, trapped, condemned, a miserable lament.

The world was different then, half a lifetime ago. The sound was there, but we did not hear it. It never even entered our minds.

Inquest

'Members of the jury, in reaching your verdict you should consider the following points carefully. For you to record a verdict of suicide you must be in no doubt that Raymond Arthur intended to take his own life. You may be persuaded by the evidence of his depression — the testimony of his doctor, for example — but that in itself does not lead automatically to the conclusion that the accident which led to his death was a deliberate act. There are a number of questions you may decide are unanswered. Why would a man intending to kill himself crash his car while wearing a safety belt? What of the absence of any suicide note, particularly of relevance given his close family ties?

'If you accept that Raymond Arthur was depressed, you must also accept that this condition had been present for many months — again, you may consider the evidence of his doctor to be persuasive in this regard. Why, then, should he choose to end his life on this of all days? You have heard evidence regarding the side effects of the medication that he had been prescribed in July, which he had not apparently taken until a few days before he died. Is there any room in your minds as to the potential for this drug to affect his driving ability? Or indeed for the work patterns of the deceased to have contributed to an overwhelming tiredness? To this end you must weigh the evidence of Mrs Powell. She testified that the deceased was alert and in control of his vehicle in the seconds before the fatal impact. Are you persuaded that this evidence was reliable? And if so, that it signified a determination to die? What of the testimony of Mr Jones, an experienced employee of the Automobile Association, who was adamant that Raymond Arthur was signalling his intention to leave the carriageway, an exit he perhaps failed, tragically, to reach?

'Finally, you must decide the weight you will accord to the evidence presented by Zoe Arthur. You have witnessed an understandable reluctance to accept that her father was depressed become modified by the evidence presented to this court. Yet you may also decide her testimony as to her father's character — his lifelong devotion to the protection of the innocent — to be a compelling reason to doubt any intention behind the accident which led to his demise.

'Your task is to decide between verdicts of

suicide and accidental death. If, after due deliberation, you find yourselves unable to arrive at either without a reasonable doubt, you should return an open verdict. That concludes my summing up. You may now retire.'

Epilogue

March

Tonight it is clients to entertain, a working supper. I can't remember the last weekday night Paul was here for Holly's bedtime. After her bath, I read her the regulation two stories, then cuddle her on my lap for a while before placing her in her cot. She is nice and drowsy, but the minute she hits the mattress she decides she's not ready for sleep and spends a quarter of an hour trying to raise herself to standing, increasingly frustrated by the limitations of her weak musculature, her still-to-develop body.

I am tired, my limbs and back ache. I spend most of the time with my head on the side of the cot. Eventually, unable to indulge her any longer, I take hold, lie her on her side, keep returning her there, covering her with her blanket in the hope that warmth will bring about a slide into unconsciousness. There is so much I still have to do — washing, supper, tidying the toys that litter the lounge. I need her to sleep.

The doorbell goes at a critical point, not long after her eyes have closed. I watch, breath held, but she doesn't stir. I hurry along

369

the hall, angry footsteps taking me out into the lobby where I open the communal door, expecting Paul minus keys. The woman there seems vaguely familiar.

'Hi. I'm Julia, Julia Graham. We bought your house?'

'Of course. I'm sorry. Do you want to come in?'

She smiles, shyly. 'No, thank you. Michael's waiting outside. I brought you this — it came a few days ago but we hadn't got round to forwarding it. We were passing so I thought I'd better drop it off.'

She hands me an envelope. I thank her, take it in my hand, wish her goodnight as she turns away. It's addressed to Dad. The redirection expired a month ago — no more Ray Arthur, redirected mail, treat as first class. The postmark is Nottingham, the writing the same as on the card sent at Christmas. I feel a flash of anger: he knows he is dead. Then it dawns on me — he has no way of knowing where I live. I realize it is intended for me, to find its way as his card once did.

Back inside, I hear Holly chatting happily in her own private language. The sound of the door, the unfamiliar voice, something has disturbed her. I don't need this, I see the evening evaporating and nothing getting done. I go in, tell her it wasn't Paul, in case she thinks she's going to get to see her daddy. I'm impatient, unable to think of anything other than opening the letter. The brusqueness in my voice, the fact that she's over-tired, she starts to cry. I shush her, try cuddling her, but it only makes it worse. She goes rigid in my arms, refuses to be held, furious now. Her cries are jagged, the envelope gets bent in my hand as I struggle to cope, I end up begging her *please* be quiet. Nothing works, I put her down, walk out, leave her in the cot, her indignation pursuing me through the flat.

I sit on the sofa, open the letter, pull out the contents. I'm so desperately weary. There's a handwritten note, folded around a couple of bits of paper. It doesn't say much, simply that if I get this would I let him know my address, there is something he may in time need to send. I shake my head. It's as vague as every other thing he has ever said. I am not sure I will even bother to reply.

One of the enclosures is a cutting from a newspaper — the *Guardian*, from the typeface. One side is part of an advert for a computer store. On the reverse is a paragraph from news in brief. A fifty-six-year-old man currently serving a sentence for dealing in child pornography has lodged an appeal

371

against a previous conviction for buggery. If successful, he stands to win considerable compensation for the years he spent inside. The case was referred by magistrates in Nottingham, where Dad lived and worked in the early days, but the name Vincent Hunter means nothing to me.

Holly's cries are beginning to subside. My frustration turns to guilt at upsetting her, abandoning her, leaving her to settle herself. I should go back, tell her I love her, that I'm sorry, Mummy's tired, that's all. But I can't. She'll start up again, I know she will, she's got herself overwrought and the only remedy is sleep. I run a hand through my hair, sink back on the sofa, feel the ache in my spine as my muscles let go. Within a minute there is silence.

I look back at the letter on my lap. The second enclosure is another of his pictures, pencil on thick textured paper. I have never seen the photograph from which it may, or may not, have been drawn.

It's an outdoor scene, tops of trees below a cloud-strewn sky. In the foreground, Dad — a younger Dad — is shown from his broad chest up, standing side on, his arms stretched high and straight, his head tilted back. His hair is thick and black and messy. He is laughing; his eyes are fixed on mine. I am two, three. I am flying in the air a couple of feet above him, my own hair sprayed in a wispy blur of frozen motion. My tiny body is curved in a concave C, my arms reaching down for him. I think I am screaming. My expression is certainly one of sheer delight. Between the tips of his fingers and the very edge of me there is a band of nothing, a strip of clear sky.

I stare at the drawing for a while then get to my feet. On the mantelpiece above the coal-effect gas fire is the better of the two photographs Paul took outside my parents' former home in Nottingham. Unbeknown to me, he made full use of the zoom. Holly and I fill the picture, there is no more than a suggestion of the house behind. Both of us were freezing cold, but the way she is perched on my hip, the way my free hand dangles loosely at my side, makes us appear relaxed and happy.

I prop Declan Barr's drawing next to the photograph, take a step back. Dad and me; me and Holly. I doubt that either picture will remain there for as long as Holly will ultimately be able to remember. But for now there is something pleasing about them, these family portraits. The flat feels like a home.

Author's Note

I gratefully acknowledge financial assistance from Southern Arts during the writing of part of this novel. I am indebted to Martyn Bedford and Jonny Geller for their critical input and support. I am especially grateful to Jason Cowley and Toby Mundy, both of whom played a significant role in developing this book. My wife, Lynn, has provided much insightful criticism as well as staunch encouragement and companionship through tricky times — thank you.

We do hope that you have enjoyed reading this large print book.

Did you know that all of our titles are available for purchase?

We publish a wide range of high quality large print books including:
Romances, Mysteries, Classics
General Fiction
Non Fiction and Westerns

Special interest titles available in large print are:
The Little Oxford Dictionary
Music Book
Song Book
Hymn Book
Service Book

Also available from us courtesy of Oxford University Press:
Young Readers' Dictionary
(large print edition)
Young Readers' Thesaurus
(large print edition)

For further information or a free brochure, please contact us at:
Ulverscroft Large Print Books Ltd.,
The Green, Bradgate Road, Anstey,
Leicester, LE7 7FU, England.
Tel: (00 44) **0116 236 4325**
Fax: (00 44) **0116 234 0205**

FIREBALL

Bob Langley

Twenty-seven years ago: the rogue shoot-down of a Soviet spacecraft on a supersecret mission. Now: the SUCHKO 17 suddenly comes back to life three thousand feet beneath the Antarctic ice cap — with terrifying implications for the entire world. The discovery triggers a dark conspiracy that reaches from the depths of the sea to the edge of space — on a satellite with nuclear capabilities. One man and one woman must find the elusive mastermind of a plot with sinister roots in the American military elite, and bring the world back from the edge . . .

STANDING IN THE SHADOWS

Michelle Spring

Laura Principal is repelled but fascinated as she investigates the case of an eleven-year-old boy who has murdered his foster mother. It is not the sort of crime one would expect in Cambridge. The child, Daryll, has confessed to the brutal killing; now his elder brother wants to find out what has turned him into a ruthless killer. Laura confronts an investigation which is increasingly tainted with violence. And that's not all. Someone with an interest in the foster mother's murder is standing in the shadows, watching her every move . . .

NORMANDY SUMMER/ LOVE'S CHARADE

Joy St.Clair

NORMANDY SUMMER — Three cousins, Helen, Tally and Rosie, joined the First Aid Nursing Yeomanry. Helen had driven ambulances through The Blitz, but it was the Summer of 1944 that would change their lives irrevocably.

LOVE'S CHARADE — A broken down car, a mix-up of addresses and soon Kimberley found she was stand-in fiancée for a man she hardly knew. What chance had the pair of them of surviving this masquerade?

THE WESTON WOMEN

Grace Thompson

Wales, 1950s: At the head of the wealthy Weston family are Arfon and Gladys, owners of a once-successful wallpaper and paint store. It had always been Gladys's dream to form a dynasty. Her twin daughters, however, had no interest, and her grandson Jack had little ambition. And so, it is on her twin granddaughters, Joan and Megan, that Gladys pins her hopes. But unbeknown to her, they are considered rather outrageous — and one of them is secretly dating Viv Lewis, who works for the Westons but is not allowed to mix with the family socially. However, it is on him they will depend to help save the business.

TIME AFTER TIME
AND OTHER STORIES

Mary Williams

In this collection of mysterious short stories the recurring theme of 'time after time' is reflected upon with varying intensity, and in several as a haunting reminder of life's immortality. Time itself has little meaning in the wheel of eternity, and it is more than possible that the vital spark or soul of any human being could by chance contact that of another known to him or her in a previous existence on earth. Some stories concentrate on the effect of wandering apparitions about the ether and in all of them can be found love, tragedy, emotional yearnings and sheer terror.

DEAD FISH

Ruth Carrington

Dr Geoffrey Quinn arrives home to find his children missing, the charred remains of his wife's body in the boiler and Chief Superintendent Manning waiting to arrest him for her murder. Alison Hope, attractive and determined, is briefed to defend him. Quinn claims he is innocent, but Alison is not so sure. The background becomes increasingly murky as she penetrates a wealthy and ruthless circle who cannot risk their secrets — sexual perversion, drugs, blackmail, illegal arms dealing and major fraud — coming to light. Can Alison unravel the mystery in time to save Quinn?